D1785030

E.R. PUNSHON
THE SECRET SEARCH

ERNEST ROBERTSON PUNSHON was born in London in 1872.

At the age of fourteen he started life in an office. His employers soon informed him that he would never make a really satisfactory clerk, and he, agreeing, spent the next few years wandering about Canada and the United States, endeavouring without great success to earn a living in any occupation that offered. Returning home by way of working a passage on a cattle boat, he began to write. He contributed to many magazines and periodicals, wrote plays, and published nearly fifty novels, among which his detective stories proved the most popular and enduring.

He died in 1956.

The Bobby Owen Mysteries

E.R. PUNSHON

THE SECRET SEARCH

With an introduction
by Curtis Evans

DEAN STREET PRESS

Published by Dean Street Press 2017

Copyright © 1951 E.R. Punshon

Introduction copyright © 2017 Curtis Evans

All Rights Reserved

Published by licence, issued under the
UK Orphan Works Licensing Scheme.

First published in 1951 by Victor Gollancz

Cover by DSP

ISBN 978 1 911413 99 8

www.deanstreetpress.co.uk

Detective Stories, the Detection Club and Death: The Final Years of E. R. Punshon

> . . . but, they dead,
> Death has so many doors to let out life,
> I will not long survive them.
>
> *The Custom of the Country* (c. 1619-23; 1647)
> JOHN FLETCHER AND PHILLIP MASSINGER

WHEN IN 1949 E.R. Punshon published *So Many Doors*, his twenty-sixth Bobby Owen detective novel, the Englishman was seventy-seven years old, with nearly a half-century of published novels behind him and a comparatively scant seven years of life and letters remaining before him. 1901, the year of the appearance of Punshon's first novel, *Earth's Great Lord*, saw the death of Queen Victoria, the long reigning granddaughter of King George III for whom a regal age of European global dominion has been named; while 1949, a year during which a convalescent Europe was still bleakly recovering from a world war that had reduced much of its civilization to ashes and rubble, saw the testing by the USSR of its first atomic bomb and the proclamation of the formation of the People's Republic of China. The world was changing with a fearsome fleetness that not merely old men who had first glimpsed light in the Victorian era were finding hard to follow.

Rapidly changing too was the craft of crime and mystery fiction that E.R. Punshon had long practiced (this admittedly a minor thing compared to unsettling phenomena like armed revolution and atom splitting). Like the once seemingly imperishable British Empire, the hegemony of the between-the-wars "Golden Age" clue-puzzle detective novel was breaking asunder, under pressure from increasingly popular rival forms of mystery fiction, such as hard-boiled, noir, psychological suspense and espionage. Already stalked by Raymond Chandler's famous gumshoe, Philip Marlowe, as well as ill-humored and hard-drinking would-be Marlowe doppelgangers like Mickey Spillane's brutish Mike Hammer, Punshon's well-born English policeman Bobby Owen, along with other of his surviving gentlemanly detective colleagues from the era of classic crime fiction, soon found himself in the sights of no less deadly a professional killer than James Bond. Agent 007's creator, Ian Fleming, who cited as his literary influences Raymond Chandler, Dashiell Hammett, Eric Ambler and Graham Greene, published his first Bond spy novel, *Casino Royale*, in the United Kingdom in 1953, where it enjoyed immediate popular and critical success. In the United States, where the novel appeared in 1954, the same year as Raymond Chandler's much-lauded *The Long Goodbye*, *Time* magazine wryly declared that "Bond . . . might well be [Philip] Marlowe's younger brother, except that he never takes coffee for a bracer, just one large martini laced with vodka."

Upon the publication of *So Many Doors* in the UK and the US (in the latter country it would prove the last Punshon mystery published during the author's lifetime), crime fiction reviewers deemed the novel and its author representatives of a vanished era. "The twenties were the plotter's heyday (consider Freeman Wills Crofts, J.J. Connington, Dorothy L. Sayers)," observed the Democratic-Socialist *London Tribune* in its review of the "well-plotted" and "studiously told" *So Many Doors*, "and to the twenties, in spirit at least, belongs Mr. Punshon." In the United States, Anthony Boucher, dean of American mystery critics, allowed in the *New York Times Book Review* that the narration of *So Many Doors* was "leisurely"; yet, after noting the seventeenth-century English stage derivation of the novel's title, he approvingly added that there "is something Elizabethan, even Jacobean, about the obscure destinies that drive [Punshon's] obsessed and tormented characters, and about the frightful violence that concludes the story." Punshon, it seemed, still had something to say in the harried and hectic atomic age, when crime fiction reviewers and readers alike seemed increasingly to believe that brevity was the soul of death.

* * * * *

To his death in 1956 E.R. Punshon maintained a loyal following in the United Kingdom among readers who staunchly adhered to the strict standard of fair play puzzle plotting associated with Golden Age detective fiction. During the Fifties the aging but seemingly indefatigable author, who still lived quietly with his wife Sarah at their house at 23 Nimrod Road, Streatham, produced, through the medium of his prestigious longtime publisher Victor Gollancz, nine new mystery titles-- *Everybody Always Tells* (1950), *The Secret Search* (1951), The Golden Dagger (1951), *The Attending Truth* (1952), *Strange Ending* (1953), *Brought to Light* (1954), *Dark Is the Clue* (1955), *Triple Quest* (1955) and *Six Were Present* (1956)— that detailed the final criminal investigations of his longtime series police detective, Bobby Owen, now risen to the august rank of Commander (unattached), Metropolitan Police. Additionally Punshon continued to remain active in his cherished Detection Club, a London-based social organization of distinguished detective novelists, in which the author had been inducted, along with Anthony Gilbert and Gladys Mitchell, in 1933, three years after the Club's founding, joining such luminaries from the crime writing world as G.K. Chesterton, Dorothy L. Sayers, Agatha Christie, E.C. Bentley, Anthony Berkeley, R. Austin Freeman and Freeman Wills Crofts.

Like other British institutions the Detection Club from 1939 to 1945 bore the bitter burdens of war, including the devastating Nazi air raids known collectively as "the Blitz." When the Club revived its meetings and annual dinners in 1946, it became immediately apparent that time had wrought cruel changes with its membership. On seeing his brother and sister detective novelists again at the Club premises after the long interval of war years, John Dickson Carr, a comparative stripling at the age of forty, recalled that he had been "shocked" by their appearance, which he had found decidedly "greyer and more worn."

By 1946 eight of the original twenty-eight Detection Club members, including G.K. Chesterton, R. Austin Freeman and Helen Simpson, had passed away and many other members were now elderly and inactive. Several more members would expire over the next few years. Even the formerly quite engaged Freeman Wills Crofts and John Rhode (Cecil John Charles Street), now in their sixties and living in the country, became markedly less involved with Club affairs, as did an increasingly infirm Henry Wade (the landed baronet Henry Lancelot Aubrey-Fletcher). For his part, John Dickson Carr, deeming British life under postwar conditions and the governance of the Labour party intolerable, would in 1948 depart for his native United States. Besides Punshon, only Christie, John Rhode and Henry Wade, among original members, and Anthony Gilbert, Gladys Mitchell, Margery Allingham, John Dickson Carr, Nicholas Blake, Christopher Bush and E.C.R. Lorac, among the smaller number of Thirties inductees, remained substantially active as crime writers into the 1950s. Of these Lorac and Wade, like Punshon, would not survive the decade, and another, John Rhode, would barely outlast it.

Clearly some new blood was badly needed. During Punshon's remaining span of life the aged and ailing Detection Club received transfusions, so to speak, from seventeen new members. Although with the deaths of Baroness Emma Orczy and A.E.W. Mason (in 1947 and 1948 respectively), Punshon became the oldest surviving member of the Detection Club, the author, who served as Club treasurer between 1946 and 1949, during the postwar years remained extensively involved in Club affairs, actively participating in hearty debates concerning prospective new members, like Christianna Brand, Michael Innes, Michael Gilbert, Elizabeth Ferrars and Julian Symons, as to whether or not they practiced fair play and sufficiently respected the King's (later Queen's) English, the Club's chief requirements for induction. (These debates are chronicled in detail in my CADS booklet *Was Corinne's Murder Clued? The Detection Club and Fair Play, 1930-1953*.)

In 1949 Punshon found himself at odds over the matter of new enrollments with the man who unquestionably was the Club's crankiest and most cantankerous member: Anthony Berkeley, famed author of *The Poisoned Chocolates Case* (1928) and, under the pseudonym Francis Iles, of *Malice Aforethought* (1931) and *Before the Fact* (1932), three of the best regarded British crime novels from the Golden Age. In April Berkeley wrote a provocative letter to Punshon in which he claimed that as the Club's "First Freeman" he possessed blanket veto power over prospective members, despite the fact that he no longer served on the membership committee. During the early days of the Detection Club, Berkeley had observed at a meeting that the Club had two "Freemans" as members (R. Austin Freeman and Freeman Wills Crofts), and he pronounced that as the person who had originally suggested forming the Club he would be its "First Freeman." To this suggestion everyone else had laughingly assented, taking the office as a joke; yet now, nearly two decades later, it seemed that Berkeley had not been joking.

Incensed by Berkeley's gambit and the rude language in which he had couched it, Punshon wrote Sayers, enclosing his antagonist's "offensive" letter (which evidently has not survived) and warning that "[Berkeley] intends to make some sort of fuss." Punshon speculated that "possibly it is better to take no notice [of the letter], except perhaps as regards the absurd claim of his to hold some special position as what he calls 'First Freeman.' I have a vague idea that once before he put forward a claim to be a permanent member of the [membership] committee on the same ground." He noted dryly that while he had forborne responding to the specifics of Berkeley's letter, he had sent the notoriously tightfisted "First Freeman" a reminder that his annual membership fee was due, to which he had received no reply.

"Bother AB!" responded Sayers in a letter to Punshon that she composed the day after receiving his missive. "I do wish he was not so rude and silly." She entirely concurred with Punshon's recollection of the once comical but now rather annoying office of First Freeman and added resignedly: "If he tries to make a fuss at the meeting, the committee will have to cope; but I hope he will have more sense. I am sorry he should have written to you so impertinently."

By the summer of 1949 the First Freeman's irksome machinations had been checked--but only, Punshon feared, for the moment. With considerable skepticism Punshon wrote Sayers, "I gather the reconciliation with Anthony Berkeley is now complete and the hatchet well and truly buried. Until dug up again." Sayers, who soon would succeed E.C. Bentley as President of the Detection Club, advised members to tread carefully around Berkeley's tender sensibilities. "Let a (more or less) sleeping Berkeley lie," she urged. Nevertheless Sayers agreed with Punshon that the Club members would have to keep Berkeley off the membership committee, because were he to be on it the Club would "never get any new member . . . he turns them all down on sight." She lamented that "Berkeley is a difficult man to work with."

Sayers found working with Punshon, whose detective fiction she had enthusiastically promoted as a book reviewer for the *Sunday Times* between 1933 and 1935, to be an altogether more pleasant experience. Surviving correspondence between the two authors suggests that Punshon was, along with Anthony Gilbert (Lucy Beatrice Malleson), the Detection Club member with whom Sayers got along most amicably at this time. The two communicated fairly frequently during the postwar years, chatting not only about Detection Club matters, but more personal affairs as well.

As treasurer of the Detection Club, Punshon gave his attention to matters large--such as any taxes the Club might have to pay to a revenue-hungry British government ("we have to remember that we may be dropped on by the Income tax people")—and matters small. As an example of the latter, Punshon advised Sayers in December 1948 that the Club should give a "small Christmas present" to Mrs. Buchanan, caretaker of the Club premises at 12 Kingly Street, Soho. ("A room and loo in a clergy house," Christianna Brand bluntly recalled of the locale.) Although payment for services was included with the rent, Punshon pointed out that "services included are very often badly neglected and so far as I have noticed in this case they have been quite well carried out and the room always seemed neat and tidy." "[E]ven in this sordid age," he reflected with characteristic gentle irony, "a few thanks and expressions of satisfaction . . . often please as much as gifts—at any rate if accompanied by a gift." A few days later Sayers gave Mrs. Buchanan a £1 Christmas tip (about £32 today).

Sadly, Punshon suffered a serious setback to his health in August 1949, not long after a busy summer that saw the English publication of *So Many Doors*, his nettlesome skirmish with Anthony Berkeley and the annual Detection Club dinner at the

Hotel Café Royal, Piccadilly. (Recorded treasurer Punshon of the latter event: "L87/9/9—Miss Gilbert paid L6/9/4 for after dinner drinks. I gave the head waiter L1. Total 95/9/1. Great success.") After writing Freeman Wills Crofts and John Rhode to inform them about the Berkeley brouhaha, Punshon went into hospital for an operation. In September Sayers wrote Punshon that she was pleased to hear from his wife that he was "making a really good convalescence," adding: "We will miss you greatly at the October meeting, but of course you must have a good long holiday and get quite fit."

By early November Punshon, recuperating at Christopher Bush's house, Little Horsepen, near Rye in East Sussex, was able to report that he was "very much better," though the same month he resigned as Detection Club treasurer. (Christopher Bush succeeded him to the office.) Later that month Punshon wrote Sayers from Bournemouth, where he was taking a "long rest." He wished her good fortune with the recently published Penguin paperback edition of her translation of Dante's *Inferno*, remarking, "I don't know any translation of Dante except the old one [1805] by [Henry Francis] Cary, and that was a fairly pedestrian performance." He also heaped praise on Penguin's ambitious paperback publishing scheme, deeming it a "very praiseworthy attempt to turn us into a nation of book buyers instead of borrowers. A Real Revolution—if they can bring it off." Punshon had particular reason to applaud Penguin's effort, as the previous year the company had issued a pair of 1930s Bobby Owen mystery titles as paperbacks. (Three more titles would follow in the next half-dozen years.)

Punshon remained active in Detection Club affairs in 1950, though he urged that Michael Gilbert be tapped to replace him on the membership committee. "Would [Anthony Berkeley] take the suggestion as an insult," he sarcastically queried Sayers, obviously still smarting over the events of the previous year. Punshon also participated in evaluations of the work of proposed new member Julian Symons (1912-1994), one of Britain's new wave of consciously self-styled "crime writers." Of Symons's recent *Bland Beginning* (1949), a novel based, as was Punshon's own *Comes a Stranger* (1938), on the Thomas J. Wise literary forgery scandal, Punshon wrote Sayers, "On the whole I should be inclined to say 'yes,' even though I think the character drawing deplorable and the construction and final explanation a bit shaky. But he does manage to produce a readable story and it is certainly an intelligent and clever book."

By 1952, Punshon's health had declined to the point where he felt unable to attend the Detection Club's annual dinner. "[A]s they used to say in the war, the situation on the (health) front has deteriorated," he mordantly wrote Sayers, adding ominously that he had scheduled an "appointment with a specialist." The next year, however, both he and his wife, now octogenarians, managed to make it to the dinner, much to the pleasure of Sayers, who promised, "you shan't be bothered with the [initiation] ceremony at all—there will be plenty of people to carry candles." Sayers promised the Punshons good seats at the High Table to hear philosopher Bertrand Russell speak, and in a contemporary letter Christianna Brand somewhat cattily reported observing Mrs. Punshon sitting "terribly close to the speakers so as not to miss a word, and sound asleep."

Sometime in the 1950s an increasingly fragile Punshon took a dreadful tumble down the landing steps at the Detection Club premises at Kingly Street, an event Christianna Brand vividly recollected many years later in 1979, with what seems rather callous amusement on her part:

My last memory, or the most abiding one, of the club room in the clergy house, was of an evening when two members were initiated there instead of at the annual dinner [possibly Glyn Carr and Roy Vickers, 1955 initiates]. As they left, they stepped over the body of an elderly gentleman lying with his head in a pool of blood, just outside the door. . . . dear old Mr. Punshon, E.R. Punshon, tottering up the stone stair steps upon his private business, had fallen all the way down again and severely lacerated his scalp. My [physician] husband, groaning, dealt with all but the gore, which remained in a slowly congealing pool upon the clergy house floor. . . . However, Miss Sayers had, predictably, just the right guest for such an event, a small, brisk lady, delighted to cope. She came out on the landing and stood for a moment peering down at the unlovely mess. Not myself one to delight in hospital matters, I hovered ineffectively as much as possible in the rear. She made up her mind. "Well, I think we can manage *that* all right. Can you find me a tablespoon?"

The club room was unaccountably lacking in tablespoons. I went out and diffidently offered a large fork. "A fork? Oh, well . . ." She bent again and studied the pool of gore. "I think we can manage," she said again, cheerfully. "It's splendidly clotted."

I returned once more to the club room and closed the door; and I can only report that when it opened again, not a sign remained of any blood, anywhere. "I thought," said my husband as we took our departure before even worse might befall, "that in your oath you foreswore vampires." "She was only a *guest*," I said apologetically.

"Dear old Mr. Punshon," no vampire he, passed through a door to death in his 84th year on 23 October 1956, four years after his elder brother, Robert Halket Punshon. On 25 January 1957 the widowed Sarah Punshon presented Dorothy L. Sayers with a copy of her husband's thirty-fifth and final Bobby Owen mystery, the charmingly retrospective *Six Were Present*. "He would like to think that you had one," wrote Sarah, warmly thanking Sayers "for your appreciation of my husband's work during his writing life" and wistfully adding that she would miss her "occasional visits to the club evenings." Sayers obligingly invited Sarah to the next Detection Club dinner as her guest, but Sarah died in May, having survived her longtime spouse by merely seven months. Sayers herself would not outlast the year. As Christianna Brand rather flippantly reports, Sayers was discovered, just a week before Christmas, collapsed dead "at the foot of the stairs in her house surrounded by bereaved cats." Having ascended and descended the stairs after a busy day of shopping, Sayers had discovered her own door to death.

* * * * *

Dorothy L. Sayers's literary reputation has risen ever higher in the years since her demise, with modern authorities like the esteemed late crime writer P.D. James particularly lauding

Sayers's ambitious penultimate Peter Wimsey mystery, *Gaudy Night*--a novel E.R. Punshon himself had lavishly praised in his review column in the *Manchester Guardian*--as not only a great detective novel but a great novel, with no delimiting qualification. Although he was one of Sayers's favorite crime writers, Punshon was not so fortunate with his own reputation, with his work falling into unmerited neglect for more than a half-century after his death. With the reprinting by Dean Street Press of Punshon's complete set of Bobby Owen mystery investigations—chronicled in 35 novels, five short stories and a radio play—this long period of neglect now happily has ended, however, allowing a major writer from the Golden Age of detective fiction a golden opportunity to receive, six decades after his death, his full and lasting due.

Crime Fiction Reviews by E.R. Punshon

E.R. PUNSHON reviewed crime fiction for the *Manchester Guardian*, a newspaper congenial to his own Liberal Party sympathies, in 70 insightful and witty columns published between 13 November 1935 and 27 May 1942. A total of 369 books were included in Punshon's near-monthly column, making his reviews one of the larger bodies of crime fiction criticism by a Golden Age detective novelist. (In Punshon's company we also find, among others, Dashiell Hammett, Anthony Boucher, Todd Downing and Punshon's Detection Club colleagues Dorothy L. Sayers, John Dickson Carr, Anthony Berkeley, Milward Kennedy, Julian Symons and Edmund Crispin.)

Punshon's crime fiction reviews, selections from which are included in Dean Street Press's new editions of the novels *So Many Doors*, *Everybody Always Tells*, *The Secret Search* and *The Golden Dagger*, indicate a partiality on the author and critic's part toward classical detective fiction, especially works by present and future Detection Club members, including, for example, both richly literary whodunits by Dorothy L. Sayers, E.C. Bentley and Michael Innes and ingenious yet austere efforts by John Rhode, J.J. Connington and Freeman Wills

Crofts. Yet though Punshon figuratively threw bouquets at the feet of Dorothy L. Sayers, whose own rave review of Punshon's first Bobby Owen detective novel, *Information Received* (1933), was a great boon to Punshon's career as a mystery writer, in his columns he forbore neither from occasionally criticizing works by other Detection Club members nor from tendering advice on improvement. He also demonstrated interest in American crime fiction, reviewing not just detective novels by classicists like S.S. Van Dine and Ellery Queen, but suspense novels by Mignon Eberhart and tougher fare like Raymond Chandler's *Farewell, My Lovely*. Altogether Punshon's crime fiction reviews offer both the mystery scholar a valuable research tool and the mystery fan wise pointers for further reading.

Curtis Evans

CHAPTER I
"MASQUERADING AS ME"

"And how," asked Olive, looking sternly at her husband across the table—"how did you like your nice whale-steak?"

"Eh, what?" asked Bobby, rousing himself from that deep abstraction in which he had been sunk during the meal. "Oh, jolly good! Yes, definitely. Jolly good!"

Olive rose to her feet, majestic in wrath.

"Heaven defend me from all men, especially husbands," she declaimed. "Here I stand hours and hours in a queue for liver: calves' liver, English calves' liver. I get it and I cook it and I serve it, and the man doesn't even know! Whale-meat indeed!"

"Oh, sorry," said Bobby, feebly apologetic. "It's only—well, I'm a bit worried."

"If you had told me," Olive retorted, unappeased, "you could have had your whale-meat, and my feet wouldn't ache the way they do."

"Sub-consciously," Bobby argued, trying to talk himself out of it, "I really did know it was something special. I did say 'Jolly good', didn't I? It shows, doesn't it?"

"Shows what?" demanded Olive; and, as Bobby didn't know, he didn't answer, but passed his cup for more coffee instead, and Olive filled it and said: "Well, what's worrying you?"

"Remember Cy King?" Bobby asked.

Olive nodded, uneasily, for Cy King was the name of a notorious gangster who for long had managed, by a combination of daring, skill and cunning, all in an unusual degree, to keep out of the hands of the police. At long last this immunity had been broken down, and, chiefly through Bobby's instrumentality, he had been convicted and sentenced. But on a comparatively minor charge, so that his term of imprisonment had lasted only a few months. His vanity, his influence among his companions, his prestige, had, however, all suffered badly from this misfortune, and prestige is as necessary to a successful gang leader as it is in any other profession. Moreover, now his finger-prints and general description were on record, his photograph had been circulated in the official 'Police Gazette', and so immunity had become merely a dream of a happier past. He now spent a good deal of time talking about all the unpleasant things he would like to do to Bobby as and when opportunity served.

"Has he been doing anything?" Olive asked.

"Apparently, according to a report from one of our contacts, getting up a pal of his to look like me," Bobby answered.

"Goodness!" exclaimed Olive. "Whatever for?"

"That's what's bothering me," Bobby told her. "I don't much like the idea of one of Cy King's lot masquerading as me. Cheek. Very likely it doesn't amount to much. Their idea of a joke, perhaps, though Cy King's notion of fun is generally anything but funny. Or it may be something serious. There's a report Cy King has been seen hanging about Southam, and that's a long way outside his usual beat. Looks like something might be brewing out there."

"Where's Southam?" Olive asked.

"Used to be a jolly little village," Bobby explained. "I've played cricket there. Now it's just another dormitory suburb—cinemas, multiple stores, tube, 'buses, all complete. The common's still there, though, just as it has been since the beginning of things, and I hope will be to the end of them. One of our chaps at Southam recognised Cy King from the photo we circulated, and he says he's seen him there twice recently. He didn't think much of it the first time, but a second time made him sit up and take notice. Especially as this time Cy was waiting in a car outside a Mr Smith's house."

"One of his friends?" Olive asked. "Receiver or something?"

"Not as far as is known," Bobby told her. "Appears to be a highly respectable, very well-to-do, retired business man. Old. In poor health. He has a niece living with him, and there's a housekeeper. Grows roses, employs a gardener, takes a mild interest in Church and politics, and subscribes liberally to any local fund. Our man—quite a young fellow, name of Ford; I shall have to ask him if he would like to apply for a transfer to C.I.D.—wondered what Cy was doing there. So he hung about round a corner somewhere, and saw a chap come out of the house, get into Cy's car, and drive off. Ford rather boggled about this part of it; finally I got it out of him that at first, just for a moment, he thought it was me."

"Why?"

"He didn't seem to know exactly. He got the impression, he said. Only for a moment. Same make of suit. My old school tie I sometimes wear. Same way of walking. So on."

"It seems most awfully funny," declared the much-puzzled Olive. "Why on earth should anyone want to look like you? Of course," she added kindly, "you can't help it, but any one else can, can't they?"

"If you are trying to make any insinuations," Bobby observed, "I would like to remind you that my looks are sufficiently up to standard for a certain young woman once to fall madly in love with me—head over heels, splash, just like that."

"Who was she?" asked Olive, interested. "You ought to have told me before."

"And for two pins," Bobby added, "I wouldn't take you to the cinema to-night."

"Oh, are we going?" Olive cried, delighted, for it was but seldom they had the chance of a night out together.

"At Southam," Bobby added. "I'll get the car."

"Southam?" repeated Olive, disappointed this time. "I thought you meant that new film at the Top-Notch in Leicester Square."

"This is official," Bobby explained. "Petrol and two cinema seats, but not yours, going down as expenses. Mr Smith and his niece go regularly every week. I want to see them. If Smith is a receiver and in with Cy King, well, I may know him—or the niece, if she's in it, as she would be most likely. In any case, when one of Cy King's friends pays an afternoon call, I want to know more about it. If Mr Smith is what he seems to be—well-to-do retired business man—he may need protection, and need it pretty badly. People often do when Cy King is around."

Accordingly, some half-hour or so later, Bobby and Olive, their car parked outside, entered a Southam cinema, one of the well-known 'Glorious' circuit, where, by good fortune, the film being shown was one Olive had long wanted to see.

A man who, umbrella under arm, though it was a fine night, had been hanging about outside, sidled up to them. He muttered to Bobby.

"To report, sir. Name of Ford."

"Right," said Bobby.

"Four-and-ninepenny circle, sir," Ford went on. "They always sit there—places kept for them regular once every week in the front row."

Bobby nodded, bought three tickets, and slipped one to Constable Ford. Together they ascended the stairway, magnificent in gilt and plush. Ford murmured:

"Housekeeper gone out, so the house is empty. We've put a man to watch, and the housekeeper's being followed."

"Good," said Bobby. "As soon as you see Mr Smith or the young lady showing any sign of leaving, let your umbrella fall to give us time to get out first. When they go, follow as close behind as possible, so I can be sure who they are, though I expect I shall be able to spot them from the description you 'phoned. Do you always carry an umbrella?"

"Well, sir," Ford answered, with some slight hesitation, "I've doctored the handle a bit. A little lead. Sort of handy if a rough house develops."

"I thought so from the way you carried it," Bobby remarked. "I should try to hold it more naturally, if I were you."

"Yes, sir," said Ford, and dropped discreetly behind, while Bobby and Olive went on to take their seats.

"Are you thinking there may be a burglary at Mr Smith's?" Olive whispered.

"Well, it all rather suggests that Mr Smith is either an accomplice or a destined victim," Bobby answered. "The latter, more likely. Possibly both. Dog very much eats dog in Cy King's world. Cy may have got to know Mr Smith keeps money by him. People do at times. Quite large sums in their bedrooms in a safe you can open with a screw-driver—or a tin-opener. And can't be covered by insurance. Or jewellery, perhaps. Some people are buying diamonds as a kind of safeguard against more devaluation. Postage stamps, too."

They settled themselves in their seats, choosing two at the back of the circle and near the gangway, so that they could get out quickly when Ford gave the dropped umbrella signal. The main feature film was followed by one of those intolerable 'shorts' with which occasionally the cinema industry insults the intelligence of even the least intelligent of its patrons. The audience began to drift away, patiently hoping for better things next time. Ford let his umbrella fall and picked it up again. Bobby nudged Olive, and they joined the outgoing trickle. In the foyer they lingered as if waiting for a friend. A little old man came out, accompanied by a tall, fair girl who overtopped him by five or six inches. Behind them came Ford, trying to dangle his umbrella as carelessly as possible. He caught Bobby's eye and nodded towards the little old man and the tall girl with him. Bobby and Olive followed them down the stairs, noting with what care and solicitude the girl watched over her companion. In the entrance hall she fussed to see he had his scarf well wrapped round his throat, his overcoat buttoned up. One of the cinema attendants watched approvingly, but the old man himself grumbled a little, protesting he wasn't a child, but all the same he was clearly not displeased. The girl said:

"Now, nunks, you mustn't risk catching cold, must you?"

They went out and disappeared in the night. Bobby and Olive found their car and waited in it. Ford appeared.

"'Phone message," he said. "Everything O.K. at the house. Mr Smith and the young lady just got back. By 'bus."

"Good," said Bobby, "keep as good a watch as you can manage for the next few days, especially if a car is seen hanging about. Day raids are almost as common now as burglaries. Easier to get away in the day-time. We don't want to hear of Mr Smith and his niece being knocked out or tied up—that sort of thing."

"No, sir. We'll keep our eyes open. I'll report what you say, sir."

Another man appeared by the side of the car. He said:

"Message received, sir. Housekeeper followed as per instructions received. Same took tube to Leicester Square and proceeded to Jimmy Joe's in Soho. Was there thirty-seven minutes.

Then left and proceeded to Tottenham Court Road, where seen to take Southam tube. Was not followed farther."

"Doesn't look too good," Bobby remarked. "Nothing we can do for the time, though, except watch."

He said good night to the two Southam men and drove away. Olive said:

"What's Jimmy Joe's?"

"Hot spot," Bobby answered and chuckled faintly. "Very hot spot," and once again he indulged in a small chuckle.

"What's the joke?" Olive inquired suspiciously.

"Well, you see," Bobby explained, "Jimmy Joe's been asking for police protection, and that tickled our people to death. The only protection they want to give him is a five-year stretch in one of His Majesty's gaols."

"What's he want protection for?" Olive asked.

"Oh, there's a queer old boy, known as Russky, hangs about Soho," answered Bobby. "Lots of queer people, young and old, in Soho, for that matter; but Jimmy Joe—he's half Italian—swears Russky has the evil eye. He complains that if Russky comes into his cafe, customers get up and go out, and if Russky is already there, then customers won't come in. Well, he was told evil eyes weren't police concern, and then he tried to make out Russky peddled drugs. Not a scrap of evidence, though it does seem Russky is a bit of a herbalist and gives treatment sometimes. But if he does, he doesn't take pay."

"He sounds rather a nice old man," remarked Olive.

"Well, I wouldn't go quite as far as that," Bobby said, "and very likely he'll be getting beaten up one of these days. They really are afraid of him, it seems, and Jimmy Joe's customers are not a nice crowd to get across. A tough lot. It's the very special private reserve of a man called Tiny Garden, as big a scoundrel as Cy King himself, but no brains. Cy has the brains and Tiny the brawn—he stands about six foot three, and probably weighs about two hundred and fifty pounds or thereabouts. I expect that's why he gets called Tiny. The point is that he is Cy King's own very special rival and enemy in gangsterdom. Cy's done him down once or twice, and Tiny is said to have tried hard to get Cy bumped off in revenge. A bit of a mix-up. I can't believe they would ever get round to doing a job together. Cy wouldn't be too sure of not getting his throat cut and Tiny would be quite sure of not getting his share of the loot. Puzzling," he said; and Olive didn't like the way he said it, for it sounded too much, she thought, as if he were setting off on a fresh trail, a new trail.

"You didn't recognize Mr Smith or the girl, did you?" she asked.

"Never seen either of them before," Bobby declared. "They didn't strike me as the criminal type, either. You can generally tell—not always, but often. Anyhow, I feel certain neither of them has ever done time."

"I thought the girl seemed rather nice," Olive remarked. "Quiet looking, and very nice with the old man."

Bobby agreed; and if it occurred to him that rich, elderly and ailing uncles are sometimes very well looked after indeed by their nephews and their nieces, he dismissed the thought as merely another example of the deplorable kind of cynicism that he feared he was tending to develop with increasing years and responsibilities.

CHAPTER II
"A MOST ADMIRABLE NIECE"

THE FOLLOWING day was Saturday, and Bobby, having enjoyed a leisurely breakfast, put his feet up to read the paper.

"Not going to the Yard this morning," he explained. "How about a run round in the car?"

"Where to?" asked Olive, patiently removing his feet from an armchair to one of more common make.

"Might go as far as the seaside and get lunch there somewhere," suggested Bobby. "How about it?"

"How about petrol?" Olive inquired cautiously, for these were days when rationing was still in force—and severe.

"Can do," Bobby assured her. "We could go through Southam on the way."

"Oh-h," cried Olive, and it was a very long-drawn 'Oh' indeed. "So that's it. Offer your poor wife a little holiday, and all the time all you want is to go running after something fresh you think you've found."

"Purely precautionary," Bobby assured her. "But I shouldn't mind having another look at rich old ailing Mr Smith and that attractive niece of his and their housekeeper, who pays visits to as nasty a thieves' kitchen as you can find in all Soho. I got one of our men to pay it a visit last night—Sergeant James."

"Jimmy Joe's?"

"Yes. They're used to it there. Wouldn't think it was anything special. Routine. Tiny Garden was there, and a man called Sunday. His real name is Sam Deedes. I don't know how he came to be nicknamed Sunday. It's not long since he finished a two-year stretch for robbery with violence. He had been rather knocked about himself this time. Black eye, mouth badly cut, so on. Sergeant James chaffed him a bit, and he said he had fallen downstairs. Tiny said it would learn him, so James asked learn him what, and another fellow there—James didn't know him—chipped in to say Sunday had been so busy talking he hadn't noticed where he was going. Tiny said Sunday wouldn't talk so much now his mouth was the way it was, and Sunday said nothing at all, but looked very sick and sulky. James thought it all added to—what?"

"To what," Olive answered promptly, "they used to call careless talk in the war. So his friends had been trying to make sure he didn't any more—poor man."

"Anything else?"

"I don't think so," Olive answered, puzzled. "Why? What?"

"Well, there is something else I noticed," Bobby told her. "Just an idea. Imagination, very likely. Have another think and see if you get it, too. If you do, I shall begin to believe there's something in it. And now, get a move on. Time we were off."

"There are just one or two things I must see to—" Olive began, but Bobby interrupted her very firmly indeed.

"No, there aren't," he said, "and, if there are, they can wait. I want you to be ready in quick time. Ten minutes, please, or else I shall shove you in the car the way you are."

"Bully," said Olive. She gave a wistful glance around, wished Bobby had to look after the flat for a few days, reflected that if he did he probably wouldn't even notice the really awful state the kitchen was in, not to mention the bedroom, and said: "Oh, all right—ten minutes, then."

"Not one second more," Bobby warned her again, and indeed it wasn't much more than three-quarters of an hour before Olive was ready to take the road.

"I want to know if there are any developments," Bobby explained as they started off, "and I would like you to have another look at the girl if possible. Somehow—"

"Somehow what?"

"I don't know—it was just a sort of vague feeling that she didn't quite fit."

"There was one thing about her that struck me," Olive remarked. "I don't suppose it meant anything."

"What was that?" Bobby asked quickly.

But Olive was gazing dreamily out of the window of the car, watching the southern suburbs slip by.

"Oh, yes," she said. "Yes. Well, have another think, Bobby, and see if you get it. If you do, I shall begin to believe there's something in it."

"Now Olive," Bobby protested reproachfully, "is that playing the game? I ask you. Besides, I'm not feeling very well this morning."

Olive was unable to resist this touching appeal. She relented. She said:

"Anyhow, I don't suppose you ever would get it. No man would. All the same, it's what you said yourself. Something wasn't right. Her frock."

"What about it?" Bobby asked. "I thought you said you liked it?"

"So I did. A nice, plain, demure little frock. Utility all over it. And a hat—the year before last, early spring. Woollen gloves. But she didn't look the woollen-glove type. I expect uncle had told her they were the only sensible wear and he always wore them himself. So she had to. And she didn't look the demure little type, either—a sort of a come-hither air about her she was doing her best to suppress, and only making it show more. Not a sign of make-up, awful plain hair-do, and yet a sort of swagger in the way she walked and the way she held her head. What about it? She seemed to be saying and trying not to. And nothing on earth will make me believe she could ever possibly have thought that hat suited her."

"I see what you mean," Bobby said thoughtfully. "Yes. Playing herself down to please the rich uncle, perhaps. You think it would go as far as wearing an out-of-date hat?"

"It might," Olive said, though with just a touch of hesitation in her voice. "Money, or the hope of it, will make almost any one do almost anything."

With this sage reflection they were in Southam. A place was found to park the car, for Bobby always liked to make his visits to police stations as unobtrusive as possible. To the Southam one he now made his way, while Olive went off to an open-air market she had spotted from afar.

Bobby was the first back, and then Olive arrived, bearing her sheaves with her in the shape of a pound of onions, some apples, and an out-size in cabbages.

"Ever so much cheaper," she declared happily. "Better quality, too. We must come again."

Bobby agreed with certain reservations in which the cost of petrol, time and a probable saving in vegetables of something under sixpence were major factors. He remarked that he hadn't learned much from his visit to the local police. Mr Smith had been living in Southam some six or seven years. It was only lately that his health had begun to fail. It was this failing health of his that had induced his niece to come from Canada, to live with him and give him the sort of care he needed. Even the best and most attentive hired housekeeper cannot feel the tie of blood and natural affection. It had been, of course, a considerable sacrifice Miss Smith made in leaving her friends and her work in Toronto, where she had a good job and good prospects. At first she had felt strange and lonely, but she had the consolation of knowing that she was doing what was right. Your own father's only brother has a claim upon you, hasn't he? And then he was the only relative she possessed in all the world, so it was natural they should like to be together.

Of course, Miss Smith herself had never said all this in so many words. But that was the general impression gathered from occasional remarks she let drop from time to time, from casual gossip with the housekeeper, Mrs Day, and from her general behaviour. It was noticeable, too, that she got on very well with Mrs Day, in spite of what sometimes happens when new brooms begin to sweep, and indeed Mrs Day had often expressed her admiration for Miss Smith and her unwearying, unselfish devotion to a, at times, tiresome old man. Apparently, however, she was quite content with the rather dull life she led alone with her ageing, semi-invalid uncle. Their weekly visit to the cinema and an occasional shopping trip she made to the West End seemed her only recreations. Her attempts to get her uncle to take a holiday now and then in the country or at the seaside had never met with any success, and now she had given up trying.

"A most admirable niece," Bobby summed up all this information he had gathered, "even if uncle's will may have something to do with it. Well, why not?" and for the rest of that trip to the sea and back to London in time for a dinner out and a theatre, there was no more mention of the Smiths, uncle or niece.

It was, in fact, three or four days later when Bobby found on his desk, among many other reports, one from Southam to the effect that Constable Ford, then in plain clothes, being off duty, had seen a man leaving Mr Smith's house rather late in the evening. Ford had not much liked the man's looks, had noticed that he was hurrying towards the tube station as though afraid he might be missing the last train. Ford had then rung up the station sergeant to suggest that this man might be met there to see if he did in fact take the London train. This had been done, and the flying-squad man who had arrived in time to see Mr Smith's visitor off recognized in him the Sam Deedes, otherwise and more widely known as Sunday, so recently out of gaol. A quick police radio call to the Yard resulted in Sunday's being met at Leicester Square, where it was guessed he might alight, and followed thence to Jimmy Joe's rather more than doubtful establishment. He had not been seen to leave again, and it had not been thought necessary to continue the watch for very long.

"I think I'll run down to Southam again to-morrow," Bobby told Olive. "I don't much like the look of things, and I shan't feel comfortable about it all till I know more, and know where Cy King comes in with his pal he seems to want to masquerade as me. I suppose there is just a chance that Tiny Garden and Cy King are working it together. And possible that there's nothing more than some silly trick they are trying to think up behind this masquerade business. But I don't much think so."

"I don't see that you have much to go on," Olive said. "Don't you think you had better wait till something more definite turns up?"

"It may be something rather nasty when it does, and I want to avoid that if possible," Bobby answered. "What I feel is that a game has been started and will have to be played out to the end—even though at present it's only P to K4, P to Q3, Kt to KB3. But I think the next move will show how the game is going to develop," and Olive, listening, was aware of a sudden chilly feeling, as though all the air around had gone suddenly cold.

CHAPTER III
"NOW THERE'S EVIDENCE"

ONCE AGAIN, therefore, Bobby drove to Southam by the road he was coming to know well. A busy day had delayed him, so that by now it was evening. Then, too, Bobby had certain rather vague plans in his mind for which the cover of night might be convenient. At the Southam police-station Constable Ford was waiting; and Bobby put him through a close examination, asking in particular many questions about Mrs Day, the housekeeper.

"There must be some connection between her and Jimmy Joe's," Bobby remarked. "It's not a place the ordinary respectable woman would know anything about. How old do you think she is?"

"I should say about sixty," Ford answered, "though she's spry and active enough. Her hair's quite grey. Very decent hard-working woman, as far as is known. She's been with Mr Smith ever since he came to live here. When Miss Smith was said to be coming to live with her uncle she spoke of getting another place. Said she didn't suppose she would be wanted any more. Miss Smith would most likely want to get rid of her, and there was talk of her going to Dr Green. Mrs Green was very disappointed when Mrs Day stayed on with Mr Smith. They seem to get along together very nicely—Mrs Day and Miss Smith, I mean. Mrs Day says Miss Smith is as nice a young lady as you would wish for. Always ready to do a little to help, and certainly between the two of them the old gentleman is very well looked after and the house like a picture."

"All sounds very satisfactory," Bobby said; "but where do Sunday and Jimmy Joe's café in Soho fit in that picture—or Cy King's visits?"

"Sunday, sir?" Ford asked, puzzled for the moment. "Oh, that's the man who was at Jimmy Joe's and here, too?"

"That's the man," Bobby agreed. "Sam Deedes is his real name. Why he gets called Sunday I don't know. Certainly not because he's either good or gay, especially not gay just now, with that face of his. Perhaps it is because he's got red hair. What I was thinking was that he might be Mrs Day's husband, but it seems he's too young and she's too old. Or he might be her son. Decent women do get at times husbands and sons who are thorough bad lots. Possibly Mrs Day may have said something about Mr Smith being well off, Sunday may have reported it to Tiny Garden, and Cy King heard, and thought it was a chance to gate-crash. That might explain Sunday's damaged face, Tiny's way of letting Sunday know he had been talking too much. Well, if you can be spared for a time, I want you to show me where Mr Smith lives. I would like a look round."

The station sergeant, appealed to, said Constable Ford was on day duty, so that would be all right as far as the daily rota was concerned. So Ford and Bobby started off, and a brisk walk of a little over a mile took them to a quiet turning off the main road. Building was going on, and older, prosperous-looking houses stood in generally large and well-kept gardens. Comfortably off, most of them, the dwellers in Acres Lane, as the road was called. Mr Smith's residence, known as 'The Haven', was a pleasant-looking abode, of moderate size, standing well back from the road. There was a large conservatory built against one side of the house, and, though it was too dark to see clearly, Bobby had none the less an impression of a garden on the upkeep of which neither expense nor trouble was spared. Ford, on being asked, said Mr Smith employed a full-time gardener, whose name incidentally was also Smith. An old and highly respectable inhabitant of Southam, where he had lived all his life. He was also, it appeared, the source of much of the information Ford had gathered about The Haven and its inhabitants.

They had been talking in low and careful tones, for Bobby had no wish to attract attention. Now he pushed open the garden gate, put on gloves, produced a screw-driver from his coat pocket and told Ford to wait where he was.

"I'm going to do a little trespassing," he said. "Against regulations, of course, but I think a prowl round might be useful. There's no dog, is there?"

"No, sir, I don't think so," Ford answered. "Mr Smith says he's not going to have his seeds dug up by dogs burying bones. There's two Persian cats, but that's all."

Bobby vanished into the darkness, walking so carefully, so silently that no sound came back to the listening Ford. Presently he returned.

"Well, that's all we can do for to-night," he remarked. "An early household, apparently. I could see a light in one of the upstairs rooms, at the back. And it's only about half-past ten. Mrs Day's still up, though. I got a peep into the kitchen. The blind doesn't quite fit. She was dozing before the fire—dozing rather deeply. A bottle of gin on the table, half empty. Of course, it may have been so before."

"I shouldn't have taken Mrs Day for a drinker," Ford observed.

"Very likely she isn't," answered Bobby. "No harm in a nip before bed, for that matter. Sedative. May help you to sleep. But also Mr Sunday's recent visits may have been worrying her, and she may have thought a little drop of something hot would be a comfort. By the way, there seems to have been some sort of an attempt made to force the back door. Distinct marks of a screw-driver or something of the sort having been used. Shouldn't wonder if a screw-driver fitting those marks isn't found lying about near by."

"Yes, sir," said Ford. "You had a screw-driver yourself, sir, hadn't you?"

"Had I?" asked Bobby absently, as he took off the gloves he had been wearing. "I think I'll be back in the morning. Mr Smith must be warned he is becoming an object of interest to doubtful characters. Only he may be a doubtful character himself—or have been."

"Well, sir," Ford protested, "he's always been thought of as one of the most respectable gentlemen in Southam."

"Very likely he is," agreed Bobby. "But retired black marketeers or receivers do attract people like Tiny Garden and Cy King. Open to blackmail, and sometimes keep money by them in notes they don't want to bank for fear of attracting attention—or in case they have to skip in a hurry. That's your black marketeer. And receivers may have jewellery not yet disposed of. I want to see him and be able to form my own judgment. If he is as respectable and honest as he probably is, then he had better be warned, and luckily there's back-door evidence now to make him take a warning seriously. Because it has to be taken seriously when Cy King and Tiny are around. And," he added thoughtfully, "I do want to know what's the idea of dressing up to look like me. Gives me a sort of personal interest."

While they had been talking, they had made their way back to the police station. There they parted, after Bobby had warned both Ford and the station sergeant to expect him back first thing in the morning—eight o'clock, most likely. "Which means," he said mournfully, "what with all I'll have to see about first, and one thing and another, that I shall have to get up at six at the latest. Who would want to be a policeman?"

"I often wonder that myself," said the station sergeant; and added, with a glance at Ford to let him understand that grumbling was a privilege reserved for seniors only: "Fine chance for young fellows, though. Very different from what it was in my young days."

Bobby nodded in grave agreement with this sentiment, that has indeed echoed down the ages ever since it was first enunciated—probably by Adam. He retired then to find his car and drive home.

Duly and reluctantly he rose from his bed next morning at the requisite hour, so as to have time to do a little 'phoning and to make sure nothing had come in by the first post requiring immediate attention. At Southam he arrived at the grim hour arranged. Constable Ford, in uniform, was waiting for him near Acres Lane. At Mr Smith's residence they knocked, and there appeared Mrs Day. She was a small, active-looking, red-faced woman, with grey hair, and a rather flat face, in which a large, well-shaped nose stood out prominently between two small, bright grey eyes, and above a big mouth with thick lips. Behind these showed strong, irregular teeth, plainly still her own. She regarded the two men with a startled, even frightened air, as would perhaps most women on finding a policeman on their door-step at so comparatively early an hour.

Bobby, at his most genial—and how hard it is to be genial when you are still half asleep and would like to be wholly so—explained that certain suspicious characters had been noticed in the vicinity and that Constable Ford had seen one in the garden of this house during the previous night.

"About ten o'clock or a little later, wasn't it, constable?" Bobby asked.

"Yes, sir, just about the half-hour," Ford agreed. "Ugly-looking customer, too. I didn't like his looks at all."

Bobby was a little inclined to consider this was a somewhat unnecessary painting of the lily, so to say. He gave Ford a sideways look, but Ford had as innocent an air as Bobby himself might once, in his younger days, have assumed in similar circumstances. But he noticed also a sudden pallor on Mrs Day's large, florid face and something like panic that seemed to show and flicker in those small grey eyes of hers. It was with some difficulty that she managed to gasp out:

"What . . . what was he like?"

"Well, ma'am—" Ford began, but here Bobby interposed:

"Smallish man, walked like a cat," he said. "Was that it?" And now it was plain that though she had not waited for Ford's reply, only by a great effort did she control herself.

"I . . . you had better see Mr Smith," she stammered, and hurried away, walking as one who only with difficulty kept balance and control.

"Put the wind up her all right, sir, that you have," Ford commented. "Were you thinking of some one in particular?"

"Cy King's a smallish man, and he walks like a cat," Bobby said. "Looks as if Mrs Day thought it might be him and knows enough of him not to like the idea. And where does that fit?"

Ford, somewhat unnecessarily, said he didn't know. They had been left standing on the doorstep, and there they had to wait some minutes before Mrs Day came back. And that she had been fortifying herself from the bottle of gin Bobby had seen on the kitchen table the previous night was fairly obvious. She said Mr Smith had not finished dressing, but would be down in a few minutes, and Bobby asked if they might have a look round outside to see, as he put it, if their nocturnal visitor had left any trace of himself or his doings? Mrs Day consented at once, and Bobby and Ford made an admiring tour of the garden. For the garden was one that was clearly kept with that kind of loving care and attention to which all created things, animate or inanimate, make their response.

"If you ask me, sir," observed Ford, more interested in allotments than in flower-gardens, "that Mrs Day was precious glad to get rid of us."

"I think so," Bobby agreed. "She wanted time to pull herself together. Had a bad scare, either for herself or for Sunday, as they call him, if he is really her son. Goes to show Cy is trying to gate-crash on something good—only what? I don't like the look of things at all."

He walked over to a greenhouse at a little distance, and picked up a small screw-driver which had evidently been lying there all night. He brought it back and gravely tried it against slight marks on the back door.

"Fits a treat, don't it, sir?" Ford remarked.

"Plainly the instrument used," Bobby agreed. "Now there's evidence to justify us in asking Mr Smith to allow us to keep a specially sharp look-out—and to justify us in asking a few questions, too."

CHAPTER IV
"NUNKS, DARLING"

THEY WENT back to the house. Mrs Day was not visible, but the front door was still open, and a voice from above, from the head of the stairs, asked them to wait in the room on the right. Mr Smith would be down in a few minutes. Bobby recognized the voice as that of the tall girl who, in the 'Glorious' cinema, had so solicitously warned Mr Smith against the risk of catching cold. A full, rich voice that with its odd, harsh undertones was not easily forgotten.

The room, that in obedience to this directive from on high Bobby and Ford now entered, was large and well proportioned, with a pleasant view over the garden, but so crammed with all sorts and kinds of furniture that the first impression was one merely of confusion. Only slowly did the visitor begin to realize that almost every bit of furniture in the room was what is called a museum piece. But all huddled together in the most glorious muddle that can be imagined of style, period and wood. No pedantic respect here for old conventions about not mixing oak and walnut, mahogany and satinwood. The chairs and table in the centre were Sheraton, in satinwood, of his best early period, their pure, clean aristocracy of line a joy to look at. The centre of this table, though, was occupied by a heavy old knife-box in mahogany. Against one wall stood a fine Welsh dresser of grand, simple old lines, and next to it was a really superb Queen Anne walnut bureau. A lovely piece. Near the fireplace was an old Elizabethan chest, bearing the original owner's arms and the date 1588, and on it was incongruously perched a jewel-cabinet by William Vile, a companion though smaller piece to that in the Rococo style made by him for a wedding present from George the Third to his bride. Then in the large bay window was a Buhl library table, dazzling in its magnificence of brass, ivory and tortoiseshell. But drawn up against it was a north-country ladder-back chair. An odd mixture, bringing together Yorkshire farmhouse and French chateau. On it, on this Buhl treasure of a table—for treasure it certainly was—stood a typewriter and a telephone, and an ancient beautifully carved Bible-box, now sadly reduced from its high estate to become a container for telephone directories.

Ford remained standing by the door, both impressed and worried by surroundings he felt he would like to understand but did not. Bobby, picking his way carefully through the maze of ancient splendour, tried, and failed, to find in so strange a medley some clue to the character and disposition of its owner. Hard to reconcile the knowledge and taste and natural instinct for the beautiful in the particular, with the curious disregard of, or lack of feeling for, essential harmony in the general. How could, he wondered, any one eager to possess such lovely old things be yet capable of throwing them all together like this—of putting an old farmhouse ladder-back chair against a Buhl library table? He reflected sagely that there's no accounting for the vagaries of human taste and character, even though environment, education, the accidents of life, can explain much.

Bobby knew something about painting, an art which he practised occasionally when he had time, but very little about old furniture. No one, however, with any feeling for line and form could fail to be impressed by the walnut bureau or fail to recognize its beauty. He was touching it for the sheer pleasure of feeling that lovely wood when the door opened and there entered the little old man of the 'Glorious' cinema. He looked more fragile now than he had done when wrapped in his overcoat and muffler, and he peered up at Bobby from watery and ageing eyes that no longer saw clearly. Nor did he look in a very good humour. Bobby, indeed, was inclined to guess that good temper was not the old gentleman's most marked characteristic and that his niece probably had her hands full in dealing with him. He was saying now in a thin, indignant voice:

"What's all this about? I don't like all these police visits. I've never had anything to do with police. Always kept myself respectable, and now there always seems to be a policeman banging at the door. Very trying, very trying indeed."

"Well, sir, I'm sorry if you've been annoyed," Bobby said in his most dulcet tones, "but surely you would prefer policemen knocking at your door to burglars coming in by the window— without knocking."

"Nonsense, rubbish!" declared Mr Smith petulantly. "Why should burglars be coming here in particular? No diamond necklaces here, no fur coats, nothing of that sort. No money even, only a little loose change. I pay everything by cheque."

"A man was in your garden last night," Bobby said. "The constable here saw him. There are marks on your back door made by a screw-driver. A screw-driver was lying near, and it fits the marks."

"Mischievous boys, most likely. Trouble enough with them," Mr Smith retorted. "Don't know what good police are if they can't look after the young scoundrels. Can't keep an apple on my trees, and all you say if I complain is that boys will be boys, but you'll do your best. Bah, if that's your best, I don't think much of it, and so I told the other fellow who came here."

"You have had a previous police visit?" Bobby asked. "I didn't know," and that remark was perfectly true, for the visit referred to had not been from the police—far from it, indeed. "Did he give his name? Did he show his credentials?"

"Called himself Owen—Bobby Owen, I think," Mr Smith answered, ignoring the last part of the question. "I didn't like him, I didn't like the questions he asked. Nosing, snooping. Said he was one of the biggest men at Scotland Yard. Told me he would issue a warrant if I didn't give him full information."

"If he talked such nonsense as that you might have guessed he was an impostor," Bobby retorted. "Did you answer his questions? What information did you give him? It's serious, perhaps very serious."

"I told him what I've told you—that there was nothing in the house to interest any burglar. If he was an impostor, how was I to know? How do I know you aren't?"

"Well, here are my credentials," Bobby said, producing them. "Also I have a uniform man with me and you have a telephone, so you can ring up the police station and ask. Mr Smith, I must warn you very seriously that for some reason this house is being an object of great interest to an expert and daring gang of thieves. I don't know why. There must be some reason. You say you can't suggest one. But it must exist. Without your co-operation there's very little we can do. Without full co-operation from the public no police force can do much. With it, we can probably assure your safety and that of your niece. Otherwise we are helpless."

"There's nothing here to interest burglars," Mr Smith persisted, though now plainly a little shaken, for Bobby had spoken gravely. "Nothing."

"There's the furniture in this room," Bobby pointed out. "Any one could see it was valuable."

"You've noticed that, have you?" the old man grumbled, as if half resentful at the discovery of his private treasure, half pleased that the worth of his possessions had been recognized. "I've had our parson in here, and he never said a word—might have been hire-purchase stuff, for all he knew. Insured for three thousand at present, item by item, and I'm having it re-valued soon. All right stuff, not a wrong item in the lot. I buy nothing till I've had it vetted by an expert."

"Very wise indeed," agreed Bobby, thinking that probably the purchased articles represented the expert's taste, and their arrangement in the room that of Mr Smith.

He wondered a little what had induced this old retired business man to take an interest in collecting furniture, and, as if answering the unspoken query, Mr Smith went on:

"Grandfather clock I had. Didn't think much of it. Big thing, rather in the way, and took a deal of winding up. It belonged to my old grannie, and she had it from her grannie. Well, a fellow came along and offered me twenty shillings for it. I said two quid and it's yours, never thinking he would pay up. But he did on the spot, and collected the clock same day. Next thing I knew there it was in a shop window, priced fifty guineas and marked sold. I wasn't going to be had again, not if I knew it."

Before Bobby could make any comment on this melancholy tale, the door opened and there appeared the tall girl Bobby had seen at the 'Glorious' cinema. Now a closer view confirmed his first impression of her as a buxom, Junoesque young woman, fair-haired, her chief claim to attractiveness lying in her youth and fine physique, and more especially in her voice—a soft, caressing voice. A coaxing sort of voice, indeed, though, too, with a rather curiously harsh undertone that might, one felt, become at times more marked. Her complexion was bad, her nose large, prominent and well shaped, her mouth soft, full, red-lipped, drooping at the corners with a hint of a tendency to pout at small provocation. A kissable mouth it might have been called. It seemed generally to be slightly open, and then it showed two rows of large, strong, slightly protuberant teeth, white and even. Of these she seemed inclined to be a little proud, for she clearly liked to display them by switching on a smile at extremely frequent intervals. At the moment this smile was in full working order, and her small grey eyes were intent on Bobby, as if on the watch for any observable reaction.

"Oh, nunks, darling," she was saying in that full, yet soft, caressing voice of hers—"oh, nunks, have they come bothering you again? I do call it a shame."

She pronounced 'shame' as if it rhymed with 'slime,' and indeed at times, but not very often, she slipped into that old cockney trick of giving the 'a' vowel an accent of the long 'i'. It is a trick of dialect that, like others of the kind, is vanishing under the steady flow, day in, day out, of 'B.B.C.' English. But though she uttered this protest against what she called a 'shime' with every appearance of fervour, the more or less dazzling smile she was bestowing on Bobby remained unchanged.

"They seem to have the idea," Mr Smith began; and then was interrupted by a fit of coughing that sent Miss Smith rushing away to fetch what she called 'your medicine, nunks, darling, you mustn't forget what the doctor said.'

'Nunks, darling' took the proffered glass, grumbled at her for 'fussing', and drank off the contents, which in fact did seem to relieve his cough.

"Elizabeth," he grumbled to Bobby, "seems to think I'm still a child—in my second childhood, I suppose."

"Well, nunks, if you are," Miss Smith protested, "I only wish I had half your second-childhood brains—and don't be an old cross-patch. You've just simply got to be looked after. I'm not going to have you ill while I'm in this house. Even though you are wonderful for your age and likely to live to be a hundred, the doctor says, and then I shall be so old you'll have to start taking care of me."

Mr Smith chuckled at this as at an old and much-appreciated joke.

"If we've not both been murdered in our beds first," he remarked, still chuckling. "They've just been telling me that some day we shall come downstairs, probably with our throats cut, and find there's been a burglar here and he's walked off with my Buhl table under one arm and my Queen Anne bureau under the other."

"Those two great things," Miss Smith exclaimed. "Oh, how silly!"

"Have you ever heard," Bobby asked, "of daylight raids by organized gangs of very unpleasant people? We really don't want to find you and Miss Smith tied up in the coal cellar while a motor-van stolen from some big West-End firm is being used to cart off all this furniture of yours. There've been one or two very nasty affairs like that. I expect you do sometimes have vans here delivering your purchases or to take away anything you want to get rid of to make room for something better. I doubt if your neighbours would even consider giving an alarm or thinking it in any way suspicious."

"Oh, how awful!" cried Miss Smith, and she turned to Mr Smith as if appealing for protection. "Oh, Uncle John, you wouldn't let them, would you?"

"Certainly not. Lot of rubbish, nonsense, perfect nonsense," declared Mr. Smith, thus appealed to. "Certainly not, my dear—nothing to be afraid of."

"Oh, I'm so glad," said Miss Smith, with a long sigh of relief.

"I've tried to warn you, as was my duty," Bobby said. "There is nothing more that can be done at present—certainly not without your full and willing co-operation. As far as our very limited man power allows, we shall continue to be on the look-out. Also I would like to advise you to install a burglar alarm—one operated from your bedroom, so that the moment you hear any suspicious sound you can give an alarm. Our men will be on the spot as quickly as possible, and they won't grumble even if it's only been the cat knocking off the dust-bin lid."

"Oh, nunks, do!" Miss Smith cried. "In my room, too. I shall feel ever so much safer. I haven't your iron nerves, you know, nunks."

"Oh, well, well, we'll see about it," was Mr Smith's response to this appeal, and he made it with a faint, slightly pathetic approach to the aged shadow of a swagger.

With that the interview ended. Bobby and Ford retired, the last sound they heard proceeding from that treasure house of old furniture, and object of strange interest to Cy King and his fellow-gangsters, being the voice of Mrs Day calling out that breakfast had been ready ages and could she serve it?

"That young lady," Ford remarked to Bobby as they walked away, "has the old boy completely under her thumb. Eats out of her hand, he does."

Bobby thought this presented rather a charming picture of some one held flat under a large and heavy thumb, and at the same time contriving to eat out of the palm of the hand appertaining to the said thumb. He remarked that Mr Smith was beginning to show his age, and Ford said he didn't suppose Miss Elizabeth Smith would have to wait long, if it was a nice little legacy in his will that she had in mind.

"Which is my idea of what she's after," Ford declared, "and, what's more, just a bit too fond of giving the glad eye all round. She tried it on you first, sir, and when you didn't catch on, then she switched to me, if you noticed."

"I did," Bobby assured him. "Just keeping herself in practice, I should say. It must be a bit dull for her, dancing attendance on the old boy all the time. What I didn't like about her," he added slowly, "was her nose."

"Her nose, sir?" asked Ford, very puzzled, inclined to think there must be some obscure joke somewhere, if only he were quick enough to see it.

But Bobby, deep in thought, made no attempt to explain.

CHAPTER V
"PLEASE COMMUNICATE"

SOME DAYS passed. No more suspicious characters were seen near The Haven, Acres Lane. No more visits were made to Jimmy Joe's in Soho. Cy King was reported harmlessly occupied in the little sweet-shop he ran with the aid of a young woman, known as Gladys, who either was or was not Mrs Cy King—no one's business which, and no one asked. One 'disincentive'—lovely word—to curious neighbourly enquiry into the matter was the fact that Mrs or Miss Gladys had a name for being handy with the end of a broken beer bottle. It was even reported that Cy King himself regarded her with a wary eye and was not much inclined to risk unnecessarily annoying her. For the jagged end of a broken beer-bottle is a horrid thing to have pushed with emphasis and vigour into your face.

At the moment, however, Gladys was away—visiting friends in Canada, it was understood. Certainly frequent letters from Canada were arriving. A devoted Gladys, evidently. During her absence her place behind the counter was being taken by her aunt, of whom no one before had heard. Why should they, for that matter? She was a ponderous, ever-smiling, middle-aged woman, who said her name was Smith—Lizzie Smith—did beautiful needlework, described herself as a qualified nurse, and in fact appeared to know something of medical matters. She was fond of saying what a lovely change it was from continually recurring sick-rooms and refractory patients, to serving the dear little children with 'all sorts', toffee apples and other delights. It was a pity that the dear little children did not seem much inclined to reciprocate. Even these tough Soho youngsters had developed an odd habit of taking their pennies elsewhere ever since Cy and Gladys had begun to occupy the shop. It was even occasionally a matter for a 'dare' to make a purchase there, though no clear reason or any shadow of a complaint had ever been suggested to account for this reluctance. It was just a general unease the children seemed to feel. Nor did this comparative absence of trade seem in any way to trouble either Cy or Gladys.

Then, Sunday—or Sam Deedes, to give him his proper name—was known to be sedulously pursuing his customary vocation of hawking in the West End such things as jumping beans or toy balloons, or, on occasion, extremely cheap nylon stockings of mysterious origin. Tiny Garden, too, seemed quite innocently and happily working in an amusement arcade, where he was remarkably successful in persuading captious visitors of the totally unfounded nature of any complaint they put forward about the working of the machines. And at The Haven the quiet, placid domestic routine continued unbroken, with Mr Smith poring over the quarterly catalogue from Christie's he subscribed for, Mrs Day out and about at her shopping, and Miss Elizabeth Smith still winning golden opinions from all by the unremitting and patient care she took of her ageing uncle. Dr Atkins, their doctor—who was also, as it happened, the police surgeon—had remarked in careless chat with the Southam inspector that Mr Smith was likely to live another five or ten years. There was nothing wrong with him except, as Dr Atkins put it, 'A.D.'. He was frail certainly, there was a growing very slow, almost imperceptible slackening of the vital processes, his chest was inclined to be troublesome. Extremes of cold or damp, or even any violent shock, might of course have immediately serious results. But nothing of that sort was likely to happen—not while he was being looked after with such loving care by his niece.

"Better luck than any crabbed old bachelor deserves," declared Dr. Atkins—"getting a niece like her to drop in on him out of the clouds, so to speak. Not every girl would put up so cheerfully with his whims and fancies and grumbling."

All this information Bobby had received, read, considered and tucked away at the back of his mind. There he hoped it would rest for ever undisturbed, as he hoped would also rest undisturbed the various reports and documents dealing with the matter he had had filed away in their appropriate pigeonhole.

At the moment, however, he was looking at an advertisement on which his eye had chanced to fall in the 'personal'—erstwhile 'agony'—column of the 'Daily Announcer'. It was quite short, and merely asked if a Miss Betty Smith, lately arrived from Canada on the liner 'Queen of the Seas', would "please communicate" with Mrs Wyllie, who had received her letter and cable, and was still expecting her. A letter box address was given, and Bobby sat and read and wondered, and all the time grew more and more uneasy.

Betty Smith? Was Betty short for Elizabeth? A second Elizabeth Smith? Well, why not? Very likely there are dozens, hundreds of them. Lizzie Smith in Cy King's sweet-shop, for example. Recently arrived from Canada? Well, Elizabeth Smith of Southam came from Toronto, and Toronto is in Canada, isn't it? But, then, she had been in England for months, certainly she had not 'recently arrived'. And Canada was where the Gladys who was or wasn't Mrs Cy King, and who had a name for being handy with broken bottles, had recently been visiting on unknown business.

Bobby didn't like it, and the more he thought about it the less he liked it. The sort of sixth sense that comes to many engaged in the war with crime, and that sometimes warns them that under the most innocent appearance may lie concealed the most sinister realities, seemed to tell him now that here were hidden dark and evil things. He sat and thought, and hesitated so long that he nearly forgot his lunch. Realizing this, and much startled thereby, he dictated a brief note to his typist to say that the advertisement had attracted attention and that Scotland Yard would be glad to have a talk with the advertiser.

For a time there was no response, though the advertisement appeared once more. Bobby did not forget, for he seldom forgot anything, but he did tuck the incident away at the back of his mind, there to remain till wanted—if ever. Then, early in the following week, a slip was brought to him to say that one Edward Wyllie, in response to a letter received, had called to see Commander Owen, as requested.

By way of a change, Bobby's desk was fairly clear, the 'In' and 'Out' trays dealt with for the time, and Bobby asked for Mr Wyllie to be shown in at once. Accordingly, there appeared a fair-haired, blue-eyed young man, tall and well-built, with an enormous mouth that utterly ruined any claims he might otherwise have had to good looks, a deep, pleasant voice, huge hands of that type which appear as if they must be extraordinarily clumsy and yet prove to be equally adept with sledge-hammers and with the tiniest of adjustments, and with a very distrustful, even sulky expression, much like that a mouse may be supposed to wear as it hesitatingly approaches the dangling, tempting morsel of cheese.

Bobby did his best to put his visitor at his ease, offering him a cigarette, waving him to a chair, saying he was glad to see him and how kind it was of him to call, commenting casually on the weather, and so on. These blandishments had small effect. If anything, they merely increased the newcomer's obvious disquiet. Only too evident that he did not at all like finding himself where he was at the moment. Bobby wondered why. For some of the underworld Scotland Yard does seem to possess that sort of fatal fascination that great depths possess for others or that the moth feels for the candle. But Bobby did not think that this young man was either of that type or that disposition, though, indeed, as Bobby well knew from his own experience, first impressions go often sadly astray. In this case it might be nothing more than shyness, though again this was not a young man Bobby took to be of a noticeably shy disposition. Finally, to bring his visitor to the point, Bobby remarked that the advertisement had appeared a second time.

"I paid for three insertions," Wyllie explained, rather with the air of regretting so lavish an expenditure. "It was my mother's idea. When I got your note I didn't know what to do. No reason why Betty should show up if she doesn't want to, and she mightn't like it one little bit if she knew we had been to the police."

"She won't learn it from us, you may be sure," Bobby declared reassuringly. "I take it, then, you are Mrs Wyllie's son, the lady whose name was in the advertisement?"

"That's right. She's rather worried. She sticks to it something must have happened, or she would have heard."

"Are you relatives?"

"No. I don't quite see we've any right to interfere. Betty may have met some one on the boat, or she may have just simply changed her mind or anything. Very likely mother will get a post-card one morning. Only she does worry so. It's upsetting her. I had to promise to do something."

"There was a cable mentioned in the advertisement. Was that from the missing young lady?"

"Yes. I don't know we ought to call her missing. She wrote to say she was coming over here on a visit, and mother wrote back to ask her to stay with her as long as she liked. Mother lives at Bournemouth, and she wanted Betty to make it her head-quarters while she was here. Betty wrote to say she would like to, but she wasn't quite sure when she could get a passage and she would send a cable to say when she was starting. Well, the cable came all right, and that's the last we've heard."

"Has Miss Betty other friends here or any relatives?"

"Not that I ever heard of—except an old uncle she's never seen and she said in her first letter she would try to look up. What's the matter?"

"Nothing," Bobby answered, annoyed that he had been betrayed into showing signs of uneasiness. No detective, he used to say in the lectures he sometimes gave both in the provinces and in London to C.I.D. aspirants, ought ever to show either surprise or any other emotion. "I just happened to remember something. Coincidence. That's all. Go on, please."

There was a short pause. The two men were looking steadily at each other. A wave of doubt and fear seemed to pass between them. Then Wyllie said:

"All? Is it all?" When Bobby did not reply at once, Wyllie went on:

"You made me think for the moment there was quite a lot more." Bobby still did not reply, but he regarded the young man with more interest. More acute than he seemed, Bobby thought. Wyllie continued: "I don't quite know what right we have to interfere."

"When a young woman," Bobby told him, "comes to this country and her friends she had arranged to stay with don't hear from her, there may be no reason for any uneasiness. As you said just now, a post-card may arrive any morning. But also there may be very good reason for uneasiness. Had she any money? Jewellery?"

"Oh, lord, no! I suppose she will have saved something, and I think her father left her a few hundreds or so. Nothing much.

Her father was a lawyer, and she has a job in what used to be his office. It was taken over by another firm when he died. In her letter to mother she said if mother really didn't mind putting her up she would be able to stay much longer than if she had to pay hotel bills, and she did want to find this old uncle of hers, if he is still alive. Some notion of taking him back with her and looking after him. Women are always wanting to look after something, and I suppose an old uncle is better than cats, anyhow. Fat-headed idea, if you ask me. She's probably got enough to do to look after herself, without taking on old pauper uncles."

"Is he a pauper? If she doesn't know him, why does she think that?"

"Well, the last they heard he was bankrupt and a warrant out against him for some bankruptcy offence or another. Trying to start again without letting on he had been there before. Betty didn't seem to know exactly. I rather imagine that a good deal of Betty's father's money went down the drain, too, in the bankruptcy, and he was more than a bit peeved about it. Thought his brother—Betty's uncle, that is—had been trying to do too much without letting on what he was up to. Changing a good sound little catering business into a string of chain shops, like Lyons, without consulting his brother. And it didn't come off."

CHAPTER VI
"YOU ARE AFRAID"

THERE WAS a long silence. From without came the murmur of traffic along the Embankment where the great stream of London's daily business flowed on by the old river's side. Bobby was lost in thought—uneasy, troubled thought. So little known, so much to fear. Young Ted Wyllie sat watching him, and in him, too, a dark, brooding fear he had till then hardly acknowledged even to himself was slowing growing, ever darker, ever heavier. His voice had become a little shrill as he burst out suddenly:

"What's it mean? What are you—afraid of? You are afraid."

"Yes," Bobby agreed. "Yes, I am. But very likely entirely without cause. Didn't somebody say once that all our worst troubles never happened? True of our fears as well, perhaps. But I think we would be justified in making a few inquiries. They'll have to be extremely discreet, extremely cautious, and we shall have to be ready to drop them instanter if it turns out that the young lady is merely staying with some other friends and has just been a little remiss in letting you know. Quite likely. Much the most likely, in fact. All the same," he added slowly, "I never did like coincidences. The most extraordinary coincidences do occur. But seldom, with any follow-up. I mean you may find sitting next to you in a restaurant neither you nor he had ever visited before an old friend you hadn't seen for thirty years. But you won't be likely to find also that that old friend had been looking for you in order to offer you the very job you wanted more than any other."

By now Bobby, as had been partly his intention, had talked away that cloud of distressed unease which had been showing signs of disturbing Ted Wyllie's self-possession. Wyllie said more quietly:

"Yes, but where does coincidence come in?"

"Only because in another case we've had our attention drawn to, there's another Elizabeth Smith who came over here to join her uncle some time ago, and we've had hints that a burglary or something of the sort may be happening soon where she and her uncle live. Just a coincidence of name," he explained, waving it airily aside. "By the way, have you any idea where this bankruptcy you mentioned occurred—in what part of the country?"

"I think it was Bristol, I think I remember hearing that. I'm not sure."

"Oh, Bristol," Bobby said, making a note. "How was it you first came to know Miss Smith? Was there any previous connection? Any introduction? Anything like that? It might give us a starting point."

"Her brother was a pal of mine in the R.A.F.," Wyllie explained. "Decent type. He had his on a bombing raid we did. We were hit by flak, and he died before we could make it. I had to tell Betty. That's all. He was the best ever—very decent type."

Wyllie spoke with a great air of hard-bitten indifference, but the still deeply felt emotion that lay beneath was easy to see. Bobby found and lighted a cigarette for himself and offered

another to Wyllie. Lighting a cigarette is sometimes a conveni-
ence—gives time for reflection or covers an awkward pause.

"And his sister?" Bobby asked. "I suppose you met her
through him?"

"Yes, she came over when he did, and she joined up with the
Waafs about the same time. She and Bill—that's her brother—
used to spend most of their leave with mother at Bournemouth.
They were there when there was the big raid on Bournemouth.
Mother always said Betty saved her life."

"Did you see much of her?"

"Well," Wyllie answered, with some slight hesitation. "Off
and on, yes. As much as mother could manage, anyhow. You
see, mother had got it into her head that she wanted me and
Betty to hitch up. I wasn't having any. Jolly nice girl and all that,
but I had made up my mind I wasn't going to leave a widow and
a baby or two to get along on the sort of pension they'd have. I
never expected to get through. None of the chaps did, though
not just yet. Only I did. Without a scratch. Besides, Betty didn't
want either. Why should she?"

"What are you doing now?"

"Toys."

"Toys?" Bobby repeated, slightly puzzled.

"I doubled up with another bloke," Wyllie explained. "Clever
type. Dolls and toy soldiers, mostly. He designs 'em. And the
dolls dressed in all the latest rig-out. Retail price a fiver or more.
You can't think where people get the money from—jolly good
thing they do. Our toy-soldier line does well in the U.S.—quite
a dollar-earner. All of 'em correct to scale in every detail. It's
damn funny, turning raw hell into toys and money. I suppose
that's life. He's going to try his hand at a toy atom-bomb next.
I said, why not a toy hell with a lot of little toy devils running
in and out? I look after the selling end. Sometimes I think I'll
get out and try farming, as the only clean job left on earth; only
we're rather booming, piling the coin up. And then you get
among farmers and hear 'em talk, and you soon find out what
they put across each other and the public."

"I'm afraid you are growing cynical, Mr Wyllie," Bobby said.

"I've been through the war," Wyllie answered simply. Then he said: "Do you really think there's any reason for mother to worry about Betty?"

"No reason at all," Bobby told him quickly. "Please tell your mother so. Still, we don't like it when a young lady comes to England on a visit and her friends she was going to stay with hear nothing of her."

"What you really mean," Wyllie remarked in his most casual, indifferent tone, "is that there's every reason to worry like hell, but I'm not to tell mother so."

"Well, I wouldn't put it so strongly as that," protested Bobby.

"What can you do, anyway?" demanded Wyllie. "Betty will give me raw hell if it's all right—you, too, if she thinks you've been meddling. She can—I've seen her go in off the deep end all right, when she found one of our chaps had been playing the fool with one of her girls."

"An unpleasant prospect," Bobby agreed, shaking his head gravely. "Nothing we dislike more than being given raw hell by an attractive young lady. But an occupational risk. Do you know if Miss Smith had any intention of staying in London before going on to your mother at Bournemouth?"

"Not that I know of. But that's what we thought at first. I thought of asking a few of them. Only there are such a lot—hotels, I mean."

"There certainly are," Bobby agreed. "Most of South Kensington is hotel and most of Bloomsbury is boarding-house. But that's a job we can easily cover. Every constable will be asked to inquire at every hotel on his beat. We'll ask at the hospitals, too. Luckily there aren't so many of them. One good thing," he added, with an air of relief, "if any young lady does turn up here to give us raw hell for not minding our own business, I can detail a sergeant to take it. What sergeants are for. I know. Not so long since I was one myself. Have you made sure Miss Smith did in fact arrive—by the 'Queen of the Seas', wasn't it?"

"Well, her name's on the passenger list. I asked."

"Are you sure it was the same Miss Smith?"

"I never thought of that," Wyllie began, and paused. "I rang up and asked, and they said a Miss Elizabeth Smith was on the passenger list, so I took it that was all right."

"We always try to check everything," Bobby explained. "If there are any developments, we shall probably check your identity and your record in the Air Force. Could you supply us with a photograph of Miss Smith and as full a description as possible?"

"Yes, but look here," Wyllie said doubtfully. "You know, I don't feel comfortable about all this."

"Isn't that precisely why you inserted your advertisement? Isn't that why you are here?"

"Oh, well, I suppose so . . . yes . . . only . . . you've never seen Betty in a paddy," he added ingenuously. "I have."

"We'll take full responsibility," Bobby said, careful not to smile. "The fact is, Mr Wyllie, some things you have told me have made me uncomfortable, too—very uncomfortable. I can't tell you the reason. I will just ask you to believe me. The only question now is whether we can have your full co-operation. Inquiry will be made. Your co-operation may make all the difference between whether that inquiry succeeds—or fails."

"Oh, all right, then," Wyllie assented, but without enthusiasm. "I've got a snap." He brightened up suddenly. "Mother's got rather a good one, I believe. I'll ask her for it."

"Ask her, too," Bobby went on, again inwardly amused, again careful not to show it, at this innocent betrayal of the boy's reluctance to part with his own snap of Betty Smith and of his relief at remembering that he could probably induce his mother to surrender hers; "ask her to give us as good a description of Miss Smith as she can. I mean the things a photo doesn't show. Personal habits. Trifles. If she prefers coffee or tea in the afternoon, perhaps. Her style of dress, her colouring, any little trick or mannerism Mrs Wyllie can remember."

"Well," Ted Wyllie answered, still very puzzled, "I do know she was rather gone on cooking. I've known her ask in a restaurant how they did something or another she thought good—it generally was good, too, believe me. She told mother she wanted to get out of being a typist and start up as a cooking instructor. That's what got mother. She said it was so nice to find a modern girl really interested in cooking. Only how's that going to help? What can it matter whether any one prefers coffee or tea?"

"It all helps to build up the picture of the person we are looking for," Bobby told him. "In this case we may possibly ask every restaurant and café in the country to let us know if one of their customers has been a young lady with a Canadian accent and who seemed interested in the dishes served."

"But, good lord!" protested Wyllie, "you can't possibly . . . millions of 'em . . . take years."

"Organization," Bobby explained. "That's detective work—not, in cold, prosaic matter of fact, identifying footmarks in the snow or examining hairs under a microscope, and so obtaining the name and address of the murderer. A dull, routine, everyday job, in fact. But don't tell any one. Why destroy glamour? And we do have our moments." He paused, and his face grew lined and hard, for he was not sure but that one of those moments was close upon him. He went on: "Have you had many replies to your advertisement?"

"Rather. Dozens. Circulars from private detectives. Most of them wanted payment in advance. I wasn't falling for that. Besides, I didn't feel like putting private detectives on Betty. Other chaps saying they thought they knew the young lady, and if I would send them their fare they would come and see me. Waste-paper-basket stuff, nearly all of it. Oh, and a few religious fanatics telling me to put my trust on High and would I come to their meeting next Sunday? One or two Spiritualists as well. Obvious fakes. One chap said he thought he could give me information if I would meet him."

"Did you?" Bobby asked.

"Yes. I thought I might as well. The letter sounded a bit as if he really might have something to say and he didn't want money in advance. It was one of those Lyons places. Tottenham Court Road."

"What was he like?"

"Well, as a matter of fact," Wyllie answered slowly, "he was a bit like you. Much the same size and make, only rather better-looking—sorry, I didn't mean that quite. Only he really was the type girls fall for. He was wearing what I took to be an old school tie of some sort. I didn't recognize it."

"Would you know it again?"

"Oh, yes. And a serge suit like yours. I noticed it as soon as I came in."

"I'll get you to do a bit of detective work," Bobby said. "If you are willing, that is. Will you go to any rather smart men's shop—Bond Street or Piccadilly—ask to look at a range of old school ties, and if you see the one this man was wearing, ask which it is. Buy anything you like—scarf, pair of gloves, shirt—to give you an opening. We'll refund whatever it cost. I shall have to ask you to hand it over, though. They keep a pretty strict eye on expense sheets here, you know."

"I'm getting a close-up on police methods, aren't I?" Wyllie grumbled. "I wish you would tell me . . . I never expected all this." He hesitated. He said abruptly: "You're giving me a scare."

"Purely precautionary," Bobby told him. "Probably a lot of fuss about nothing. Work of supererogation. Most detective work is. So don't worry, and don't let Mrs Wyllie worry."

"Just you try and stop her when she's that way," her son retorted.

"What did this man you met have to say?" Bobby asked next, showing no inclination to accept the task offered.

"Oh, he asked a lot of footling questions—just like you. Sorry again. I didn't mean it like that."

"Possibly both his questions and ours may be less footling than they seem," Bobby answered, a little grimly, for he liked not at all this reminder of that companion of Cy King's who, together with Cy, had visited the house where resided the other and earlier Betty Smith.

"I told him," Wyllie went on, "I was willing to pay for any information likely to be useful, but not till I had tried it out, and till then it was no good wasting any more time talking. He looked a bit peeved. I gave him my name and address, and told him to ring me any time he had anything to say, and then I paid for my own bun and coffee and told the girl he could pay for his. He looked quite a lot more peeved then."

With that the interview ended, Bobby promising to let Wyllie know in due time of any results achieved—or not achieved. Nor had Wyllie long been gone before one of the C.I.D. men appeared.

"It's about the gentleman that's just been in," he explained. "I've been on duty keeping an eye on Jimmy Joe's in Soho. You know the place, sir?"

"What about it?" Bobby asked.

"Gentleman that's just gone out been there once or twice, seen in company with Tiny Garden."

"Thank you," Bobby said. "Positive identification? Yes, I'll remember. It may be very important. Glad you spotted it. Good work."

CHAPTER VII
"ME? O.K."

"IT'S AN extraordinarily difficult case," Bobby remarked discontentedly to Olive that evening. "All sorts of hints and possibilities, and yet nothing you can be sure of. Just a mass of shifting sands of suspicion. There's this Wyllie lad. Favourable impression made, as we say, but, then, it's the job of a confidence man to make a favourable impression, and what was Wyllie doing at Jimmy Joe's, also recently visited by Mr Smith's housekeeper? It's like trying to make a sketch of a landscape in a fog that keeps thickening and clearing. And always in the background Cy King and his pal he seems to want to get up as a kind of," said Bobby indignantly, "imitation me. And of all the cheek—"

He left the sentence unfinished, brooding in angry silence on what he felt was deliberate insolence and—much more important—contained hidden within it some sort of challenge, perhaps merely impudent, perhaps much more serious.

For Bobby had no thought of under-valuing Cy, in whom he recognized an unusual combination of cunning and of reckless daring.

"What about making inquiries in Canada?" Olive asked.

"We could," Bobby agreed. "We could ask for information about a Betty Smith who left Toronto some months ago to join an uncle in England. They would probably tell us that hunting for needles in haystacks was what they loved above all else, but they did prefer some sort of hint as to size and kind of needle required, there being many different needles or Betty Smiths in and around Toronto. I do suspect the Southam girl of being a fake, but she has been recognized and accepted by old Mr Smith, and he ought to know. Anyhow, if mischief is really intended we've given warning that we are there."

"What sort of mischief?" Olive asked.

"Well, what?" Bobby asked, and Olive did not answer. Bobby went on: "If the girl is no more Mr Smith's niece than I am, it's quite plain the idea is to get hold of his money. That can only be done by inducing him to make a will in her favour. What would be his expectation of life once that was properly signed and witnessed?"

But Olive shook her head.

"I don't believe that girl's the murder kind," she said slowly and thoughtfully. "More what you would call a good-time girl. Remember her mouth—soft and drooping, a sort of perpetual pout to it. There's not a hard line in her face, and I thought she was trying her best to look after the old man, and rather enjoying doing it, too."

"Well, I don't know," Bobby said doubtfully. "You may be right, but it's a big thing they're on. That is, if I'm right. And Cy King dodging about in the background."

"Yes, yes," Olive said, and looked less comfortable. "I wish you could get rid of him somehow."

"Then," Bobby continued, "there's this story about another Betty Smith her friends haven't heard of since she landed. She comes from Canada, too, and she has an old uncle somewhere, she says, though apparently her old uncle is, or was, a bankrupt. But bankrupts sometimes made good and turn into rich men. Suppose it's the same uncle, and the missing niece is the right niece? And suppose she's being kept out of the way? And if it's like that—well, it doesn't look too good."

"But all that's only guesswork," Olive protested uneasily.

"Oh, yes, nothing solid to go on. But you can't forget all this about a girl who never turns up at the friends she was going to stay with. Precious little to go on there. No real proof she is missing in any police sense of the word." He took a photograph from his pocket. He said: "Wyllie wired his mother to bring it up and leave it at the Yard. I got it just before I left."

He handed it to Olive. It showed a young woman in the uniform of a junior officer of the women's branch of the Royal Air Force. Olive studied it long and carefully.

"She looks a nice girl," she pronounced finally. "Nice-looking, too, and if her colouring and complexion are all right, a little more than only nice-looking. I wonder if she knows how to dress. I do think uniforms are horrid for women, don't you? You can't tell, can you?"

"Tell what?" Bobby asked.

"Well, anything. I mean, the way a girl dresses shows . . ."

"Does it?" said Bobby.

"Well, of course," said Olive. She studied the photograph again. "What did you say?" she asked.

"Me? Nothing," Bobby answered.

Olive looked up with a slightly startled air.

"I thought I heard you say: 'Me. O.K.'"

"You're dreaming, my girl," Bobby told her. "Time you were in bed." He took the photograph, and in his turn studied it long and thoughtfully. He found himself wondering if this pleasant-looking young girl were indeed in danger of her life, or whether there was a perfectly good, simple reason for her failure to get in touch with her friends. Not, he thought, as far as one can judge from a photograph, the sort of girl who would unnecessarily cause worry and inconvenience to other people. It was pure fancy, of course, that made the photograph seem to take on an air of appeal, as of one crying desperately for help, from out of the uttermost depths. Too late, perhaps. Who could tell? He put it down impatiently, angry with the sick fancies that seemed invading his mind. "Time we were in bed," he declared again, and added in accents of profound gloom: "I don't suppose I shall sleep a wink all night worrying about what it all means and—and—"

He left the sentence unfinished, but Olive knew well that what was in his mind was the gnawing, dreadful doubt whether two lives were not in imminent danger, if indeed, for that matter, it was not already too late to take effective measures to help and to protect.

Not that Olive was unduly worried by the prospect of Bobby's possible sleepless night. She had heard that forecast made before, but had never known it fulfilled. For indeed he possessed that almost priceless gift of being able to put out of his conscious mind for the time all doubts and difficulties till the hour came to give them fresh attention.

Next morning—after, by the way, nearly eight hours' dreamless slumber—there was brought to Bobby, busy in his room at the Yard, a letter addressed to the Commissioner and endorsed in that gentleman's familiar and crabbed handwriting:

"What's all this about?"

What it was about was Mr Smith's violent indignation at the annoyance he was suffering at the hands of the Southam police, apparently instigated thereto by an individual calling himself Bobby Owen, representing himself, most likely untruthfully, as employed at Scotland Yard, and not fit to be employed anywhere. After this genial introduction, the letter went on to say that Mr Smith did not wish it to be thought by his neighbours that he was under the supervision of the police. He considered it damaging to his character and reputation to have plain-clothes police any one could tell at a glance were police—if only, said the letter spitefully, by the size of their boots—always hanging about his house or banging at his door. Unless he received an immediate apology and a promise that the annoyance would cease immediately he would be forced to instruct his lawyer to commence proceedings with a view to obtaining an injunction and damages. There was also a specially vicious suggestion that certain marks on the back door of 'The Haven' had been made deliberately by the police themselves in order to give them an excuse to come snooping.

"Be sure your breach of regulations will find you out," murmured Bobby sadly, and went off to see the Commissioner, to whom he told the whole story.

"You'll have to drop it," decreed that dignitary. "We can't afford to have proceedings like that started against us, farcical, of course, and dismissed on sight, I hope. I don't know, though. You can't trust lawyers. They might dig up some old witchcraft act or another, just for the fun of the thing, and try to make it apply. Anyhow, think how the papers would revel in it. The headlines, the screams of 'Gestapo in London.' Won't do, Owen won't do at all. The ancient Egyptians didn't know their luck."

"Ancient Egyptians, sir?" asked Bobby, puzzled by this somewhat abrupt change of subject.

"Ancient Egyptians," repeated the Commissioner firmly. "They only had ten plagues. Trifles—locusts and that sort of thing." The Commissioner, his memory failing him, did not attempt to go into further details. He went on: "The whole bunch of them a flea-bite compared with the eleventh they never knew—the Press," he concluded dramatically.

"Well, sir—yes, of course," agreed Bobby and added, for he knew the 'Daily Announcer' was the Commissioner's favourite paper, read every day from first page to last: "We might rather miss the 'Daily Announcer', though."

"Oh, well, the 'Daily Announcer'" grumbled the Commissioner, and left it at that. "We'll have to apologize," he went on— "talk about perhaps too great zeal shown in this case, but there were very real grounds for uneasiness, but now the matter may be considered closed."

"Yes, sir," said Bobby doubtfully.

"Well, if people want to be murdered," snapped the Commissioner—"well, there you are. You can't protect people if they won't co-operate."

"No, sir," agreed Bobby, less doubtfully.

"Chiefly applies to this Smith bloke," the Commissioner went on. "Not to the missing girl you talk about. If she is missing. No reason why you shouldn't look into that. Discreetly, of course."

"Yes, sir," said Bobby.

"You can't help wondering," said the Commissioner.

"No, sir," said Bobby.

The Commissioner was studying the photograph from Bournemouth.

"Pleasant-looking girl," he said. "Sort of frank, jolly look about her. Got two daughters myself. Don't let anything happen to the kid if you can help it."

"No, sir," said Bobby stolidly, and wondered how he was to help it.

"By the way," the Commissioner added, "I rang up Southam about this plain-clothes-man story. They said none of their plain-clothes men had been near the place. Said they had done no more than instruct the man on the beat to keep a special eye on the house. Of course," he added sorrowfully, "the most truthful blokes think it's all right to pull wool over the boss's eye—and, what's more, they think he swallows it all. But Southam did seem to be in earnest this time."

"I can't say I like this plain-clothes-man story," Bobby said. "It's just possible that what it means is that Cy King and his pals—or Tiny Garden and his pals—have been hanging about again." He picked up Mr Smith's letter and read it once more. "Probably that's the explanation," he repeated, "and I don't like it."

"Nothing we can do," said the Commissioner; and, in hushed and awe-stricken tones, went on: "There might be a Question in Parliament if we aren't careful."

"We don't want that," agreed Bobby, himself shaken to the depths by this suggestion, which few indeed can hear unmoved.

The Commissioner was still staring at the photograph, which to him also had now taken on an air as of one crying for help and crying without hope. Rather shyly, for he was always a little scared of his subordinates, most of whom had so much greater experience in criminal matters than he had himself, he said:

"Do you think it possible this girl at Mr Smith's is not only not his niece but that he knows she isn't? Just calls her his niece to make it more respectable."

"It might be," Bobby agreed. "It's possible, certainly. One thing, I wouldn't mind betting is that Miss Smith's behind this letter. To my mind, there's more than a touch of sly feminine spite about it. Old Mr Smith would have been less catty and more abusive."

The Commissioner said he was inclined to think so, too, and repeated that you couldn't do much to protect or help people who wouldn't co-operate.

"If they want to be murdered, they've got to be murdered, I suppose," he declared; and Bobby said he thought so, too, but he didn't want it to happen, all the same.

CHAPTER VIII
"UNKNOWN DESTINATION"

EARLY THE following week there arrived from Liverpool a report which in no way lessened the latent unease in Bobby's mind, but yet did not seem to help in any way or to suggest any action that could usefully be taken.

"Doesn't make it any easier," Bobby told himself, and then he picked up the 'phone and made an appointment with Ted Wyllie for that afternoon.

Ted arrived punctually. He looked tired and worried, and he admitted, when Bobby said something to that effect, that he had been sleeping badly and having bad dreams, though what they were he could never remember.

"Sort of being in a hole somewhere and not able to get out," he said. "Never dreamt much in my life before. It's not knowing, I suppose. You've no news, I take it, from what you said when you rang me?"

"No, only an inconclusive report from Liverpool," Bobby told him. "Doesn't take us much farther forward."

"I don't believe," Ted said slowly and deliberately, almost as if he were reciting something he had learnt by heart but all the same was not quite sure of—"I don't believe Betty would be here all this time—it's three weeks now—without letting mother know. Not if she could help it. It's not like her. A letter might go wrong, but there's the 'phone. Mother's got one. Betty often used it when she was there. Even if she had forgotten the number she could easily look it up. It's second nature to Canadians. You said you had a report from Liverpool?"

"Yes. It confirms that Miss Betty Smith landed from the 'Queen of the Seas' on the date you gave us. We had the photograph we got from you reproduced, and it was identified by two or three of the staff. She is remembered by them as a very pleasant, friendly girl, full of fun. And it seems that none of the travellers' cheques issued to her in Canada have been cashed. They come to a substantial amount—about a hundred pounds."

"Well, what's she doing for money?" Ted said. He went on: "Mother's been wanting me to come to see you. She says—"

"Yes," Bobby prompted.

"I expect you'll laugh."

"Why?"

"Well, it sounds so cracked. I told mother you would only think me a fool. She started to cry." With that he started to wriggle on his chair. His face was more than red—crimson. "When a chap's mother starts crying . . ."

"Yes, of course," said Bobby.

"I had to promise. What she says is she's twice heard a voice when there was no one there. Well, you can't, can you? I mean to say, hear what isn't there to hear? But she sticks to it."

"What does Mrs Wyllie think the voice said you think she didn't hear?" Bobby asked.

This way of putting it seemed to puzzle Ted, who remained silent, regarding Bobby with a very worried air. It was some moments before he spoke. Bobby waited patiently. Then Ted said:

"She sticks to it the first time was in the middle of the night, when she was lying awake worrying about Betty and what could have happened, and she heard quite clearly, and it was Betty's voice, she says, and it said: 'Me, O.K.' Mother says she went to sleep then. Then two days later she heard it again when she wasn't doing anything in particular, but it was quite loud and clear, and it said the same thing: 'Me, O.K.'"

"'Me, O.K.'" Bobby repeated; and this time, being better prepared, he showed no sign of surprise or special interest. "You are sure those were the exact words? And Mrs Wyllie is sure she heard them?"

"Swears to it," Ted answered, a little relieved that Bobby had neither burst into loud guffaws nor given the quiet cynical, politely superior smile Ted had unconsciously dreaded still more. But, then, Bobby had not felt in the least like either the loud guffaw or the superior, cynical smile. Ted went on: "What do you make of it?"

"Nothing," Bobby answered promptly. "Not enough to go on. Quite likely it's only that Mrs Wyllie is badly worried and so she's imagining things. May be some sort of telepathy or thought-reading or something like that, I suppose. Even if it is, it doesn't take us much further forward. All the same, if Mrs Wyllie hears, or thinks she hears, anything more, let me know at once. 'Me, O.K.,'" he repeated. "Seems more reassuring than anything else."

"Yes, that's what I thought at first," Ted agreed. "Only I don't now, and you don't either, do you?"

Bobby was a trifle taken back by this remark, and by the suggestion thus conveyed once again of the unexpected and shrewd insight Ted seemed able to display at times. Bobby knew that in his heart he believed this message—if message it were—to be profoundly ominous, and yet he could not have told why. No sensible officer of police could allow himself to be affected in any way by the workings of the imagination of an elderly woman. Yet Olive also had heard or thought she heard. He knew that henceforth he was going to give to this problem a concentration of attention he had not till now felt able to afford. Answering Ted's remark, he said:

"Anyhow, it says 'O.K.'"

"That's what I told mother," Ted answered. "She wasn't having any," and the plain implication in his voice was that he wasn't either. "Look. Betty's got to be found."

"You may depend upon it that no effort will be spared," Bobby said, becoming as coldly official as he only did when he was deeply moved and didn't want any one to know. "At present it is not easy to say what the next step should be. Publicity might be dangerous, and publicity is often our greatest help in such cases."

"Why should it be dangerous?" Ted asked, but it was evident he neither expected nor wished for a reply, since also he already knew what it would be.

"Our Liverpool report," Bobby went on, "states that no trace of Miss Smith has been found further than that she took a taxi to Lime Street. Presumably she caught the London train. Fortunately at Euston a porter has been found who thinks he remembers her arrival. But he's not sure of the date. However, he was able to pick out her photograph from several we showed him. He remembers her because she seemed rather surprised at being met, and even a little doubtful about it."

"Who was it met her?" Ted asked quickly. "I don't see how any one could. No one knew she was coming except us. We didn't till we got her cable."

"You can't be sure about that, can you?" Bobby said. "She was met by a young man described by the porter as tall, as wearing a raincoat, as having his hat pulled down over his face, so that the porter didn't see him very clearly. But, then, he didn't take much notice. There was a car waiting. They drove off together in it. The porter didn't notice either the number of the car or the make. You couldn't expect him to."

"I don't see who it could have been—or why," Ted muttered. "It all sounds screwy . . . screwy," he repeated, but clearly that was not the word that was in his mind. "I don't understand it," he said, very loudly, almost defiantly.

"You didn't think of meeting her yourself?" Bobby asked.

"I should have if I had known in time," Ted answered, and he showed no sign of seeing that this question might have underlying implications. "I was in Ireland, trying to fix up an order for a big supply of Irish soldiers, all in correct Eire uniform, and after that I did a run round to our agents and customers. Mother wired me as soon as she got the cable saying Betty had sailed, but it followed me all round the place, from one hotel to another, till in the end it was sent back to our London office. If it had reached me in time I could have met her all right, but it didn't."

"That seems, then, as far as we can trace her," Bobby said. "She is met by an unknown young man for some unknown reason, since apparently no one but you knew she was coming, and together she and this unknown young man drive off together to an unknown destination."

"It doesn't sound too good," Ted muttered, "We've got to do something."

"Not much to go on," Bobby said. "I suppose the young lady wasn't a vegetarian?"

"Why, no. What's that got to do with it?"

"Well, presumably, if she wasn't vegetarian, some butcher somewhere will have a new customer. Grocers, too. A slender line, but it might work," and the thought in his mind, though he did not give it words, was that perhaps this young girl had now no further need of such things as meat and groceries.

"I don't know what to think," Ted said in the same low, muttering voice, and he had become so pale that clearly this time he understood better what was in Bobby's mind.

"You can't suggest," Bobby went on, "any other friend or acquaintance of hers she might have gone to or who might know something about her?"

"Not that I can think of," Ted answered. "There may be, of course. Look. It's all pretty upsetting. Only why? I mean—well, if something's happened—well, why should it?"

"The first thing is to find her," Bobby said, avoiding a direct answer, for at present he did not wish to mention Southam or that other Betty Smith, who also had left Canada to find or join an uncle. In her case, though, a rich uncle, not one to be described as an undischarged bankrupt. "We'll do everything we can. We may be able to dig up something to help. It won't be for want of trying if we fail. I don't like any more than you do this story of her being met by and driving off with some young man or another. But there's always the possibility of that post-card arriving some morning or a 'phone call to clear it all up. Let us know at once if anything out of the ordinary turns up, no matter what it is. By the way, did you do what I asked about identifying the tie you mentioned?"

"Oh yes. I bought a shirt. I'll keep it; it'll come in all right. They showed me some old school ties. It was a St. Dominic's the chap was wearing."

"An old school-fellow of mine, then," Bobby observed. "I wear it sometimes. Inspires confidence in those who know, and those who don't only think what rotten bad taste I have to wear such a sort of fiery cross, all the colours swearing at each other."

With that the interview ended, and Bobby sat for long in thought. He had asked the young man to call very largely because he wanted to form a fresh judgment of him. In that he had not had much success. Ted Wyllie gave the impression of being simple and straightforward, and yet at times he showed an unexpected subtlety of insight. There might well be in him depths he had not yet allowed to appear. As a business man he appeared energetic and successful, for even in what is called a 'sellers' market', it is not too easy to build up a new and prosperous business.

Could it possibly, Bobby asked himself, have been Ted himself who had met the lost girl? A bit of a dark horse, Mr Ted Wyllie, and not so simple as he seemed. It had sounded from the porter's account that the young man was a stranger to her, since she had shown surprise and some reluctance to accompany him. But the porter's account had been naturally somewhat vague; the surprise might simply have been surprise at seeing Ted, the reluctance to accompany him due to the abrupt change of plan, since presumably she had been intending to go on to Bournemouth. Ted had admitted he could have met her if he had received his mother's wire in time. Well, had he?

Not difficult to imagine a motive. Miss Betty Smith might have come not merely or chiefly to find an old and apparently bankrupt uncle, but for some other reason inconvenient to Mr Ted Wyllie. There had been, according to him, some sort of a suggestion of a marriage between them. Suppose there had been more than talk—promises, for instance. Or even a marriage that had been kept secret? And did she now wish it acknowledged, and would that be inconvenient to Wyllie?

No use, Bobby told himself, pursuing these vague speculations, but they would have to be kept in mind. By his own evidence Ted and his mother were the only people in England who could have known of the girl's arrival by that ship on that voyage, and the description the porter had given answered well enough to Ted, who also was young and tall. But, then, so were several hundred thousand others in the country.

The 'phone rang. Bobby picked it up. It was Constable Ford of Southam, whose application for a transfer to the C.I.D. Bobby only that morning had endorsed with a strong recommendation.

"I hope you don't mind, sir," Ford was saying. "I asked to be put through direct to you. Said it was urgent."

"That's all right," Bobby answered. "What is it?"

"Mr Smith and the young lady have gone off for a holiday, Mrs. Day says, and she says they haven't told her where, because they don't know yet, and they don't want any one else to know, because Mr Smith needs a complete rest. They'll let her know when they're settled, but she's not to tell."

"Thank you," Bobby said. "I rather wonder what that means. Let me know if there's any further development," and to himself as he hung up, he murmured: "Altogether too much unknown destination about all this for my liking."

CHAPTER IX
"IT'S A BAD SET-UP"

ON BOBBY'S desk lay plenty of work, awaiting attention. But very little of it got done that afternoon, as Bobby sat and mused on what he had just heard.

So much to fear, two lives that might well lie in the balance, so little on which firm action could be taken.

On the face of it, only an old man who had gone away for a quiet holiday and asked no more than to be left in peace and quiet; only a young woman who had preferred during a visit to England not to stay with former friends, having perhaps found others.

Yet that ignored so much. It ignored the sinister, fleeting appearances in Southam of Cy King and his satellite made up for some reason to resemble Bobby himself. What legitimate cause could there be for that or for the call on old Mr Smith? It ignored the recent visit to Canada made by Gladys, Cy's feminine companion of the moment; it ignored the arrival of the old fat woman, Mrs Lizzie Smith, to take charge of Cy King's sweet-shop; and is not Lizzie, like Betty, short for Elizabeth?

Had all that no significance? Bobby asked himself, brooding uneasily in his room and letting lie unheeded on his desk the papers and the letters and the reports with which it was strewn.

Altogether too high a proportion of Smiths, he decided, and was it decently probable that two Betty Smiths from Canada should arrive in England within six months of each other, each in search of an uncle, even though one uncle was certainly rich and the other reputed to be poor? But, then, the first Betty Smith had been accepted as genuine by an uncle, and presumably an uncle does not need to be really very wise in order to know his own niece.

Nor did Bobby feel very happy about Ted Wyllie, who, by his own showing, had alone, with his mother, known the time of the second Betty Smith's arrival, and who therefore, again by his own account, was the only person in a position to meet her. Had he done so? And was it with him she had gone away and not been heard of since? For Bobby knew how often an uneasy and a questioning conscience, driven by the urge to know what was happening, what was being said and done and thought and planned, had brought to the police, on one pretext or another, those of whose activities nothing would otherwise have been heard.

Bobby picked up the house-'phone and asked if Sergeant James was in the building. Fortunately he was. From him, who had the reputation of knowing more about the night clubs, and, in general, the haunts of Soho than any one else in the force, Bobby had already received valuable information. Now he soon appeared in Bobby's room. Then, the sergeant comfortably seated and provided with the inevitable cigarette, Bobby explained what he wanted.

"Your considered opinion," he said. "Is it possible that Tiny Garden and his pals can be working in on some long-term job with Cy King and his pals?"

"Work together?" repeated the sergeant. "Them? Like hell they would. I mean that. Like hell, I mean. Cutting each other's throats they would be before a week was past. Even if they tried, meaning it, they couldn't. Dead sure they would be all the time that each of 'em was selling the other out. The whole lot of 'em will most likely be doing themselves in some day because of not able to trust their own selves any longer."

"That was rather my own idea," Bobby remarked. "But Cy King has been to the Jimmy Joe café, hasn't he?"

"And got away alive," admitted the sergeant in a faintly surprised tone. "Most likely because he came unexpected, kept out of that upstairs room, and there hadn't been time to arrange for getting rid of the body. Tiny always swears he'll do Cy in some day, and Cy says the same, but means it more. I'm all for letting them carry on according. Wouldn't be proper official, though."

"Being proper official is a big handicap," Bobby agreed, "but we have to put up with it. There's some idea that Cy may be gate-crashing on one of Tiny's biggest jobs."

"Lummy," said the sergeant simply.

"That," said Bobby approvingly, "is exactly what I thought."

"Wild cats won't be in it," Sergeant James declared with almost equal approval. "Can't we let it rip?"

"Unfortunately, no," Bobby said. "There's a girl's life may come into it—or her death."

"That's bad," said the sergeant, looking grave. "You don't mean Gladys?" he asked, almost hopefully. Bobby shook his head. The sergeant said: "May be that's why Cy has closed down his sweet-shop and cleared out."

"To an unknown destination?" Bobby asked.

"That's right," agreed the sergeant, slightly surprised. "Him and that Gladys girl of his, and the old woman he had in to look after the business while Gladys was away—and said to be Gladys's mother, which is as may be. And a hanger-on of his from the East End somewhere—Bill Bright. I don't know anything about him. But all four of 'em piled into a taxi and went off together just like that. Shut the shop with a notice on the door—'Closed temporarily'."

"There's a Mr Smith," Bobby said. "He and a niece of his have gone off on a holiday, they said, and without saying where. It's possible Cy and his friends have gone after them. Cy may have kept a closer watch in Southam than we could do, and he may know."

"What's the idea?" James asked, as Bobby paused, lost in uncomfortable thought.

"Mr Smith is a retired business man, very well off," Bobby explained. "Cy may have plans for getting hold of his money, and possibly Tiny Garden is on the same track."

"Lummy," said James.

"You said that before," Bobby pointed out. "Cy's going off may be a help. We can't very well circulate descriptions of a perfectly respectable, law-abiding citizen and his niece on holiday, but we can of Cy King. Luckily he has a record. We can put a full description in the 'Gazette' and ask for a look-out for him to be kept, especially in watering-places, spas and seaside towns—holiday resorts generally. If we do hear of him, that's where Smith and his niece will be."

"Is the niece the girl you said might be in danger?"

"No," Bobby said. He opened a drawer of his desk and took out a copy of the photograph supplied by Mrs Wyllie. "That's the one I'm worried about," he said. "Landed a little while ago from Canada, was going to stay with friends, and hasn't been heard of since she was seen to leave Euston with an unidentified young man who met her there."

James had been studying the photograph carefully. He laid it down on the desk and then picked it up again.

"Nice-looking kid," he said. "Sort of jolly look about her, as if she enjoyed life. Is it her? She may be in their way?"

"It's a possibility," Bobby said. "Nothing known for certain yet. There's an old man, too. His life will be just as precious to him, and our duty to him is just the same. Only when it's a girl . . ."

"Yes, sir," said the sergeant soberly. "Some of us are fathers. Looks about the age of my Jenny. It'll be the old man's money they're after?"

"Looks like it," Bobby said. "Too many Smiths, too much money, too much Canada, too much unknown destination. A bad set-up, and yet too little to be sure of or to act on. It's always like that. The gang has the initiative, and until something breaks, nothing we can do. And then it's too late." He picked up the photograph still lying where James had laid it down. He said: "It may be too late for her, for all we know."

"Canada, sir?" asked James. "That's where Cy's girl friend Gladys has been. Visiting friends, she said. More like trying to get rid of loot if you ask me. She's been back two or three weeks. Came on the 'Queen of the Seas'."

Bobby asked the date. The sergeant gave it. Bobby said:

"The same boat and the same date as the girl whose friends have never heard of her since she landed."

"Lummy," said the sergeant for the third time, but in a different tone. "If you ask me . . ."

But Bobby did not ask him, nor did the sergeant show any desire that he should do so. Instead he listened carefully while Bobby gave him a brief account of recent happenings.

"It's a bad set-up," he agreed when Bobby had finished. He picked up once again the photograph Bobby had shown him and laid it down once more. "Poor kid!" he said softly. "Bad luck," he said, and then he went away, promising to do his best to pick up any piece of information he could about either Cy King or Tiny Garden or any of their associates.

Indeed, it was hardly more than an hour before James was ringing up to confirm that Tiny Garden and his associates had, like Cy King and his friends, vanished from their usual haunts. In their case, too, no one seemed to have any idea where they had gone and why.

"If you authorize it, sir," added Sergeant James, "I'll promise five or ten bob to any of our contacts who can tell us."

Bobby said he thought it would be money well spent, and the sergeant said he would ring up the moment he got results—if any. He wasn't very hopeful, though. Both Cy King and Tiny Garden were gentlemen of reputation, and no one was very anxious to interfere with any plans of theirs. More especially, and emphatically, not with Cy King's. To do so was apt to be a short road to the river.

This talk had, as it happened, interrupted Bobby as he was in the act of putting through a call to Southam. Now he did so, asking for Constable Ford, whose transfer to the C.I.D. had not yet been completed. Ford was at the moment out on his beat, his tour of duty this week being from two to ten in the evening. Bobby asked that Ford should be told to ring him up as soon as possible. It was not much more than half an hour before Ford was on the line.

"I've a little job for you," Bobby told him. "Confidential. Off the record. Of course we would never dare open a letter—worse than high treason. Couldn't do that even to save the country from immediate ruin. But I think we might risk looking at a post-mark."

"Looking at a post-mark, sir? Yes, sir," said Ford, very much puzzled.

"I want to know where our Mr Smith has gone for his holiday," Bobby continued. "Both Tiny Garden and Cy King have vanished in the last few days, and I don't like it. May mean things are coming to a head, and if it's that way, Mr Smith may be in real danger. He's an obstinate old ass, but we've got to do our best for him, not to mention that we've plenty to see to without having to set to work to chase any more murderers."

"Do you think it's as bad as that?" Ford asked.

"I do indeed," Bobby answered. "I may be all wrong, of course. What I want you to do is to see if you can get the postman delivering Mr Smith's letters to notice post-marks. If Mrs Day gets one from any holiday resort, that's most likely where Mr Smith has gone for what he calls peace and quiet. If he isn't careful, it's a peace and quiet he may find in his grave before long. Do you think you could manage that for me?"

"Oh, yes, sir, I think so," Ford answered confidently.

"Have to be careful, you know," Bobby warned him. "If it got out we should probably be told that even the Gestapo at its worst would never have done a thing like that. Looking at post-marks! So mind your step."

"It'll be all right, sir," Ford assured him. "I know the chap on that round—Andy Stokes. He is opening batsman for Southam first eleven. Very steady bat. You can always trust him."

"Good," said Bobby, as he hung up, reflecting that cricket was a great game and only in the Empire did they know how to play it.

He wondered if Ford also was a good steady bat. The C.I.D. first eleven badly needed a man to go in first.

CHAPTER X
"IS IT A MR SMITH?"

NEARLY A week passed before Bobby heard anything more. As completely as the second Betty Smith from Canada had vanished after her arrival in England, so now it seemed had vanished also not only old Mr Smith and Betty Smith I., but also both Cy King and Tiny Garden as well as their companions. Not a situation Bobby liked to contemplate; and yet, with so little that was definite to go on, and with hardly any one but himself convinced of the desperate need for speed in action, there was very, very little he could do.

Then, one morning as he was busy in his room, word was brought to him that Constable Ford, on transfer from Southam (O Division) to the C.I.D., was asking for permission to see Commander Owen. Bobby sent for him at once, and there appeared a somewhat apologetic Ford—in plain clothes, as his posting had not yet come through. For his desire to make a personal report he excused himself on the ground that he thought Bobby might wish to give him fresh instructions. So Bobby said that was all right and to get on with it, and Ford explained that the trustworthy Stokes had told him that by the last post on the previous afternoon he had delivered at 'The Haven' a post-card he would certainly in any case have noticed, since it had on it no writing whatever, other than the address. Nor had there been any need to notice the post-mark, since the photograph on the reverse side was of Seemouth Castle, the ancient fortress dominating the little seaside town of Seemouth. It had been built according to the records by Simon de Montford to stop penetration by French invaders up the See, in those days a river navigable for twenty or thirty miles inland, though now sadly shrunken.

"Looks as if a blank post-card had some sort of pre-arranged meaning," Bobby remarked. "Anyhow, that's probably where they are. Seemouth is about half-way between Bournemouth and Weymouth, isn't it? Play a lot of golf there."

"Yes, sir, so I believe," Ford answered with the properly tolerant contempt of a pucka cricketer for that alien intruder from the north, "and not a decent cricket-pitch in the whole place," he added, this time with less tolerance and more severity.

"Tut, tut," said Bobby. "Bad that. I had better ring them up and ask them to keep their eyes open. Not very much we can do though except wait and watch while Cy and Tiny get their plans nice and ready. Our best hope is that they'll soon start double-crossing each other."

He spoke with some despondency, for he was, he felt, in a singularly helpless position, obliged to stand idly watching the approach of a catastrophe he could do little or nothing to avert.

He tried to cheer himself by the reflection that quite possibly his fears were groundless and that everything that had happened bore some perfectly simple, perfectly harmless explanation. None the less, there still haunted him, coming between him and his work, that photograph lying in a drawer of his desk—the photograph of a gay and eager, happy seeming young girl, who was one felt welcoming with open arms the full life she saw stretching before her.

He did his best to put that troubling image out of his thoughts and to get on with his work. Then again, late that night, after Bobby had returned home, and indeed as he was beginning to think of bed, Ford was on the 'phone.

"I hope you don't mind me ringing up so late, sir," he said, "but Andy Stokes has just been round, and I thought you might like to know. He says when he was making his last delivery he saw Miss Smith coming back home, and he says she looked something terrible. I couldn't get out of him exactly what he meant. He says he saw her first almost running up the road, and she looked like death, he says. She didn't notice him, but he had a circular to deliver, so he followed her to the front door, and when Mrs Day opened it, Miss Smith sort of tumbled into her arms and then had hysterics, right there on the floor of the hall, kicking and laughing and screaming. Stokes says he stood there staring till Mrs Day banged the door right in his face. I thought perhaps I had better let you know, sir."

"Quite right," Bobby said. "Disturbing. Something happened at Seemouth to upset the young woman. Too late to do anything to-night, when we don't know their address at Seemouth, or, for that matter, if it really is Seemouth she's come from. I'll get on to them in the morning."

He hung up then. Too late for action that night, he told himself again. Too late also, he feared, it might well prove to be for old Mr Smith. Was it too late also for the unknown girl of whom nothing had been heard for so long?

In the morning, as soon as he got to his office, the first thing he did was to put through a call to Seemouth, and ask if anything had been seen of the suspicious characters for whom it had been asked that a look-out should be kept.

The Seemouth station sergeant who took his call replied that no report of that kind had been received. He added with a touch of complacency that they kept a sharp look-out for such. Seemouth visitors were high class and often possessed valuable jewellery. So a close watch was kept for hotel thieves, and all hotels were reminded each season to report at once anything doubtful or suspicious.

"Which they never do," the station sergeant said, "being so afraid of giving offence. Besides which there's the bungalows on Under Castle Shore. Not so classy there by a long way, and we've had a case of a woman in an hotel making the plans and a bloke from the bungalows carrying 'em out. But we watch 'em close. There's a spot of trouble there this morning though. Old gentleman found dead in his bath. It's making us busy. Have to be an inquest."

"Is it a Mr Smith—Mr John Smith? From Southam?" Bobby asked, but he knew already what the reply would be.

"That's right," the sergeant said, and his voice sounded very surprised as he wondered whether Scotland Yard knew something, or whether it was just a lucky guess. "Not one of the suspicious characters you were asking about, was he?"

"No," Bobby answered heavily, "thank you. Good-bye"; and then he hung up, aware now that it was in fact too late to save the obstinate old man who had refused to take any notice of the warnings given him.

He went then to see his closest associate in the hierarchy of Scotland Yard.

"It looks to me like murder, almost certainly murder," he told his colleague. "The girl was probably sent back to Southam to get her out of the way, but she guessed what was going to happen. That'll account for her hysterics the postman told Ford about. She may not have bargained for murder. It'll pass for a natural death unless we do something."

"What do you think of doing?" the other asked.

"There's the second girl, too," Bobby went on, unheeding this question. "Betty Smith II. What's become of her?"

"If you're right," his colleague answered, and now his voice, too, had grown heavy and sombre—"If you are—too late for her as well?"

"It may be," Bobby agreed. "But possibly not too late to see her murderers don't go unpunished—or Mr Smith's either. And, after all, there is a chance she may still be alive. It may be she is being kept as a kind of hostage to make sure Mr Smith's money, if they do get hold of it, is divided equally. And of course there is always the possibility that she is keeping out of the way for her own private reasons."

But neither of the two men believed this for one moment.

"You mean locked up in an attic somewhere?" the colleague asked doubtfully. "Is that possible nowadays? What about neighbours? What about food, with rationing and all the rest of it?"

"I think it would be possible, especially in London or one of the big towns, where neighbours don't take much interest in each other," Bobby answered. "Or even in the country, where anything any one noticed would simply be put down to the odd ways of visitors from a town. And there's plenty of food off the ration you can get now."

"I take it it's Mr Smith's money they mean to try to get hold of?" the other man asked.

"Most likely they've got the old man to make a will in the girl's favour," Bobby said. "They are playing for big stakes. I don't know how much Mr Smith will have left, but he seemed to be very well off."

"Well, what's to be done now?" was the next question, after a long and troubled pause while the two men contemplated grimly the task that lay before them.

"Eh? What? Do now?" Bobby asked, roused abruptly from his thoughts. "Oh, I thought I would ring up Seemouth and ask them if they would mind if I ran down to make sure their Mr Smith is the same Mr Smith we've been worried about. I'll tell them there's a background to the case I think they ought to know about."

"Going to say you believe it's murder?"

"Not till I'm sure it is," Bobby answered. "There may still be one chance in a million it's natural death."

"Long odds," the other said. "Oh, by the way, who is going to do your work while you're gallivanting by the sea?"

"You," answered Bobby, and the other sighed heavily and said he had had a premonition that was coming.

So Bobby congratulated him on his foresight and went away to put through his call to Seemouth.

CHAPTER XI
"ELEVEN BOTTLES?"

HE GOT his call through without difficulty, and Seemouth's reply was prompt and cordial. The Seemouth chief constable would be delighted to welcome Commander Owen, and would much like to know if the Mr Smith found dead in his bath in one of the Seemouth Castle Shore bungalows was identical with the Mr Smith in whom the Yard had found reason to be interested. Nothing even remotely suspicious, though, about the death. Heart failure, the doctor said. No, there was no sign of drowning, nor had the water in the bath been at all deep. A post-mortem would be carried out, however, though more as a matter of routine than for any other reason. Bad luck, certainly, that the old gentleman had been alone in the bungalow at the time. If help had been at hand the unfortunate man's life might have been saved. Of course, no blame attached to any one on that account.

Bobby expressed his thanks for all this information and asked if, as far as possible, everything in the bungalow could remain exactly as it was till he arrived. The smallest detail, he said, might be a help to obtaining information about the dead man's connections and past life.

To this Seemouth replied, of course, of course, and Bobby said good-bye and rang off, to be immediately rung up in his turn from Sidmouth, where apparently they had been waiting some time to get through to him.

"We thought you might like to know for what it's worth— which don't seem much," explained the Sidmouth sergeant at the other end of the line. "It's about information asked for re Cy King and unknown companion, as you said you would like us to look out for. Well, they've turned up here all right, and there's a bit of a smell about it. The two of them were playing darts at the 'Green Dragon', being noisy like and very liberal standing drinks. No way offensive or quarrelsome, just making themselves conspicuous. After closing time they went down to the front for a breath of fresh air, they said. One of our men noticed them, thought they had had enough to drink, and told them to go home. They said they would, but later on he found them sound asleep in one of the shelters. He asked them where they were staying, and they told him. They said they supposed they must have had a drop too much, but they were all right now, and he saw them start off. Next thing he heard a lot of shouting, and when he went to see what was up, he found one of them had been a bit knocked about. Pretty sick he looked. Their story was that going up Fore Street on their way home to their lodgings they saw a man hanging about near the entrance to one of the shops. By way of a joke more than anything else, both of 'em still feeling a bit jolly like, they asked him if he was going to do a smash and grab. The chap turned round and slugged them—good and hard, too—and did a bunk. By the time our man got there, not a sign of him."

"There wouldn't be," said Bobby. "What about the whole thing being faked?"

"Oh, lord, no!" came the answer from Sidmouth. "You wouldn't think so if you saw the face of one of 'em."

"Did they give their names?"

"Both had their identity cards, all proper and complete. That's how we knew it was the same asked about—Cyrus King and William Bright, addresses in Soho and Stepney."

"Half a crown to nothing at all," Bobby said, "that it was Mr William Bright who had been knocked about."

"That's right," Sidmouth replied, a little surprised now, like Seemouth previously. "Had a bloody nose and his mouth cut. Knocked him flat, he said, being taken unsuspecting, and fell on top of King, so as King hadn't a chance to do anything before the bloke got away in the dark. Maybe King wasn't too anxious to try, seeing what his pal had had. He was given a spot of first aid, and they were both sent off in one of our cars to where they said they were staying, just to be sure. That was O.K., and their landlady gave them notice on the spot to clear out next day. Said it wasn't respectable and she wasn't going to be knocked up out of her bed in the middle of the night any more."

"It may have been even less respectable than she thought," Bobby remarked. "Sounds very much to me as if they had been putting up an act to provide themselves with a good sound alibi."

"Well, sir," the Sidmouth sergeant answered very doubtfully. "You wouldn't hardly think so if you had seen Bright's face."

"An occupational risk," Bobby remarked, "if you go along with Cy. You didn't look at Cy's knuckles, did you?"

"You don't mean as he may have knocked out his pal himself?" asked the sergeant. "There wasn't a word said like that."

"There wouldn't be," Bobby answered. "The Bright gentleman knew better. Well, thanks for what you've told me. Very interesting, and may be very useful, too. Help us in an investigation we have on hand you may hear more about. How far is Seemouth from you? Is there a good straight road?"

"Seemouth?" repeated the Sidmouth man, rather as if he had hardly heard of a place that, because of a practically prehistoric ruin and an absurdly over-rated links, succeeded in attracting to itself a number of the visitors who ought by rights to be coming to Sidmouth. "Well, I should say it's all of twenty-five miles and the road's good enough, except for a very dangerous double turn to avoid the links they make such a to do about—more than one accident there," said Sidmouth, and evidently thought it served the victims right.

Bobby rang off then and, by hurrying, was just able to catch the next train for Seemouth—a good, direct, fast service. He had sent a telegram to say he was coming, and on his arrival he was met by the Seemouth chief constable, Mr Perkins, a veteran who had risen from the ranks.

An exchange of courtesies and Bobby was soon in Mr Perkins's car on the way to the Bungalow Beach. Seemouth station is a considerable distance from the town, and to reach the bungalows a long detour has to be made to avoid the channel of the See, now only a foot or two deep, but running between steep banks.

"First thing we did was to wire for the niece," Mr Perkins explained. "Most unfortunate she was away. Very likely it wouldn't have happened if she had been there. I hope she's not blaming herself, but there's a reply from a Mrs Day to say Miss Smith has collapsed, but Mr Smith's lawyer—a Mr Moon—is coming at once. I expect he was on your train, but I didn't wait to see. I thought you might like a bit of a chat first. Something a bit screwy about Mr Smith?"

"I wouldn't like to say that," Bobby answered. "We've every reason to think he was a most respectable, law-abiding citizen, quite above reproach. Very well-to-do, apparently. Sold his business to a limited company and retired. But we've been worried to find that some of our London gangsters seem to be rather too much interested in him. Much too much for our liking. We tried to warn him, but he wouldn't listen. Took offence, in fact, and complained. You remember we asked to be told if two rather dangerous characters we are interested in turned up here. Well, it seems they were in Sidmouth last night."

"In Sidmouth?" Mr Perkins repeated; and his tone suggested that in his opinion it was much more likely for dangerous characters to turn up there rather than in Seemouth. He went on: "Did Sidmouth let you know about them? But they can't have anything to do with this if they were there."

"Who made the discovery?" Bobby asked without disputing this proposition.

"A lady in the next bungalow—Mrs White. Miss Smith—that's the niece—asked her to go in this morning just to see everything was all right. She said she was a little nervous at leaving her uncle alone at his age, but there was some business he wanted her to attend to, and he was touchy about any suggestion he couldn't look after himself. Mrs White couldn't get any answer when she knocked, and she could see a light was still burning. She waited a bit, and then she told one or two of the neighbours, and they found the back door wasn't locked. So they went in—and got the shock of their lives. And here we are."

The car had drawn up before one of a cluster of bungalows, extending for some half-mile or a little more beneath the great rock on which still stood the old castle that once had kept watch and ward against raiders from across the sea. Now, after near-ly half a thousand years of calm, it had once again served the same purpose when anti-aircraft guns had blazed their wrath at German aircraft and old battlements built for protection against arrow and cross-bow bolt had been shaken, but no more, by the blast of falling bombs.

It was a sprawling, unkempt, untidy scene, yet not unpleasant in its suggestion of a holiday atmosphere and general relaxation of too much care for everyday respectability—a kind of carpet-slipper, shirt-sleeve, who-cares-what-the-neighbours-think, sort of atmosphere. A few children were playing on the sands, a few people were sitting about. The arrival of the car produced a general stir and turning of heads, but no one seemed unduly interested. It was very sad, of course, that an old man on a holiday should die so suddenly. But we all have to go one day, people were telling each other, confident that for them that day was still far distant.

"Put up for summer visitors," Mr Perkins was explaining. "A good many permanents as well now, though. Because of the housing shortage. Very bad here indeed, very bad."

A uniformed constable opened the door for them, and they went in. The plan of the bungalow was quite simple, its best feature the wide veranda facing the sea. Inside there were three small bedrooms, a lounge, a tiny kitchen, and the usual offices, including the bathroom which death had visited so suddenly, so recently. Gas and water were laid on, and the furniture seemed adequate, even though it did appear to contain a somewhat high proportion of deck chairs and bamboo tables.

"Most of the visitors like to take their meals outside on the veranda," Mr Perkins explained.

Bobby was looking at the table in the lounge, on which still stood the remnants of a meal. It had consisted of cold chicken, bread, butter, cheese, and a tomato salad.

"Looks like his supper," Mr Perkins remarked, "he hadn't troubled to clear away. Nothing been touched."

"Some of the chicken still on his plate," Bobby observed. "Bread and cheese not touched. Almost looks as if he had stopped eating in the middle of his meal."

"Yes, we noticed that," Mr Perkins said. "I said to the doctor that it looked as if he had been feeling unwell and not wanting to eat any more, and then he had the idea that a hot bath might do him good."

"Dropped a fork on the floor," the constable said. "That one." He pointed to one on the table. "Felt sick or giddy, maybe. If the lady had been here, most like it wouldn't never have happened."

"I don't suppose it would," Bobby agreed. "No, probably not." He was still staring at the table. Mr Perkins looked at him, wondering what was interesting him so much. The constable waited, all stolid patience. Bobby said: "There doesn't seem to be anything to drink."

"Beer in the kitchen," the constable said. "Eleven bottles."

"Eleven bottles?" Bobby repeated. "Not twelve? People generally get in a dozen at a time. I wonder what's become of the twelfth?"

CHAPTER XII
"THE PERFECT MURDER"

IT WAS a wonder very evidently shared neither by Mr Perkins nor by his constable. Difficult to see, they were both thinking, what an empty beer-bottle had to do with it, one way or the other. However, though more to please Bobby and out of deference for his rank and reputation than for any other reason, the constable was instructed to make a thorough search.

"Look everywhere," Mr Perkins ordered. "Inside and out."

The constable said "Yes, sir", and began his search, while Mr Perkins showed Bobby the bathroom.

"Gas heater, I see," Bobby remarked, and Mr Perkins said there was no electricity yet in this part of Seemouth. Due to the war, he said. Bobby went on: "If we are right in thinking it's Mr Smith's supper on the table in the lounge, then presumably death occurred last night. What's the doctor say?"

"Much the same. He thinks death took place about twelve hours before found," Mr Perkins answered. "The probable cause was exposure—him lying there all night in the bath with the water getting colder all the time. Fainted probably, and if he did come to, too weak and numbed to move. Sort of coma."

"Twelve hours like that enough to kill any one," Bobby agreed. "I take it there's no question of drowning? Do you know how much water was in the bath?"

"Well, we can't say for certain," Mr Perkins answered. "Mrs White and the others all got rather excited—a bit hysterical, one or two of them. Can't wonder, I suppose. Bad shock finding the poor old boy like that. It's all a bit confused what they say—in details that is. Difficult to get it all straight. But they do all of them agree the bath was nothing like full. First thing they did was to let the water out, and it was quite dry by the time we got here. Six or seven inches most likely, from what they say, or maybe a little more. No telling for sure. Doesn't matter much, as drowning doesn't come into it, and anyhow you couldn't rely on anything any of the four of 'em said being exact. Too upset they were. Why, one of them wanted to tell me she saw a young woman going into the bathroom just before Mrs White opened the door. No one there, though, she admits, so I don't know what she thinks became of the woman she sticks to it she saw. Funny what tricks imagination plays you at times like that. There's even one of the others backs her up."

"What do they say this woman was like?" Bobby asked.

"Oh, they say they only had a glimpse as she went into the bathroom just ahead of Mrs White. They don't explain why Mrs White didn't see her and why Mrs White had to open the door again if some one else had just that minute opened it before her."

"Mrs White didn't see anything?"

"Not a thing; says it's all nonsense," Mr Perkins answered. "You can see what happened. They saw Mrs White going in, and afterwards, what with the shock and the excitement and all the rest of it, they managed to get it into their heads they had seen some one else first. Never get them to think different either."

"Well, I daresay that might explain it," Bobby agreed. "Two of them tell the same story? Mrs White says it's nonsense? Who else was with them?"

"Mrs White's sister, staying with her. Her story is she heard somebody say 'Me, O.K.', like a whisper in her ear. All worked up, all of 'em. Any one would be."

"A bit curious," Bobby said. "It's an expression I've come across before in this case. Doesn't make sense, but it's odd, all the same. Can't mean anything, though."

"Everybody goes to the pictures," Mr Perkins pointed out. "I do myself when I've time, and that's not so often. Pick up American slang without knowing it. I'm always saying 'O.K.'. Sort of reflex action. Probably that's what happened. Somebody said 'O.K.', without even knowing she was speaking, and this girl heard it, and it stuck somehow."

"It might be that," Bobby agreed. "I noticed there was a slot-meter in the kitchen. Do you think the gas people could tell us exactly how much gas was used last night?"

"You mean the water might have been too hot and that was what caused it?" Mr Perkins asked. "There's no sign of scalding or anything of the sort."

"I wasn't thinking of that so much—" Bobby began, and then was interrupted by the reappearance of the constable who had been conducting a careful search outside as well as in.

"Can't see any empty anywhere," he reported. "I've rung up the shop, and they say they delivered a dozen yesterday in the afternoon. Taken in by an old gentleman and paid for. Discount allowed on empties returned. Must have been broke and the bits thrown away. Nothing in the dustbin or anywhere."

"If it was broken before Mr Smith had his supper last night," Bobby said, "it doesn't explain why there's no sign of anything he was going to have to drink with his meal. If it was broken during the meal there would be something to show. You can't imagine he would leave his supper half eaten while he cleared up the mess so carefully there's no sign of it left. Especially if he wasn't feeling well. And then what was he going to drink his beer from? No glass."

"Yes, but does it matter?" Mr Perkins asked. "I don't quite see where all this is going to get us."

"I only wish I did," Bobby said. "Not an idea at present. I'm only noticing details. Irrelevant, perhaps. You never know. One beer-bottle and contents vanished without trace. Glass tumbler ditto. We could check up on that with the inventory, if there is one. There generally is with these furnished places. I would like to know, though, if the gas-people could give us any idea how much gas was used to heat the bathwater last night."

"Well, we could ask them," Mr Perkins said tolerantly, not quite sure whether to be amused or annoyed by so much meticulous attention to detail.

The constable was therefore sent off once more, this time to ring up the gas show-room. He returned almost at once with the information that the meter inspector was at that moment somewhere on Bungalow Beach, busy collecting the contents of the slot-meters. So now the constable's next errand was to find him and bring him along, and meanwhile Bobby wandered restlessly to and fro, his mind full of many thoughts. It was not long before the constable returned, bringing the meter inspector with him.

"I cleared the meter here late yesterday afternoon," the inspector told them. "Almost the last job I did before knocking off. The old gent was here, and he was all spry and lively then."

"That means," Bobby said, "you can tell us at once how many shillings have been put in since then and about how much gas has been used."

"That's right," agreed the inspector. He went to the meter and opened it. "Nothing here," he said. "Not been used. I remember the old gent asked me to change him a ten-bob note along of being short of shillings and not having been able to get hot water when he wanted it. But he's put none in, and no gas been burned."

"But that's not possible," protested Mr Perkins. "He must have used some gas. For his bath. He had to."

"I don't know anything about that," the inspector said. "But there's been no shillings put in, and consequently no gas—no shilling, no gas. Look for yourself."

Mr Perkins did so. He said:

"All the same . . ."

The constable said:

"Silver found in deceased's possession included ten one-shilling pieces."

"There you are," said the inspector. "Sort it out anyway you want, but there's been no gas burned since I was here last thing yesterday. And that's gospel."

"The water for the bath must have been heated somehow," Mr Perkins persisted. "Mr Smith can't have wanted a cold bath—not at that time, not at his age."

"I'm beginning to think," Bobby said, "that a cold bath is what he had, but not what he wanted."

Mr Perkins said nothing. The constable remained stolid and unmoved. Not his to reason why. His pay didn't run to it. The gas inspector told them again to sort it out any way they liked, and so departed. Bobby was deep in thought—not too pleasant thought.

"You know," he said, "I don't like that story about some one thinking she saw a young woman who can't have been there."

"Crazy," said Mr Perkins. "It's all crazy. Stands to reason no man of that age would leave a supper half eaten to have a cold bath. And why," he demanded, "should he have it if he didn't want it?"

"Yes. Why?" Bobby said.

"Well, then," said Mr Perkins.

"Perhaps the perfect murder," Bobby said.

Mr Perkins was silent. Half unconsciously he had been afraid this was coming, and he didn't like it. Bobby had often been obliged to make himself unpopular with many people for many reasons. Seldom had he been more unpopular with any one than he was with Mr Perkins at this moment. What had been a simple, though unfortunate, accidental death, a mere matter of routine to be comfortably disposed of according to settled form and precedent, appeared to be transforming itself under his eyes to a highly complicated, sensational, mysterious case of murder—the sort of thing to give an elderly, peace-loving chief constable on the verge of retirement endless trouble, worry, responsibility. Swarms of Pressmen badgering him day and night, afternoon and evening, for information. If he gave it, he would be blamed for talking too much. If he didn't, then probably the 'Daily Popular' and the 'Weekly Chatter' would be making caustic remarks about the incompetent Seemouth police. No time to do his own work either, and the Watch Committee very likely pointing out that sensational murders did high-class seaside resorts like Seemouth no good at all, and hinting that really competent chief constables would see that they didn't happen.

He took a sudden and desperate decision without caring a bit what an economically minded Watch Committee might have to say about the expense involved.

"If it's murder—and I don't see why you think it," he said, "then it's you say-so, and you're from the Yard, so you had better take over and handle it—murder," he repeated, and now his tone was of utter disbelief.

Before Bobby could reply, a taxi drew up outside and there alighted an elderly man, carrying a brief-case. Mr Perkins looked relieved.

"That'll be the lawyer Mrs Day's wire spoke of," he remarked. "Name of Moon."

CHAPTER XIII
"WATER-TIGHT ALIBI"

MR MOON seemed a little relieved to find he was expected. Also he seemed more than a little surprised when Mr Perkins, after introducing himself as the Seemouth chief constable, went on to introduce Bobby as Commander Owen of Scotland Yard.

"I don't quite understand," he said. "Is there any reason why Mr Owen should be interested?"

"There are some unusual features about the case," Bobby answered. "You have been acting for Mr Smith, and were no doubt in his confidence. You probably knew that he considered he had grounds for complaint over police action?"

"Certainly. He consulted me, and I advised him to write to the Commissioner. He received a satisfactory apology."

"And now he's dead," Bobby said grimly. "Just possibly if he had been more ready to listen to us he might still be alive."

"What does that mean?" Mr Moon asked, frowning at what he felt was an implied criticism of himself and his advice.

"I will try to explain," Bobby told him. "We found that some criminal elements in London were showing much too much interest in Mr Smith for our liking. We tried to warn him. He refused to listen." Mr Moon's frown deepened. Bobby continued: "He and his niece came here for a holiday as he put it, for a little rest and peace and to avoid being worried by us. Before I go on, will you tell me if I am right in believing that Mr Smith was well off and that recently he made a will leaving his money, or a large share of it, to Miss Elizabeth Smith, the young lady who has been living with him since she arrived from Canada?"

Mr Moon pursed his lips and did not answer at once. He was evidently considering how far he was justified in giving any information whatever about his client's affairs. Bobby murmured something about an inquest being held soon—possibly next day. Questions might be asked, Bobby observed, as to the ceiling. Mr Moon appeared not to hear, but said, still plainly weighing each word before utterance:

"Mr Smith was a man of some wealth. The personal estate will probably be in the neighbourhood of two hundred thousand pounds. Most wisely invested. Chiefly in Government stock. His will—the Great Southern Bank and myself are the executors—names his niece, Miss Elizabeth Smith, now resident with him, as principal legatee."

"Does Miss Smith know?"

"I can't tell you that. She was not present when I received my instructions or when the will was executed. Two of my clerks were witnesses. The will is perfectly in order. No doubt Miss Smith, whether her uncle told her or not, would have a reasonable expectation of being mentioned in it. I don't think that she had any idea of the amount of Mr Smith's wealth. He lived in comparatively modest circumstances. Even the purchases of antique furniture he made were, he told me once, in the nature of an investment. A precaution against any further risk of devaluation. I may add," Mr. Moon went on, "that what I have seen of Miss Smith has made a very favourable impression on me. Her devotion to her uncle was evident, and her thought and care for him most marked. A most sensible, level-headed young woman. I only wish," he added with a faint sigh as at the thought of troubles, past, present and to come, "one could say as much of all the young women one is forced to employ in these days. So—I can only say frivolous. Frivolous," he repeated, with grave and measured condemnation, and on his lips it sounded as if a new and still more deadly sin had been added to the other seven. "This terribly sudden event," he went on, "has shaken her profoundly. She collapsed so entirely that their doctor had to be sent for. He has insisted on rest and quiet for the time. That is why I am here alone as her representative."

"Yes, I heard she had broken down," Bobby said. "Our information is, indeed, that she had a fit of hysterics even before Mr Smith's death had taken place."

"I must ask you to explain what you mean by that statement," Mr Moon said. "Be pleased to remember that you are speaking of my client, whose interests I am here to defend. What reasons have you for making such a very remarkable statement? I hope they are substantial."

"The evidence of an eye-witness," Bobby answered. "May I go on with what I was saying? I was going to explain why I find some of the set-up here more than disturbing. What seems to be Mr Smith's supper is still on the table, and he appears to have left it unfinished. Why? People generally have something to drink with a meal. There is no sign of anything of the sort on the table, and a bottle of beer and a glass seem to be missing. Why? It appears to be certain that the water for the bath hadn't been heated. Why? I can't imagine why a man of Mr Smith's age should leave his supper unfinished in order to take a cold bath."

"I don't in the least understand all this," Mr Moon protested. "Not in the least. Most disturbing. Are you hinting there's reason to suspect foul play?"

"I am saying quite plainly, I hope," Bobby answered, "that Mr Perkins and myself are not satisfied."

"Not satisfied at all," declared Mr Perkins, rallying bravely from his first moment of surprise when he heard this. "Of course," he added, hedging a little, "there may be some explanation. I'm not ruling that out. But there it is."

"Exactly," said Bobby, though what was 'exactly', he didn't quite know. "All we are saying is that further investigation is necessary."

"Very necessary," said Mr Perkins, loudly and firmly.

Mr Moon had seated himself. He was looking pale and disturbed, and it was a moment or two before he spoke. Then he said:

"All this is most unexpected—most unexpected. Are you suggesting that Miss Smith had reason to believe her uncle was in some kind of danger? It seems incredible—utterly incredible."

"I'm suggesting nothing," Bobby answered, "beyond what I've already said—that we think further inquiries are necessary. The more so as it is possible that another life may be involved—that of a young woman. If it's not too late already."

"Good God!" cried Mr Moon, jumping to his feet. "You don't mean that Miss Smith—really, I can't believe all this. I don't understand. I protest—I demand that you speak more plainly. Is Miss Smith in any danger? If so, what steps do you propose, and what are your reasons?"

"I don't think your client is in the least danger just now," Bobby answered. "She may be presently, but not now. I was not thinking of her. What I think happened here is that the beer put out for Mr Smith's supper was drugged. I think that is why the bottle itself and the glass used have both disappeared. I think after drinking some of the beer Mr Smith became unconscious. A heavy sleep, possibly. I think he was then undressed and placed in the bath in cold water. I think the calculation was that cold and exposure for twelve hours at least would kill him. He was an old man, not very strong, and to all appearance it would seem a natural death. The perfect murder. I think it would certainly have passed as natural had we not known of the interest being shown by suspected persons in Mr Smith and had not Mr Perkins and myself noticed the suspicious circumstances I've mentioned."

"Very suspicions indeed, in my opinion," said Mr Perkins. "But we are, of course, ready to accept any reasonable explanation."

Mr Moon had rallied a little by now, and was beginning to show fight.

"No," he said firmly, "I don't accept all this, not for a moment. I suggest that everything you have said is susceptible of a perfectly simple explanation. There's no proof. None whatever. Drugged beer and all the rest of it. A cold bath! There's no motive. The only person to benefit is my client, Miss Smith. She left her uncle in good health. I trust you do not intend to suggest that even the shadow of suspicion rests on her?"

"I have never suggested," Bobby answered, "that she had any part in the actual murder, if I am right in thinking it is a case of murder—an exceptionally cruel and cunning murder. For one thing, her alibi is unquestionable—unquestioned. Other people have taken pains to provide themselves with a complete alibi."

"Who? What other people?"

"A man named Cy King who has a record and a man named Bright—Bill Bright he is known as. We don't know much about him. There are also two women: Gladys King and a Mrs Elizabeth Smith, an older woman. We want to get in touch with them if we can."

"Elizabeth Smith? The same name? What's that mean?"

"I am only stating a fact," Bobby answered. "So far as our information goes, these four people have nothing to do with the young lady who is your client."

"I shall defend her interests," Mr Moon broke in.

"I am helping you to do so by explaining what we know and think—and what we fear," Bobby said. "Like yourself, I am an officer of justice, and our duty, for both of us, is to see that justice is done as far as possible."

"I don't need to be told what my duty is," Mr Moon said, very angrily indeed.

"All I want to say," Bobby went on, unheeding this outburst, "is that at present the utmost caution is necessary. There is some reason to believe that another young woman—shall I call her Miss X?—is involved. All we know about her is that she had arranged to stay with some friends. They have not seen or heard of her, and they have made inquiries of us. I had, of course, no idea that Mr Smith was such a wealthy man. In the event of anything happening to your client, to Miss Smith, do you know who would inherit?"

"I understand there are no relatives. I'll try to make sure. All this is most disturbing."

"If Miss Smith died intestate, the money would go to the Crown?"

"Unless, of course, any relatives appeared to claim," Mr Moon answered. "I shall advise her to make a will leaving everything to charity. Most unnecessary, but you have disturbed me greatly, very greatly indeed." Since his arrival, Mr Moon had been in succession surprised, indignant, bewildered, alarmed, angry, disturbed. Now he decided to be severe. "In my opinion—my considered opinion," he said impressively, "I should have been informed of these facts before."

"Well, we could hardly inform you of Mr Smith's death before it occurred," Bobby observed mildly. "Nor can we very well consult a lawyer over his client's head—especially if we have no means of knowing who that lawyer is. That is for the private judgment of the person concerned, as Mr Smith consulted you and was advised to demand an apology—a satisfactory apology. I can't help thinking he might be inclined to regard it as less satisfactory now."

Mr Moon frowned as he had seldom frowned before, not even at those 'frivolous' typists who were the bane of his life. In silence—dignified silence—he collected his hat, umbrella and brief-case. Still severe, and even more so, he said:

"I am gravely dissatisfied with the whole of your handling of this affair. I shall not hesitate to say so. I presume you will be in charge here for the present. I shall hold you responsible for the safety of the contents of the bungalow. I am returning to town. I shall get in touch with my client, and I shall return by the first train in the morning. In view of what has been said, I must take time to consider my course of action. I may consider it advisable to secure counsel to represent us at the inquest."

With that he wished them a stately and aloof 'good afternoon' and retired to the still-waiting taxi. Mr Perkins, watching this ominous and reserved departure, said uneasily:

"Old boy going to make a stink, do you think?"

"Not he," Bobby answered. "He won't want anything to come out about that 'satisfactory' apology he advised poor old Smith to demand. Not that he is in any way to blame, of course, but all the same he won't want it mentioned."

Mr Perkins looked relieved. There was nothing he disliked and dreaded more than a 'stink', upsetting that peaceful routine he was accustomed to and that both Bobby and the lawyer seemed bent on destroying. The constable, who during the recent colloquy had been stationed outside to keep moving the small groups of spectators still apt at times to cluster near by, appeared in the doorway.

"Beg pardon, sir," he said, "there's two suspicious-looking blokes hanging about outside. One of 'em been in a fight, if his face is anything to go by. I asked them if they were residents, and they answered, impudent like, as that was their affair. But they moved off, and now they're back again."

Bobby went to the door and looked.

"Oh, yes," he said. "Cy King and Bill Bright, secure in the pure panoply of a water-tight alibi."

CHAPTER XIV
"TWO HUNDRED THOUSAND POUNDS"

BOBBY WATCHED for a moment in silence. Then he strolled towards where Cy King and his companion were standing talking together. As Bobby drew nearer, Cy's teeth showed in what might have been either a snarl or a smile. In his small, shifting eyes showed both threat and fear. He had a little the air of a watchful fox that knew well the hounds were close, but was not sure whether they were on its own trail or on that of another. Cy's companion drew back a yard or two, and, though he was a much bigger man than Cy, he gave an impression of trying to shelter behind him. In his most dulcet tones—those he kept for moments when he felt the need was greatest—Bobby said:

"Well, Cy, this is an unexpected meeting—at least on my side. What's brought you around?"

"Heard a poor old gent had died very sudden like in his bath," Cy answered. "Is it the Mr Smith as lived at Southam?—that's where we heard he came from. If it's the same gent, I tried to do a deal with him once. It didn't come off. Nice old gent, too, even though he wouldn't bite."

"What sort of deal was it?" Bobby asked.

"Some of that old antique furniture he was so keen on," Cy explained. "Time of Henry the Eighth—the bloke with the wives. Best solid mahogany, all of it."

"Well, that ought to have been valuable," Bobby agreed gravely. "Mahogany furniture of that date is extremely rare. If genuine."

"Oh, it was O.K. all right," Cy declared. "Quite O.K."

"Me, O.K.," Bobby said on an impulse, and saw the sudden startled jump Cy gave, and saw how his companion flinched and paled and turned as if to run.

But Cy's gesture stopped him, though Cy's voice was still shaken and uneven as he stammered:

"What . . . what's that for? Why . . . I mean . . ."

He subsided into silence. His hands were shaking, and his companion still seemed poised on the edge of precipitate flight. Bobby made no attempt to answer. He waited. Cy seemed to recover himself, and he put on a slight swagger as he said:

"Gave me a bit of a start for the moment. I mean what you said. Reminded me of an old pal of mine. He used to say that. He's dead now."

Bobby was looking at him thoughtfully, remembering that odd incident when Olive had insisted that she, too, had heard the same curious phrase used, though certainly there had been no one there to speak it. Cy stared back at him defiantly, as if challenging him to make of it what he could. Bobby said:

"You mean you think you've heard it said when no one was present to say it? What was it in the first place? A trick of speech? A sort of watchword—or password, perhaps? It might be overheard, I suppose, caught up, remembered, repeated. Only how could that be if there was no one there?"

"For God's sake," muttered Cy's companion from behind, and his face was ghastly.

Cy was licking dry lips. He, too, was clearly badly shaken, and not least by the questions Bobby had just asked. Cy turned abruptly on his companion.

"Shut it!" he said to him in a fierce whisper. To Bobby he said: "I don't fall for that nursery stuff—not me. If things can't happen, they don't happen. See? And that's all there's to it. Imagination," he said loudly. "Like a bloke with the D.T.'s. We'll be going."

"Won't you introduce me to your friend first?" Bobby asked. "I don't think we've ever met, have we? Had a bit of an accident, I see. Argument with a tram-car or something like that? I've not often seen two lovelier black eyes."

"Injuries received," Cy explained, while the victim himself scowled, but said nothing, "doing his duty as a man and citizen helping the police, and not so much as a word of thanks. You tell them at Sidmouth if they expect help they did ought to acknowledge it when given. Me and my pal were going home last night when we saw a bloke acting suspicious, so we spoke to him warning like, and afore you could say Jack Robinson he up and outed Bill with a quick left, right. Bill, that's my friend here—Mr Bright's his name: Bill Bright, Esquire. Bill, meet Mr Owen, a Yard bloke. Awful popular." And into those last two words Cy packed all the venom, hatred, malice, lust for revenge he had cherished, dwelt upon, fanned to increase by day and by night, ever since his proud immunity from a police record had been broken and his underworld prestige destroyed, by the prison sentence—too short, too lenient—he had received through Bobby's instrumentality.

"Glad to meet you, Mr Bright," Bobby said. "I'm sure you won't misunderstand me if I say I hope we shall have no occasion to meet again. I'm sorry for the way you've got knocked about—helping us. Too bad. I expect you are thinking you had a jolly sight rather it had been Cy."

Bill shuffled his feet, looked sulkier than ever, and made no reply. Cy gave Bobby another vicious look and said:

"Me and Bill pals. See? Now it's one, now it's the other."

"But generally the other," Bobby suggested. "I wonder if it's true there is a strong likeness between Bill and me. Can't tell very well the way it is at present." He turned swiftly on Cy. "You used my name that day you called to see Mr Smith in Southam—and it wasn't about antique furniture. Look up dates before you talk nonsense about mahogany furniture dating from the time of Henry the Eighth. Why did you tell that particular lie—about Bright being me?"

"Just our bit of fun," Cy explained. "The old gent wanted to be sure the stuff was genuine true, which it was, and I said if he didn't trust me he could ask my friend, Mr Bobby Owen of Scotland Yard. That was Bill, I meant, only him being so like you, as you'll see when he's more like himself than he is just now, he often gets called Bobby Owen. So I said the same to the old gent by way of a joke. Flattered like, Bill is, you being so well known."

"Flattered he may have been, but flattened now, as far as his face is concerned," Bobby observed. "A warning to mind his step, was it?"

The silent Mr Bright scowled more deeply than ever. Cy said they must be getting along, as they had to find lodgings. Their Sidmouth landlady had given them notice simply because they had come home a little late and in the company of police. So they had decided to push on to Seemouth to finish their holiday there.

"I'm not blaming the old girl for giving us the 'go' sign," Cy went on. "No one wants bogies about, and she may have thought us the same—you being took as according to the company kept. Suppose there'll be an inquest on the old gent?"

"It's usual in such cases," Bobby answered.

"Matter of form like?" suggested Cy.

"You can attend if you like," Bobby told him. "Inquests are public. Then you'll know as much as any one else."

Cy gave him another of those vicious scowls of his. Bobby nodded a farewell and went back to where Mr Perkins had been watching this colloquy from the bungalow veranda. Cy and Bill Bright walked away. Bobby said to Mr Perkins:

"Those two are mixed up in it somehow. Nothing yet to show how or in what way. I think they must have known Mr Smith's murder had been planned for last night, or else why the alibi they arranged? Now they want to know what we think or if we are going to let it slip through as a natural death."

"Did you say anything?"

"No. Obviously, every one will know at once if we ask for the inquest to be adjourned. That'll make it plain we aren't satisfied."

"Moon may bring a K.C. down," Perkins said gloomily. He was not looking forward to the kind of questions K.C.s sometimes put to inoffensive, long-suffering policemen—even when chief constables. "Then the cat will be among the pigeons all right. You don't bring K.C.s along for natural deaths—or even accidentals. I wasn't expecting you would tell Mr Moon quite so much. Generally speaking, the less said the better."

"Oh, yes, certainly," Bobby agreed. "Quite right. But if I hadn't told Mr Moon what I did, he would have been asking questions at the inquest, and a lot would have come out I think had better not be made public just yet. There's a good deal at stake."

"Two hundred thousand pounds, Mr Moon said," Perkins remarked. "A lot of money. There's plenty wouldn't stick at much to get their hands on it."

"One death already," Bobby said, "and I don't think it is going to stop there. I don't know. But it's begun, and it'll be apt to go on. Unless we can act in time—one chance in ten thousand."

"You mean the girl who gets the money? Is she next?"

"I wasn't thinking of her," Bobby answered once again. "I imagine she's safe—for the present. But I'm sure there's a plan to get hold of the Smith fortune and I'm sure it's not for her sole benefit—or chief benefit, for that matter. It may be worked by marrying her to this Bill Bright."

"What him? With a mug like his?"

"Oh, he's not so bad—quite good-looking, really. Must be," Bobby explained modestly, "because they say he's rather like me. If his nose wasn't swollen and his mouth a bit tidier and his eyes more as nature intended, he could pass. But I doubt if that's the idea. They wouldn't be likely to trust Mr Bill quite that far. He's been warned, though. The alibi could have been fixed up just as well without knocking him about. I should guess he's been showing signs of rebellion. Possibly draws the line at murder. You can't tell. It may be anything. What is curious is the odd kind of parallelism that seems to be running through all this. Cy and our friend Bill with his damaged face; and in the background the girl Gladys and the older woman, Mrs Elizabeth Smith. If that's her real name, as it almost certainly isn't. Possibly Gladys's mother. My daughter's my daughter all her life, you know. And then there's Tiny Garden with his satellite, Sam Deedes—Sunday, they call him—also with a badly battered face in the interests of discipline. Also in the background the girl, Betty Smith—if that's her real name, as it probably isn't— and the older woman, Mrs Day. Possibly the mother again. My daughter as before. They have the same shape nose, for what that's worth. What we've got to work out if we can is the interplay between the two groups, what they're each planning, who actually committed the murder. It may have been Gladys and the other woman after Cy had done the preliminary work. Or it may have been the second, Tiny Garden's group, hurrying the pace because of knowing Cy was preparing to gate-crash on the Smith money when the time's ripe."

"If it's like that," Perkins said thoughtfully, "then they are sure to fall out, and that'll be our chance."

"Yes, there's that," Bobby agreed. "But Cy has brains, and for the sake of half of that two hundred thousand—it's a big prize—he and Tiny Garden may manage to work in together. But there's something much more important, much more pressing. We've got to find out what has become of the other girl I spoke of just now. A second Betty Smith who came over from Canada recently in the 'Queen of the Seas' and hasn't been heard of since. Vanished without trace. So is she alive or is she dead? And how we're ever going to know I've no idea."

CHAPTER XV
"NO ANSWER"

IT WAS not a point on which the very much worried Mr Perkins had any advice to offer, so Bobby asked him how long it would take to get to Bournemouth.

"A lady there I think I ought to see," he explained. "The lady the missing girl was going to stay with. It's just on the cards she may be able to tell us something useful. A forlorn sort of hope, I'm afraid. Generally, if a person goes missing there's something to work from. But here we've a strange girl in a strange country where she knew no one and no one knew her, except this lady she was going to and the son. All we know is that she got to Euston and was met by a young man, drove away with him, and has never been heard of since."

"If no one knew about her except this Bournemouth lady and her son," remarked Mr. Perkins; "and the last heard of her is driving away with a young man, and the son is a young man—well, it doesn't sound too good to me."

"Nor to me," agreed Bobby.

"Are they after the Smith two hundred thousand as well?" Perkins asked. "Bit of a mix-up."

"Needs sorting out," Bobby replied. "One thing, we've got a starting point, now there's a dead man to show. I can't be told any more there's no proof anything's wrong. A man dead as poor Mr Smith died is sufficient cause, as they say."

"It was this young man gave information about the girl being missing, wasn't it?" Perkins asked. "But they do sometimes. Come and talk. Got it so much on their minds they can't keep away."

"I know," Bobby said. "It may be like that. About getting to Bournemouth?"

"You could do it in about an hour and a half fast driving," Perkins told him. "It's a good straight road. Take you all day by rail, and anyhow it's too late now to make connections."

"Could you spare me a car and a driver?" Bobby asked. "If you can, I'll get on the 'phone to Bournemouth and tell them I'm butting in, and ask them to get me a room somewhere."

Mr Perkins said he thought they could manage the car and a driver, short of men as they were. Privately he was wishing that the starting point Bobby talked about had been anywhere but in the select and fashionable resort of Seemouth, where, apart from the language occasionally heard on the famous links, so little ever occurred to trouble the soft, warm, yet bracing breezes for which the resort was so widely renowned. Some consolation, though, that now they were going to see the last of Bobby—at any rate for the time. Goodness only knew what else the fellow would be rooting up if he hung around much longer, and to the constable driver he chose to take Bobby to Bournemouth, Mr Perkins said confidentially:

"Mind you see every drop of petrol you use is charged to the Yard. No reason why we should pay for their car jaunts."

So Bobby was soon on the way to Bournemouth, and when he got there found a comfortable room had been booked for him in one of the hotels, and was also informed that Mrs Wyllie lived at some considerable distance from the centre of the town, in an outlying district.

By this time it was late, and Bobby was hungry, so he decided to get his dinner, and call on Mrs Wyllie in the morning. It would be less disturbing for her, and she would perhaps be more willing to talk than if visited so near bed-time—very possibly after her bed-time, for that matter. He rang up the Yard, therefore, to report, and at the same time put through a call to Olive, was asked in melancholy tones by the Yard if he didn't think they had enough on their hands as it was, without his going on seaside trips to dig up mysterious murders, was informed in even more melancholy tones by Olive that she was contemplating writing her reminiscences under the title 'Wife of a Perambulating Husband', made appropriate soothing replies in both cases, and went up to his room fully determined to spend the whole night in wakeful meditation, thinking and thinking and thinking till by sheer force of thought he had wrested some meaning from the chaos of events with which he was confronted.

However, he went to sleep instead, and next morning felt terribly ashamed of himself for such weak yielding to nature. But that's the way it was, and in fact not only had he slept soundly, but also he now enjoyed a leisurely breakfast, and even made quite a leisurely stroll of his progress to the outlying district where stood the small house occupied by Mrs Wyllie. It was a comfortable-looking semi-detached dwelling in a neighbourhood, Bobby guessed, where most of the inhabitants were pensioners or retired business men living on their savings. An equalitarian society, in fact, where extremes of wealth and poverty were alike unknown, and where life passed quietly, the full force of its fever far behind.

Bobby walked up the garden path. A milk-bottle stood on the door-step, and a morning paper was sticking half-way through the letter-box. Looked as if the inmates were not up yet, he thought idly, and time they were. So he had no hesitation in knocking and ringing, and as the electric bell happened to be in order, he could hear it sounding shrilly through the house. There was no answer. He tried again, knocking more loudly this time, and keeping his finger longer on the bell. Still no answer, and for the first time a faint unease began to invade his mind, and rather more than a faint regret that he had not paid his visit the night before, no matter how late the hour. Once more he tried, knocking still more loudly, ringing longer still. A woman who had come out next door to sweep the front looked at him curiously. He called to her to ask if she knew if Mrs Wyllie were away, as he could get no answer.

"They were both there yesterday," she answered. "They may have gone out."

"They?" Bobby repeated. "Is Mr Wyllie here—her son, I mean?"

"Oh, no, he's in business in London. I don't think she was expecting him. It's Miss Poore. She lives with Mrs Wyllie—her housekeeper."

"I'll have to try again later on," Bobby said. "They may be back soon."

He went away then, but this time not strolling. There was a call-box near. From it he rang up the Bournemouth police.

"I can't get any reply at Mrs Wyllie's," he explained. "No one there, apparently. Will you ring up and see if you can get through? I'm going back to the house. I want to know if I can hear the 'phone going."

He returned accordingly. The 'phone was ringing vigorously, but there seemed no response. He went back to the call-box and reported that the 'phone was in order but no notice had been taken of its summons.

"No one there," he repeated. "No answer. I don't like it. Could you send a plain-clothes man to watch the place, do you think? I'm coming round to see you. I want to put a call through to London to ask them to get in touch with the son and get his consent to our breaking in."

All this took time. It was nearly noon before Ted Wyllie rang up to say he was catching the next train, due in shortly before three and would go at once to the house.

"Have to wait, I suppose," Bobby said. "If it's all right and they've just been out somewhere, I expect there'll be a nice little row and more letters of complaint demanding apologies. There's been one already."

"You think there's a tie-up with the Seemouth murder?" the Bournemouth man asked. "We've no report of the men you wanted us to keep a look-out for."

"They may have been careful to keep under cover," Bobby said. "Easy in a town this size."

So Bobby got his lunch, relaxed on the front for a time, then took a 'bus to the district where Mrs Wyllie lived, and found waiting for him the Bournemouth inspector he had arranged to meet. Punctually a taxi arrived. Ted Wyllie alighted. Bobby and his companion were standing close by. Ted glanced at them, but did not speak, nor did they. Bobby noticed that the young man was looking pale and tired, with red-rimmed eyes, as though recently he had had little sleep. It was so marked that even the inspector, who had never seen him before, noticed it, and said to Bobby:

"Looks bad—something on his mind. Nervous."

Bobby nodded agreement. Ted had paid and dismissed the taxi-man, and was now walking up the garden path. Bobby and the inspector followed. Ted took no notice. He produced a key and opened the door and entered. They still followed, and he still took no notice. He shouted:

"Mother! Mother! Are you there?"

There was no reply. He opened the door of the nearest room, the front sitting-room. He stood for a moment, and then drew back. The room was in complete disorder. Evidently it had been thoroughly ransacked. Without a word Ted turned and ran first to the other rooms on the ground floor and then upstairs. He was down again almost at once. He said to Bobby, speaking for the first time:

"She's not here. Miss Poore, too. What's happened?"

Bobby and his companion had been looking at the other rooms in Ted's wake, though not quite with his swift and fearful speed. All the rooms showed the same signs of having been thoroughly searched, except the kitchen, which was neat and tidy and had been in no way disturbed. Bobby noticed on the kitchen table two empty hot-water bottles. He saw the inspector looking at them. They went upstairs. The bedrooms were in the same state of confusion as the downstairs rooms. Drawers emptied and their contents thrown about. A hasty, impatient and yet efficient search, Bobby thought.

"The beds have been made," Ted said to him. "They can't have been gone long. They must be all right. They'll be back soon."

"The beds may never have been slept in," Bobby said. "Can you tell if any of Mrs Wyllie's outdoor clothing is missing?"

"I don't know," Ted answered. "Her fur coat's there." He pointed to it lying on the floor. "For God's sake, do something!" he burst out.

"Seems to me," the inspector said, "as if what's happened was late last night. Beds not slept in, two hot-water bottles in kitchen waiting to be filled, supper-things washed up and put away, and no sign of breakfast."

Bobby nodded agreement, and went back to the kitchen. Their first hurried glance had shown him a door opposite the window. He said to Ted:

"What's that door?"

"The cellar. It's empty. The coal's kept outside. Mother didn't like the cellar steps, carrying the coal up. It's kept locked. The key ought to be there. It always is."

"I'll open it, if you don't mind," Bobby said.

It was a simple lock, and Bobby had previously had occasion to use his quite unofficial skill as a locksmith. In a minute or two he had it open. Within there showed the head of a steep flight of steps. Bobby switched on the torch he always had with him. Ted said:

"Mother had the shoot blocked up in the war. She was afraid of poison gas."

At the foot of the stairs was a strong door. It had been securely fastened by a wedge thrust beneath it and by two screws driven into the door-post. Bobby removed the wedge and turned his attention to the hinges. He thought them more vulnerable than the screws. Soon he had them wrenched away and the door forced back. Within, the light of his torch showed two women, one standing up before another, who was half sitting, half lying on the cellar floor. Ted pushed past Bobby. He called:

"Mother! Are you all right? Mother!"

"No thanks to you if she isn't, Master Ted, and you so long coming," snapped the standing woman. "Help me get her to bed, and then put the kettle on."

CHAPTER XVI
"SHE THOUGHT SHE WAS THERE"

THE LITTLE house became all bustle and activity. A small crowd gathered outside, stared, obeyed a request to move on, re-gathered, continued staring. Indoors Mrs Wyllie had to be got to bed. A doctor had to be sent for, though Miss Poore made it plain she had a very low opinion of doctors and a very high opinion of her own home-made remedies. Miss Poore herself had to be almost forced to sit down and rest and take some food, with the result that she nearly collapsed, whereas before she had seemed prepared to take full charge of everything—including, and especially, the police. Of them she expressed the opinion that she didn't want a lot of men trapesing all over the place now, when there had been no sign of them when wanted. As soon as she had emerged from the darkness of the cellar into daylight it was seen that her face was badly bruised and swollen, but for these injuries she firmly refused attention. She knew what to do for them, she declared. Cold water and a preparation of her own were all that was required. No doctor's stuff for her. Indeed, she seemed to have suffered very much less than had Mrs Wyllie from the treatment they had received and their long confinement.

Then, too, the team of police whose arrival had drawn from Miss Poore the already noted protest was showing itself extremely active, while Ted had been asked to make a careful examination of the contents of the house, so that it could be known what was missing.

At last, however, Bobby was able to find time to question Miss Poore. She was in the kitchen, whence she had just driven the doctor with the remark that she had done without doctors for sixty years and wasn't going to start now. She was heating some concoction of her own in a saucepan on the gas, and when Bobby tried to say something sympathetic about the injuries to her face, she observed that anyhow it hadn't spoiled her beauty, she having none nor ever had.

"Could you tell us just what happened last night?" asked Bobby, who was accompanied by the Bournemouth inspector.

"It was when we were listening to the wireless," she said. "The mistress likes to listen, and it isn't such a waste of time as you might think, because of being able to do your sewing and not pay attention. Most like along of the noise the wireless was making I never heard a thing till the mistress started to scream, and I turned round, and there was a man in the door with a bit of stuff over his face so as to hide his ugly mug. He said to put our hands up, and I tried to get at the poker, but he hit me first, and, I suppose," admitted Miss Poore reluctantly, "I must have tumbled down, and then somehow—I don't quite remember how—we were being pushed along into the kitchen and down the cellar." She paused and fixed a severe and exceedingly swollen eye on Bobby. "Young man," she said, "are you police?"

"Well, yes," Bobby admitted, somewhat apprehensively.

"What for?" demanded Miss Poore.

"But not Bournemouth," Bobby explained, hurriedly and pusillanimously. "My friend here is from the Bournemouth force."

"Oh, is he?" said Miss Poore. "And what's the good of you if you let decent respectable people be put in cellars in their own houses, and might be there still, only for being let out?"

"We are very sorry indeed about that, ma'am," said the Bournemouth man meekly, far too prudent to attempt any defence. "We'll do our best to see it doesn't happen again. And then, of course," he added, getting a little of his own back, "we didn't know anything about it till Mr Owen told us. He's from London."

"From London?" repeated Miss Poore, and her tone made it plain what she thought of London and those who came therefrom. She surveyed the two of them with impartial disapproval, and indeed they had rather the air of two small boys each trying to excuse himself and put the blame on the other. "I never did think police were much good," she remarked. "A lot of men! Except for asking the way," she added, trying to be fair.

Bobby, a little afraid of drawing fresh fire, inquired cautiously if she could give any further description of their assailant.

Any, even the smallest, detail would be helpful, he said. But she shook her head. She had had, she said, only the merest glimpse of him before diving for the poker and getting knocked out. She was not even sure if he had been alone or if he had a companion, though her impression was that that there had been a second man. It was plain that as a result of the brutal and stunning blow she had received her memory of subsequent events was very hazy. Nothing more emerged than the statement already made—that the intruder had been a very big man.

Bobby went on to ask if she or Mrs Wyllie could tell him anything more about the young lady, a Miss Betty Smith, who had been coming to stay with them but had never arrived.

"She stayed with you during the war at different times, I understand," Bobby said.

"And her room ready this time and all," Miss Poore said, "and then she never came. And don't tell me she wouldn't if she could have helped. Something happened. There's been an accident, or she's ill. She wasn't one to do a thing like that if she could help it."

"What makes you say that?" Bobby asked.

"Because she wasn't," Miss Poore answered conclusively. "Not like most of the girls to-day, all paint and silliness and powder, and not an idea in their heads except their boys. She had a way of cheering you up, somehow—had you laughing when you didn't want." Miss Poore pursed her lips and shook her head, evidently feeling it a duty to condemn the memory of a cheerfulness she had nevertheless enjoyed at the time. "Always ready to help, and wanted me to sit down while she did the washing-up. As if I would. The mistress thought a deal of her, and all last night kept talking to her off and on. She thought she was there."

"Thought she was there?" Bobby repeated, puzzled. "Who do you mean?"

"Miss Betty," snapped Miss Poore. "That's what I said, isn't it? A bit light-headed she was, and so would you, if you had been knocked about unexpected in your own house and pushed in the cellar, and the air so you could cut it with a knife."

"Do you mean Mrs Wyllie thought she saw her? Did she say she did?"

"She wouldn't have been trying to talk to her if she hadn't thought she was there, would she?" Miss Poore retorted. "Kept asking her where she had been and why she had been so long, and things like that, and I couldn't hush her, though I tried."

"Did she seem to get any reply?"

"How could she when I keep telling you there was no one there and it was all because of being treated the way she was?"

"Me, O.K.," Bobby said.

"What's that mean?" Miss Poore asked suspiciously, and Bobby's Bournemouth colleague gave him a surprised stare.

"Oh, nothing," Bobby answered quickly. "Just a sort of catch-word I seem to have picked up somehow. About Miss Smith. Do you think there was anything between her and Mr Wyllie?"

"That's for them to say," Miss Poore answered severely. "She might have done worse, and so might Master Ted. I'll tell you one thing. It's a lie about her meeting a strange young man in London and going off with him. She wouldn't ever. Not that sort—not with a young man she didn't know."

"But it might have been some one she did know?" Bobby suggested.

"There wasn't any," Miss Poore answered. "She said in her letter there wasn't any she knew any more in England except us. And if it was—though it couldn't be when no one knew she was coming—she would never have gone off without letting us know, not when she had told us to expect her, and knew we were."

Miss Poore was beginning to show signs of exhaustion, and Bobby suggested she would be better in bed. She snapped out a demand to be told who was going to look after the house and the mistress and Master Ted and all if she was in bed, where she said, with great firmness, she had no intention of going. With even greater firmness, Bobby told her to bed she was going, if he had to carry her there, and that the attendance had been arranged for of a nurse, who would be arriving almost any minute. Miss Poore told him sharply that she didn't hold with nurses, whom she described as a lot of simpering minxes, and she wasn't going to have them in her house.

However, the conflict thus threatened between Bobby, irresistible, and herself, unmoveable, was resolved when Miss Poore suddenly collapsed into a half faint. Before she had fully recovered the expected nurse appeared, as tart, resolute and efficient as Miss Poore herself. The ensuing battle was short, ending in complete victory for the nurse, though it is only fair to remember Miss Poore was by no means up to her usual fighting form. Before she well knew what was happening she was in bed, her bruised face was being attended to—and with 'doctor's stuff', her own cherished concoction having gone contemptuously into the sink—she had been given a pill so briskly she hardly knew she had taken it before, as a result, she was sound asleep, and the nurse set free to organise fresh victories.

Bobby, meanwhile, relieved at this happy outcome, went to look for the sergeant who had been in charge of the examination of the house. From him Bobby learned that no 'dabs' had been discovered, nor anything else of interest. The weather had been dry, and the garden showed no footprints. The back door had been found locked, but the lock was one, according to the sergeant, that a ten-year-old could pick with a match stalk. The key had been picked up lying on the floor near the door, and it looked as if the door had been locked on the outside and the key then pushed beneath it. There didn't seem to be anything much missing, or so the young gentleman said. He was in the front sitting-room now, and there accordingly Bobby found Ted.

"Nothing missing, as far as I can tell," he repeated to Bobby. "Mother hadn't much jewellery, but it's all there, I think. So is what silver she had—a tea-set and some other things. It all seems all right, in spite of the way everything's been thrown about. I can't make it out."

"Would Mrs Wyllie be likely to have any money by her?" Bobby asked.

"No, just the housekeeping. Anything big she pays by cheque. There's four or five pounds in her handbag, and that hasn't been taken either. There's one thing, but mother may have put it away—a photo of Betty she sent from Canada. It used to be in a silver frame on the piano, but it's not there now."

"That's very important," Bobby said. "Helps to make the picture a lot clearer."

CHAPTER XVII
"THE ONE THING MISSING"

LATER ON the same day Bobby returned to London. For there it was, he felt, that the main investigation would have to be carried out. Seemouth and Bournemouth could be left to attend to the routine inquiries necessary on the spot, but it was highly improbable that anything very useful would be discovered in either locality. Not there, but in London, was to be sought the cause, the perpetrators, of both crimes, and only there could be found the evidence and the proof required to bring the criminals to justice. Even more important, only in London was there, Bobby felt, much hope of securing the information necessary to prevent the success of what it now seemed certain was a daring and ruthless scheme to obtain possession of the Smith fortune. Already one life had been sacrificed in that aim, and it was heavy on Bobby's mind that more were in the balance.

His responsibility it was, he told himself unhappily, to save those endangered—a heavier responsibility by far than merely to avenge a life already lost.

"If, that is," he said to Olive, "it isn't in fact too late. There is one hopeful sign—the photograph missing from Bournemouth."

"The one taken from Mrs Wyllie's?" Olive asked.

"The one thing missing," Bobby said. "Bournemouth has confirmed from her that it was in the front sitting-room and that now it isn't."

"All that just to get hold of a photograph?" Olive asked, a little doubtfully.

"And felt to be so important that jewellery and cash and silver were all left alone," Bobby said. "There's only one explanation for a photograph being wanted so badly as all that—to identify somebody. And that means that that somebody must be still alive. And that's what's troubled me ever since I knew the second Betty Smith had disappeared. Easier to hide the dead than the living," he said grimly.

Olive said don't and it gave her the shivers when he talked like that. Then she said:

"Suppose these people do find her now they've got her photograph to work from?"

"Now you give *me* the shivers," Bobby told her, and there was silence for a time. Then he said: "Gay and happy, every one said, even Miss Poore, and it must have been a bit of a job to make that old battle-axe laugh."

"Bobby," Olive said, "you just simply must."

"I tell myself that," Bobby answered. "I don't know that it helps. It's time that matters. If we had all the time, we could be sure of finding her in the end, even if we had to go all over the country with a fine tooth-comb. It's not only finding her, but finding her first. There's so little that we know."

"You do know it must have been Tiny Garden who was at Bournemouth?"

"Oh, yes," Bobby agreed. "We can work on that. Description agrees well enough, and the whole thing is like him. Unnecessary and stupid brutality. And there's no doubt about his being guilty of the murder of old Mr Smith. Cy King has established his alibi. He knew, or guessed, what was going to happen, but he has made it plain he had no part in it. Ted Wyllie has an alibi, too. He was in London."

"But you don't suspect him, surely?" Olive protested.

"Why not? He seems to have been the only person in a position to know when the second Miss Smith from Canada would arrive, and therefore apparently the only person in a position to meet her—as she was met. And Miss Poore says she would never have gone away with a stranger, so it must have been some one she knew."

"But why? Why should he?"

"The whole thing is obviously aimed at getting hold of the Smith fortune—two hundred thousand pounds," Bobby told her. "The only way of doing that is through the first Betty Smith. She inherits the money by a will no one would even think of disputing, since she passes as the only living relative. The easiest way of getting hold of the money after that is by marrying her. After which, again, she may meet with a sudden death. Oh, yes, it's on the cards," he added, as he saw Olive about to protest. "She may be induced to hand it over or share it out, and she may refuse.

Plenty of possibilities there. She may find herself in deeper water than she ever thought of when it began. There's this story of the fit of hysterics as soon as she got back from Seemouth, which does rather suggest that she hadn't been contemplating murder, and had a shock when she found others were."

"You feel sure she is an impostor?"

"Nothing else makes sense," Bobby said. "My idea is that she is really the daughter of old Mrs Day, the housekeeper. There is a certain family resemblance. They've both the same shaped, rather prominent noses. Nothing very marked, but it's there. Probably Mrs Day discovered that the old man was feeling very much alone in the world, and found out he had a niece in Canada he had never seen. Or heard of for years. What easier than to provide him with this unknown niece in the form of her own daughter? So the girl is sent off to Canada to find out details and get the necessary local colour. She comes back, introduces herself, and is welcomed. Some one of his family to look after him in his old age, Mr Smith must have felt, and didn't dream it was his own swift and sudden death that he was welcoming. I don't expect either Mrs Day or the girl were thinking of murder at first. Their idea was probably a good fat cheque on some pretext—buying a business for the girl or something like that—and then disappearing with a small but quite satisfactory loot. But she got such a warm welcome and was soon so well established that bigger possibilities began to show up. Still, very likely no thought of murder yet. Then the man called Sunday comes on the scene. Pretty clear he is Mrs Day's son and the girl's brother. Quite a family affair. Notice the 'day' termination? The 'Sun' may come from his red hair, or maybe because he is Mrs Day's son. Anyhow, it's clear he soon got to know their plans. Couldn't keep it to themselves. Felt it a bit too big for them to handle, and wanted help probably. And Sunday would want quick results. Mrs Day had a good job as housekeeper, and the girl was comfortably fixed as favourite niece. So they two may have been ready to wait, even though it's weary waiting for dead men's shoes. But not Sunday. Or again, the girl may have wanted action. She may have got tired dancing attendance on an old man and humouring and flattering him all day—a change she may have found intolerably dull after the sort of life she had probably been leading."

"I don't think it was like that," Olive interposed. "I think she was growing quite fond of him. You could tell. Why couldn't she find being dull and safe much nicer than being not dull and very unsafe? It's comforting to know you've nothing to worry about. And then it was worth while being a little patient. All that money to get, and no risk or danger, only waiting a little for it to come to you quite naturally."

"With the full approval and kind assistance of Mr Moon," Bobby remarked. "You can't tell. Anyhow, either because the girl or her brother or one or both wanted quicker results, Tiny Garden comes in. Or else—which I think is more likely—because Sunday was too big a fool to keep his tongue still, and started boasting about the good thing he was in on. Tiny Garden gets to hear. Even then they may still not have meant murder, or else kept it at the back of their minds as a last resource. But then the fatal complication. The genuine niece is going to visit England, and suppose she turns up at her uncle's?"

"But how could they know?" Olive asked.

"Mrs Day would be sure to keep an eye on all letters, and if one came from Canada, she would open it at once."

"But you said Mr Smith hadn't heard from her for years?"

"Yes, there's that," Bobby agreed. "The Wyllies knew about her, of course, but there's nothing to show they had ever heard of the uncle, or knew where he lived. But she may have talked about her English uncle, and the Wyllies may possibly have got his address somehow. Not too likely, but we must consider the possibility that Ted Wyllie did know, that he made inquiries when he heard the real Betty Smith was coming, discovered there was a fake niece in possession. We don't know what his business position is. We don't know if he wanted to marry the genuine Betty. She may have turned him down flat before, and not been very likely to change her mind. He may have seen a chance to gate-crash. He gets the genuine Betty out of the way and tells the fake she's got to marry him or be exposed. If it was that way, he may be in more danger than he knows. Gate-crashing isn't always a very healthy occupation."

"But how could he?" Olive asked. "How could he keep her out of the way?"

"Yes, I know," Bobby said sombrely. "There's that, isn't there? But, then Cy King and his friends have to be brought into the picture somehow. It's clear Cy got to know something big was in the wind. That may explain why Sunday was knocked about. Been shooting off his tongue too much, and let out something that got passed on to Cy. Cy thinks he would like to know what's on. He hears it's a likely job at Southam, and he finds out that it's to do with an old man who has a lot of money and lives alone with two women. Must have looked an easy break-in job, and Cy may have thought at first it was merely who got in first. Then he began to guess again. What interested me was the getting up of one of Cy's pals to look like me. My first idea was that Cy meant to get admission to the house by pretending that a burglary was being planned and a police ambush was to be ready."

"Headed by you?" Olive asked. "And the local police to know nothing about it? It could have been made to sound quite plausible."

"So it could," agreed Bobby. "The cheek of it. Get admission to the house like that. No fuss or noise. Line the inmates up, tie them up, or push them in the cellar out of the way, and then make a comfortable get-away with everything in the house worth taking. And all by using my name. Well, I wasn't going to have that happening if I could help it, so I went along, and soon got the idea it wasn't so simple as all that. Then I saw the advertisement in the 'Daily Announcer' about a Betty Smith from Canada her friends hadn't heard of since her arrival. That made me really uneasy."

"Do you mean you think Ted Wyllie and Cy King are both in it?" Olive asked.

"Not together. I'm working on the theory that there are three separate gangs—or rather two gangs: Cy King's and Tiny Garden's, and Ted Wyllie on his own. Mrs Day started it, and brought in her son and daughter, and was joined, whether she liked it or not, by Tiny Garden."

"And it's they killed poor Mr Smith?"

"Yes. It wasn't Cy King. His alibi proves that. It also proves he knew what was going to happen; or why the alibi? It wasn't young Wyllie, because he has an alibi, too. He was in London at the time. We've checked that. It wasn't Mrs Day—at least actively, because she was in Southam as usual. And the girl's attack of hysteria the postman told us about suggests she didn't know till the last moment what was going to happen. Perhaps she didn't know, only guessed. Anyhow, she wasn't actively concerned, as there's evidence the old man saw her off from Seemouth by a late train before he went back home to his supper and his death. And over it all the question of what has become of the genuine Betty Smith."

"But if they wanted her photograph so much they had to break into Mrs Wyllie's house to get it, that shows she is still alive, doesn't it?"

"It suggests the Tiny Garden gang thinks so," Bobby agreed. "The ransacking the house may have been in the hope of finding out something about her and where she was. In any case, it seems to prove they had nothing to do actively with her disappearance, just as Cy and his gang had nothing to do actively with the Smith murder. But it does leave open the possibility that Ted Wyllie is behind it all—even the murder. His alibi may be less water-tight than it seems. That's how it all looks to me, and I think it's all clear logical reasoning."

"Ye-es," said Olive, "I suppose so," and would have liked to contradict instead of agreeing, because she had a poor opinion of logic, which, she said, derives from reason, and has therefore nothing to do with life, which is never reasonable.

And if that, she used to say triumphantly, isn't sound logic, what is?

Bobby went on:

"If Ted Wyllie is really pulling the strings from behind, then I haven't much hope of saving the girl. Too late. On his own, he would never be able to keep her hidden for long. If it's Cy, then he and his friends may be holding her alive, in reserve, to produce if a proper share of the Smith fortune isn't handed over. After that . . . or if Tiny can find her before we do . . . well, there it is."

CHAPTER XVIII
"WHAT SHOULD I CARE?"

THERE WAS a conference at Scotland Yard, and it was agreed that, in current officialese, 'top priority' must be given to the problem of what had become of the second, and now believed to be the genuine, Betty Smith.

"Nice-looking girl, not so much being so awfully pretty as the 'isn't-life-fun?' sort of look she's got somehow," observed the senior of those present, putting down the photograph he had been studying. "Give it all your attention, Owen. Anything else—well, pass it on to the next man."

"Me," said Bobby's colleague sighing. "Don't mind that. Makes life real fun, doing two men's work."

But this sad note of resignation passed unnoticed, for the senior officer was repeating very gravely:

"Give it all you have, Owen. But keep it quiet what you're doing. Won't do to let it be known she's being looked for. Too dangerous. You've been working on those lines? Rub it in to every one else."

Bobby nodded assent. But was it possible? To search with eagerness and passion, and yet to let no sign appear of what it was was being sought. Or, indeed, that any search or special activity of any kind was in progress.

But the attempt had to be made, and from this moment dates the beginning of that strange, secret search which still is spoken of by those who shared in it with a kind of wonder, almost of awe.

Henceforth a feverish eager activity prevailed all through the C.I.D., and not in London alone, and yet everywhere routine remained to all appearance undisturbed. Suspects were questioned, watched, examined, found themselves the objects of increased attention, and yet got no hint of the reason. Nothing was allowed to escape of the real purpose and intention of it all, and indeed some of the C.I.D. men employed knew no more than that they were to be on the look-out for and report at once anything unusual, and that to do so was of extreme importance. Some odd stories were dug up in fact—a rather specially cunning dog-racing swindle, an elaborate scheme for smuggling watches from the Continent. But nothing anywhere to throw light upon the fate of a missing girl.

Once, indeed, Sergeant James came in some excitement to see Bobby. There was a report of a girl said to be held in an attic in Penge. She had been seen at the window in an attitude of supplication, and the occupants of the house refused to answer questions. But it was a case of which Bobby had already heard. A young woman was suffering from an acute form of religious mania, and had shut herself up to wait for a divine revelation. Her relatives, naturally distressed, had no wish to relieve the curiosity of neighbours, though now it was becoming a question whether she would not soon be certifiable.

There was one other item James had to report.

"That Mr Ted Wyllie," James said. "One of my men says a young gent answering his description was at Jimmy Joe's café again, which isn't any place for young gents, and was seen to leave same in company of Tiny Garden. He put in a special report."

"Yes, I've seen it," Bobby said. "Doesn't look too good. It may mean Mr Wyllie is in with the gang, or it may mean he's playing detective."

"Oh, lord!" said James.

"I know," Bobby said sympathetically. "Either way he's liable to get his throat cut, and it's up to us to stop it, of course. Everything is always up to us. How is young Fred Ford getting along?"

"Might be worse," pronounced the sergeant. "I will say he does seem to understand a C.I.D. man's week is twenty-four hours a day, seven days a week. Some of these youngsters," complained the sergeant bitterly, "talk about dates with their girls or going to the pictures. I tell 'em to get a job in the building trade. I've had Ford meet one of our contacts, Ally Hidd. Ally's a shy bird, and he's more likely to talk to a new man. He won't talk to me, except on the 'phone, for fear of being seen. Thinks he'll be corpsed in double quick time if spotted."

"He's probably right," commented Bobby.

"Generally O.K. what he does pass on," the sergeant remarked. "I would as soon trust him as any contact man."

"He's an old scoundrel," Bobby said, "and he wouldn't be a contact man if he wasn't too old to burgle any more."

With that James departed, and Bobby, when lunch-time came, took a bus to King's Cross, where he entered a crowded tea-shop caféteria. He found himself a table, and was soon busy with a frugal lunch—total cost 1s. 7½d., and no doubt as many proteins and vitamins as any West-End restaurant would have provided for six or seven times the money. He had nearly finished when another customer came in, secured his lunch, looked round for a vacant seat, saw one at Bobby's table and joined him.

"Sausage," he said approvingly, "and jam roll. Not too bad."

"Expecting a friend, Ford?" Bobby asked, observing that on the tray were two plates of sausage and two other plates, each with its appropriate share of jam roll.

"I hope they think so at the counter," Ford answered unblushingly. "I generally double at these places. Nice thing about the 'Help Yourself' counter idea. No waiter to notice things."

"Great advantage," agreed Bobby, and retired behind his paper, while he looked round to make sure no one, waiter or other, was paying them any attention. Then he emerged again, and to Ford, now busy with sausage plate number two, he said: "Seen Ally Hidd?"

"Can't get much out of him" Ford complained. "All of a tremble. Jumpy as a cat on hot bricks. First thing he said was he was going to Brighton to get a job there and be out of it."

"Sounds as if he knew something," Bobby remarked. "You gave him my message?"

"And the pound note," said Ford, who had now gone on to the first jam-roll plate. "Funny thing, sir. When I told him you said he could name almost any figure in reason if he helped us find the girl, he said what would be the good if he had his throat cut, and he wasn't getting across Cy King or Tiny Garden, not if we offered him the Crown jewels in a paper bag. I showed him the young lady's photo, and he looked at it, and he used some language such as you don't often hear, and then he looked at it and used some more, quite different, and then he said 'O.K.' He supposed he would have to croak some day, and it might as well be soon as late, only why the hell couldn't I keep my damn photos to myself? He went off, still cursing and swearing quite out of the common; and then he came back and said to look out, and if any kid asked me to tell him the wrong time, then I was to tell him to run off and not be cheeky, and after that follow him, only be sure not to be seen. And the same for you, sir."

"I'll remember," Bobby said. "Ally's a worthless old scoundrel, but—somehow there's always a 'but'. One way or the other. I don't suppose there ever was any one yet without a 'but'."

"No, sir," said Ford, slightly puzzled. "I mean, yes, sir."

"Anyhow, you'll get ten times the help from him now he's produced a 'but'," Bobby said, "than you ever would for any tenner or more you gave him."

"Yes, sir," said Ford, still puzzled. "One other thing Ally said was that there's a young gent hanging round what'll get put away if he don't mind. Asking too many questions. Ally said to tell him blooming amateurs had best keep away from jobs of this sort."

To Bobby this advice from Ally Hidd seemed good advice, and so, instead of returning direct to his desk, he took another 'bus to the City, and then called at the office of the General Consolidated Toy Manufacturing Company—two or three rooms on the third floor of a tall office building. There a very smart, efficient-looking young lady informed him that Mr Wyllie was in, indicated a door marked: 'Private. Sales Manager,' and returned to her typing. As he was, it appeared, intended to knock and enter, Bobby did so.

A small room, almost entirely occupied by two large desks. At one of these Ted Wyllie was sitting, his desk covered with papers, and he himself apparently occupied staring at the blank wall opposite. But when Bobby entered he half rose from his seat.

"Yes. Well?" he asked. "Have you—?" And there he stopped, as if he knew at once the answer to his unspoken question.

"I just thought I would look in," Bobby said. "May I sit down? I thought a little chat might be helpful."

"God in Heaven, man!" Ted cried, and so loudly that the rattle of the machine stopped for a moment, as if startled into silence, and then resumed again, "What's the good of a little chat? Why don't you do something?"

Bobby did not answer immediately. He was thinking that he had seldom seen a man look so strained and worn, so pale, so haggard, with such bloodshot, red-rimmed eyes, with every nerve so clearly stretched to breaking point.

"We are doing our best," he said at last.

"Mother says she's dead," Wyllie said.

"Does she give any reason?" asked Bobby.

"She says she saw her that night—saw her plainly."

"Mrs Wyllie was hardly in a normal state," Bobby reminded him. "Naturally. Miss Poore saw nothing. I don't think we can attach much importance to what your mother thought she saw—not after the shock she had suffered."

"If Betty's alive, where is she?" Ted asked.

"We are doing our best to find out," Bobby answered. "Believe me, we are doing everything we can."

"You don't seem to be getting anywhere," Ted told him sullenly. He leaned across his desk. He said in an odd, croaking voice: "For God's sake, do something. Sit there and talk; that's no good. What's it matter to you? I shall go off my head soon, I think." He struck his fist with violence on his desk, as if he meant to split the surface. He said: "Just another case. File 2002, Class XY, No 66. That's all it means to you. All very smart and efficient, and gets you nowhere."

"It means a good deal to you?" Bobby asked gently.

"I never knew how much till now," Ted answered; and quite suddenly broke down and began to sob. Bobby took out a cigarette and became busy lighting it. Ted controlled himself. "Sorry," he mumbled. "It's the waiting and not knowing, and then you come, so damn calm and official and efficient, you and your 'little chat'. Sorry. Quite natural, of course. You never heard her laugh—it bubbled up so God himself had to smile just to hear her. Look. Did you ever hear of a man called Tiny Garden?"

"You mean the man who broke into Mrs Wyllie's house and took away the missing photograph?" Bobby said. "We know him all right."

"Well, then, why don't you arrest him?"

"Because we hope by watching him we may find out what's become of Miss Betty. How did you come to hear of him?"

"He wrote to me. He said it was him had answered my advertisement and made an appointment to meet me at a place at Soho, and did I remember? He said he had been prevented from turning up, but now he could, and would I come?"

"At Jimmy Joe's café?" Bobby asked. "Did you go?"

"Yes. How did you know it was there?"

"What had he to say?" Bobby asked, not replying to the other's question.

"Nothing much. It sounded more as if he were trying to find out what I knew. He wanted to know if I would give him her photograph."

"Did you?"

"No. I didn't trust him, somehow. I wasn't sure what he wanted it for."

"He wanted it so badly he broke into Mrs Wyllie's to get it," Bobby remarked. "It was about him I came to see you. With a message. You've been noticed talking to him. You've been seen at Jimmy Joe's place. And I've been asked to give you a warning. It comes from a man who knows Tiny Garden. It is: 'Blooming amateurs had best keep out of a job like this.' It's a warning I want you to take pretty seriously. Leave it to us. I don't want to have the further job of finding out who it was cut your throat and dumped you in the Thames. Please believe me when I say that's a possibility you must consider very seriously."

Ted leaned back in his chair. He was smiling a little now. He looked much more normal. Imitating Bobby, he took out a cigarette and lighted it, and Bobby noticed with surprise that his previously shaking hands were now quite steady. Ted said:

"Will you take a return message? Tell them that throat-cutting is a game two can play at. If anything's happened to Betty, I'll take a hand myself, and that goes for every man-jack of them."

"Don't talk like a fool," Bobby said, startled and angry, for there was that in Ted's voice, now very quiet and low, that made him feel Ted meant it and would do it. "Do you want to get hanged yourself?"

"What should I care?" Ted asked.

CHAPTER XIX
"ANYTHING IS POSSIBLE"

BOBBY WENT away then, more worried and troubled even than he had been on arrival. To Olive that evening he said:

"Means I've not only to take care that Wyllie doesn't get murdered himself, but also that he doesn't murder any one else. I've told Sergeant James and young Ford to keep a sharp lookout and let me know at once if they see him anywhere in the Jimmy Joe café neighbourhood. I wish now I hadn't mentioned Ally Hidd's message."

"Why?" Olive asked. "What's that matter?"

"I don't know, but Wyllie is nearly off his head, and you can't tell what he may not be up to next. He looks it, too—off his head, I mean. James has noticed that. Only—"

"Only what?"

"Well," Bobby answered, half apologetically, "it's rather far-fetched, but all the same it's got to be considered. James put it to me that the only man he has ever seen with that sort of wild, distraught look of Ted Wyllie's, was a man who had murdered his sweetheart and was being driven slowly mad by the memory. So James is saying it may be like that this time, and he thinks possibly Mrs Wyllie more or less unconsciously suspects that that's what's happened, and that's why she keeps thinking she sees or hears the dead girl. Her subconscious presenting her secret hidden fears to herself in visual form."

"He's been reading psycho-analysis books," Olive commented.

"We all do," Bobby answered. "There's something in them if you observingly distil it forth. My own idea was that it might be some form of spontaneous thought-reading, like that broadcast, you remember, the other day. Quite outside police routine, though. Not the sort of thing you would ever dare put in an official report."

"If it was thought-reading—and after that broadcast, you can believe anything," Olive said musingly—"wouldn't that mean that she is still alive?"

"I don't know," Bobby answered. "I don't think it follows. If thought-reading is possible . . ."

He left the sentence unfinished, and they were both silent for a time. Olive looked at the clock and said it was bed-time. Then she said:

"If it's Mr Wyllie, why should he be going to these places, trying to find out things when he knows all about it and they don't? And why should that bother them so much that Ally Hidd thinks they may do something to him?"

"Well, anyhow," Bobby pointed out, "there's no doubt about the plot to get hold of the Smith money, and no doubt about there having been one murder already. If Wyllie starts hanging about and asking questions, it's quite likely they may think he's after the Smith money and had better be got rid of. But there's always the hope that the real Betty Smith is still alive, being held as a kind of hostage to make sure that when the Smith money is secured, it's shared out."

"But could any one be kept shut up like that nowadays?" Olive asked. "Is it possible?"

"Anything is possible to-day," Bobby told her. "We don't live in a nice, safe, comfy Victorian world. Our world is all violent melodrama, with bits of dead bodies dropped out of aeroplanes and other bodies destroyed in quiet suburban cellars in sulphuric acid. And communists dreaming of seizing the government of the country by force, and quite capable of having a try some day—with tommy-guns, and not votes, to decide. Not that I mean any one could be kept shut up for very long. If we had time we would go over the country with a small tooth-comb. But for a few weeks all you want is a good lock on an attic or a cellar and take care never to leave your prisoner alone for long. Or you could use drugs, or put your prisoner's legs in plaster-of-paris and explain they had been broken in an accident. Something of that sort. Ted Wyllie couldn't do it, not by himself. No one could. But Cy King has two women to help, and that makes all the difference."

"But surely no woman would—not when it's a girl."

"That wouldn't bother our Gladys one little bit," Bobby retorted. "Especially not, when it is a girl. She'll hate her all the more for reminding her of what she herself was once. If she has anything to do with it, all the less hope."

Olive lapsed into a distressed silence, and no more was said that night. Next morning Bobby was at the Yard a good deal earlier than usual, and found waiting for him a report from Sergeant James. It was to the effect that Cy King was back at his sweet-shop, though this had not been reopened for trade. There was still a notice in the window 'Reopening shortly under New Management.' It did not seem that the two women—Gladys and the older woman who called herself Mrs Elizabeth Smith—were with him, and no one seemed to know anything about them. But, then, no one in the underworld was very anxious to supply information about any of Cy King's doings. Not very safe. A disturbing item in the report was that Ally Hidd had been seen the previous night talking to Ted Wyllie and had then failed to meet Fred Ford, as had been arranged. Of the other suspects—Tiny Garden and his associates—the only thing noted about them was that they were to be found back in their usual haunts, but appeared to be drinking even more freely than usual.

Bobby's first job was to supervise and, in one or two details, to tighten up the arrangements for picking up every crumb of relevant information. Seemouth had been able to secure evidence that two men answering the description of Tiny Garden and Sunday had been seen in the Castle Beach district. But that was hardly matter for an arrest, and Bobby felt that the simplicity and ease with which the crime had been committed were going to make proof of guilt extremely difficult to secure. Then he drove to Southam in the hope of seeing the sham Betty. He thought it possible that if she were in a state of real distress or fear as a result of finding herself concerned in a brutal murder she had never contemplated, she might be willing to talk. The one weak point, he thought, in Tiny Garden's plans. It was a hope soon dispelled. Mrs Day, watchful, suspicious and resolute, told him that by doctor's orders Miss Smith was not to be in any way disturbed or worried. He had forbidden her to attend the inquest, and indeed the police had agreed that her presence was not necessary—at any rate, not yet. Evidence of identification was satisfactory, and there was ample further evidence that Mr Smith had been in good health and spirits when she left Seemouth.

So Bobby had to be content with leaving a message that if she needed help in any way he was always and entirely at her service. As was the whole of the police force of the country, since their purpose and duty was not only to bring the guilty to justice, but also, and even more, to protect the innocent, including of course the not wholly innocent who had somehow got themselves more deeply involved than they had ever expected or intended.

Not that Bobby thought this hint was very likely to be taken up. Of that, Mrs Day's stony features and stubborn eyes gave little hope. Perhaps she knew her son—if Sunday were her son—had gone too far for there to be any hope of mercy for him.

Bobby went away then. Once more he warned the Southam police to be on the watch for any developments. Then he returned to town, feeling rather helpless. It seemed a dead end had been reached, and that there was little more to be done till the organization he had set on foot secured definite information on which action could be taken.

Back in his office, he turned to other matters, till presently James appeared with little to report but much to say on the difficulty of keeping watch on suspects who knew very well they were being followed.

"In and out of tubes and lifts at the last moment," James complained. "Up one escalator and down the other, and grin at you as you pass each other. Stores with half a dozen doors, in at one, out the other."

"Got to go on trying," Bobby told him. "Till we know different. We must work on the idea that the real Betty is being held somewhere. If it's like that, our best hope is that some of these people may give us a lead. Or there may be a general blow-up."

"Well, if they start doing each other in, that'll be different," James remarked, but not very hopefully. "Only, if there are corpses, corpses can't tell, and those that aren't corpsed will talk less than ever. Suppose I put it about there's money waiting for any information about a girl believed to be held somewhere?"

But Bobby shook his head.

"Too dangerous," he said. "Remember we've got to find her before Tiny Garden does—and he's probably working as hard as we are. I don't want Cy to know we're on the same track. One reason why I'm worried about young Wyllie. So far as I can see, Cy knows nothing about him. He may now. And he may begin to feel it's too dangerous to keep her alive and much too dangerous to let her go."

"Hands tied all along the line," James grumbled.

"The girl's safety has to be put before everything," Bobby repeated once more. "If it's not too late already. Has Ally Hidd turned up yet?"

"Not a sign."

"I've rung up Mr Wyllie's office," Bobby said. "They've had a 'phone call to say he won't be there for a day or two. That's all they know, and they seem a bit peeved about it. Anyhow, the 'phone call shows he's quite safe up to the present."

"Serve him right if he wasn't," grumbled James, with all a professional's contempt for amateur interference. "Got enough on our hands without him."

"About Cy's sweet-shop?" Bobby asked. "What's the layout? Back way in?"

"Not regular, no back door," James explained. "It's one of a block of shops in a turning out of Main Street. They all have backyards, and the walls between aren't too high. Easy to climb both ways, and from Main Street only three back yards to cross. More the other way. At the rear there used to be a church. Badly blitzed. Dead easy to slip across the blitzed area—it's been cleared, but that's about all—make sure no one's followed you and then skip over the back wall into Cy's yard. No trouble at all. Overhead premises let off in flats. All respectable people, as far as known. Cy's premises are the shop, a sort of back parlour, and a big storeroom. There's cellars, good size."

"Cellars?" Bobby repeated. "We've got to get a look at them."

"I was thinking that," James said. "Warn Cy, though."

"Work it through the Gas Board," Bobby told him. "I'll get their co-operation. They'll have to say a leak's been reported. They can start at the Main Street end and go through the motions till they get to Cy's. Then they must examine every inch of the floor. Under a microscope. Two of our best men must go with them, got up as Gas Board workers. Every inch of the floor," Bobby repeated. "And have a close watch kept, just in case there's any attempt to smuggle the girl away if she's alive and that's where they've had her. But I don't expect that."

"No, sir," agreed James. "We'll take care of the cellar floor all right," he added grimly.

CHAPTER XX
"RING ME WHEN HE'S GONE"

THE NEXT day this operation was carried out. Without result. Bobby was hardly disappointed. He had not expected more. It wasn't going to be as simple as all that. Whether Cy's suspicions had been aroused it was impossible to say. He had not seemed much interested in the proceedings, and though, to add a touch of verisimilitude to an otherwise bald and unconvincing performance, a gas-cylinder had been cautiously opened so that escaping gas could be smelt above, he had made no comment.

So once again it seemed a dead end had been reached. Cy King on the one hand, Tiny Garden on the other, appeared to be behaving in their normal manner. Ally Hidd was still missing from his usual haunts, and Ted Wyllie had still not returned to business. But he was being 'tailed' by a plain-clothes man, and since he was unaware of the fact, and in any case would have had no experience in how to throw off those following him, the task was not difficult. He had been indoors all morning. About two in the afternoon of this day he came out and took a 'bus to Baker Street. His 'tail' travelled on the same 'bus, and followed him to a tea-shop. There he provided himself with a cup of coffee and a bun, and as he seemed settled for a time, the plain-clothes man risked leaving him long enough to ring up the Yard and ask that Bobby should be informed.

"Looks like he was expecting some one," the message said, and as Bobby thought that sounded likely enough he got a police car to take him to the indicated spot.

"He's still there," the plain-clothes man told him on his arrival. "Just been joined by a party answering the description given of Ally Hidd."

Bobby nodded, and went into the tea-shop. The two of them, Ted and Ally, were too deep in conversation to notice him. He provided himself at the 'self-help' counter with a cup of coffee and crossed to their table.

"Mind if I join you?" he asked amiably as he seated himself.

Ally half rose from his chair as if minded to make a bolt for it, but sat down again abruptly when Bobby looked at him.

"I ain't doing nothing about nothing," he muttered.

"Aren't you?" Bobby said, and turned to Ted. "And you?" he asked.

"Do you expect me to sit still while you mess about and get nowhere?" Ted retorted, with dark anger in his eyes, hot and inflamed and bloodshot.

"Are you getting anywhere?" Bobby asked.

"At any rate I'm not sitting on my behind, doing nothing," Ted answered in the same angry tones, and Bobby smiled wryly as he thought of all that hidden, intense activity, that secret search, of which it was so important no sign should be shown. Ted saw that smile and misinterpreted it, and said with even greater anger: "Nothing to grin about." Then he asked: "How did you know I was here?"

"Oh, we have our methods," Bobby retorted. "I am afraid you do not feel much inclined to trust us, Mr Wyllie."

"It's not that," Ted replied, though somewhat grudgingly. He was staring hard at Bobby. He seemed to hesitate. "Where are your results?" he demanded. "If my salesmen don't show results, I want to know why. I'm having a try myself. Where's Betty?"

"You should learn to swim before you dive into deep waters," Bobby told him, and then turned sharply on Ally. "Well," he said, and managed to make that simple word sound like a warning and a threat.

"S'elp me," Ally protested, "that's what I been saying. Wasn't it me said to tell him to keep out? How was I to know he would come right straight to Jimmy Joe and hand him a one spot to put him on me? Which Jimmy Joe didn't ought to do, not to a pal, and never would, only for seeing Mr Wyllie wasn't a busy, and thinking to do me a good turn."

"I suppose you mean Mr Wyllie promised to pay you well?" Bobby suggested.

"I told him I might wring his neck for him if he didn't mind," Ted interposed.

"There you are," complained Ally. "What did I tell you? That's him all over. So what was I to do when he comes along?"

"Your methods, Mr Wyllie are just a trifle crude," Bobby said. "I think you had better be careful—very careful." Ted's scowl indicated that he had no intention of being anything of the sort. "I had occasion," Bobby went on, "to say much the same to Mr Smith. He wouldn't listen. Now he's dead."

"What was I to do?" Ally repeated plaintively. "I ain't so keen on getting across these blokes what's working it. I don't want to be mixed up in nothing. All for a quiet life, I am, and here's this gent, talking violent like, only offering good money, and I don't hold with murder, or young ladies what nobody knows what's become of them, especially when she's sort of smiling and nice like, as if it was all a bit of fun, and Mr Wyllie don't take no notice when he's told to keep out, but back again, asking his damfool questions same as before, so as every one knows and Tiny Garden and all—well, what was I to do, only try to keep him out of trouble?"

"I promised to pay his passage to New York and give him something over to start with when he got there," Ted said.

"They wouldn't let him in, not with his record," Bobby said.

"Now, guv'nor, you know better'n that," Ally protested. "You know same as me there's places where they'll give you an A.1 passport all complete, everything O.K.—very reasonable, too, mostly."

Ted had seemed to lose interest in what the other two had been saying. He spoke now, his tone and manner suddenly changed:

"Miss Poore thinks Betty's dead and it was her ghost mother saw."

"Ghosts," Ally repeated, and looked very uncomfortable. "I don't hold with ghosts," he said.

"I shouldn't pay any attention to that," Bobby said to Ted. "The shock to Mrs Wyllie is quite enough to account for her being a little delirious."

"Miss Poore says she wasn't—delirious, I mean," Ted said. Then he added, with a slight return to his earlier hostile manner, "What are you doing except talk? That's what I want to know."

"We are collecting every scrap of information we can," Bobby answered. "You are making our job more difficult because you are making it necessary for us to watch you as well." He changed his own manner abruptly, and with a sudden heat of anger he said: "Are you too big a fool to understand that your blundering in like this may cost the girl her life? That's what we are afraid of all the time. That whoever is keeping her out of the way may take alarm at any moment and decide to end it."

"What I want them to know," Ted said quietly, "is what I told you—that if anything happens to her, I'll see the same happens to them—and I shan't worry about legal proof, either. But if she returns safe and sound, nothing more will be said—and any money asked for will be paid without any trouble."

"Have you two hundred thousand pounds?" Bobby asked. "For that is what these people plan to get hold of—the Smith fortune. And it doesn't depend on you to decide whether anything more will be said."

"Which I told him," Ally interposed. "Nothing stops a bogey—puts it all down on paper and it's there for keeps. Tells all about," he said feelingly, "what you did when you was a kid. Rake it all up because it's always there. On paper. Police ain't nothing without paper."

"Out of the mouths of—" Bobby said, and left the quotation uncompleted, since the last words hardly seemed appropriate. Then he said, as Ally was obviously waiting for him to continue: "Who told you that one?"

"What do you mean, told me?" Ally asked suspiciously. "Look at that there 'Police Gazette'." He mused bitterly for a moment on those issues of the past in which he had figured with some prominence. "Keep 'em all on tap," he said as a culmination of injustice.

Ted got suddenly to his feet.

"I've had enough of this," he said angrily. To Ally he said: "Come along."

"Stay where you are," Bobby said. "I want to talk to you."

Ted glared. Ally wriggled. He wanted very much to 'come along', but Bobby's eye was stern and watchful. Ted walked away. Then he came back and said to Ally:

"Ring me when he's gone."

With that he walked away again, and this time did not return. Ally, watching him go, said:

"He's dangerous."

"So he is," said Bobby.

"All worked up," Ally said. "He thinks she's dead. Or else he knows."

"Why do you say that?"

"He sort of . . ." Ally began, and paused. "I don't know," he said. "He don't seem to care about nothing no more, and the way he sits and stares or talks to himself only so quiet like you can't hear. It ain't natural, like, and sometimes I get to thinking as it might be him done her in and now it's on his mind so he can't do nothing but remember."

"Well," Bobby said slowly, a good deal startled that this idea should have occurred independently both to Sergeant James and to Ally, "I don't know. Why should he?"

"Any bloke always liable to do in any skirt he's fallen for but not her for him," Ally said simply. "You see it happen."

"Got to take it into account, I suppose," Bobby said.

"What's a bit of news worth?" asked Ally.

"What it is worth," Bobby answered. "No more, no less."

"I'm getting out," Ally said. "Dublin. Not too far, not too near. Too hot for me here, and getting hotter, what with him half off his chump, and Cy King doing nothing same as a cat watching a mouse-hole, and Tiny Garden with one killing done and all set for more, and you on the pounce and all."

"Aren't you going to help find the girl?" Bobby asked. "I thought you didn't hold with that sort of thing."

"Same as I don't," Ally answered. "But I got to think of myself, ain't I? If I don't, no one else will."

"Oh, I think of you quite a lot," Bobby told him sweetly.

Ally scowled. He didn't like the remark. He liked even less the tone in which it had been uttered. He said:

"Anyway, not a chance in a million she's still alive. I'll give you one tip, though. Cy's Gladys ain't around any more. Nor the old fatty who was helping in his sweet-shop and loved the dear little kiddies so much none of 'em wanted to go near her. Find 'em, and it's on the cards you'll find the girl, too, if she's still there to be found."

"We thought that one out for ourselves," Bobby said. "The other tip is worth more."

"Now you're kidding," Ally told him. "There wasn't any other."

"Well, so long," Bobby said. "See you later very likely, even if we have to go to Dublin to find you."

With that he nodded and departed, leaving Ally looking sulkily and uneasily at the empty coffee-cups before him.

CHAPTER XXI
"AT THE SAME PLACE"

As it happened, there was a call-box only a few yards away. Bobby went across to it and rang up the Yard.

"Seemouth Beach bungalow case," he said. "Ted Wyllie, tailed in connection. I want him picked up and detained for an hour at least. Oh, on any pretext you can think up. Complaint received that he has been heard uttering threats involving a breach of the peace. What's that? Who is complaining? Why, I am, aren't I? But don't say so, say 'Information received'. Well, if you can't find him, you can't, but I expect you to, and he is almost certainly on his way back to his boarding-house. I heard him say 'Ring up'. Useful tip. He'll want to be there to take the call. As soon as you've got hold of him, send a plain-clothes man to the boarding house—young Ford if he is handy. Ford can explain he has to take a 'phone message. I don't suppose the hotel people will object, but if they do, Ford must flash his warrant card. Tell them it may be a matter of life and death—that goes for Wyllie, too. It's important to know who is speaking and what is said. My good man, of course it's most irregular and improper. No, it is not like opening a letter. Lord, no! I wouldn't dare do that—probably a breach of Magna Carta or something. But I don't think there's anything in it against taking a 'phone message intended for some one else. Yes, I take the responsibility. I always do. Get the sack for it some day, most likely."

He hung up then and walked on to where he had left his car in a side street near by. He found the driver busily investigating the engine, the bonnet up and tools spread out.

"What's wrong?" he asked.

"Nothing, sir," the driver answered, without looking up. "Wanted an excuse to report. Man on beat saw me, and says Cy King is hanging about. He saw him talking to two toughs in a car cruising round here. One of them got out and had a look in the tea-shop. Then he gave an O.K. sign to his pal, and he's still there, waiting near the door."

"Did he seem to know me when I left?" Bobby asked.

"No, sir. Took no notice."

"Bit of luck," Bobby said. "Looks as if it were Ally Hidd is wanted. Been asking too many questions for their liking. Your wireless working? Good! Send a call for a flying-squad car to come along and collect Ally. Tell them to put him down, where he likes, only near a 'phone-box. I suppose we have to see he doesn't get his throat cut, which is very likely what is intended. He wouldn't be the first found in the river and nothing to show how he got there, only that Cy had stopped liking him. Where is Cy? Seen him yourself?"

"No, sir," the driver answered. "He was in the street first on right when seen. The cruising car comes down it. They don't take any notice of each other, him and the driver."

"Oh, they wouldn't," Bobby said. "I'll go along and have a bit of a chat."

"Think it's safe, sir?" the driver asked, a little uneasily. "He's still awful sore about your getting him sent up, after all his boasting no one ever would. Bears a grudge somehow, as if it wasn't our job," and now he was speaking with some indignation, for this was an unusual breach of the generally accepted convention that police and crook each do their own job and no hard feelings.

"He's a vicious brute," Bobby said. "But he'll think twice before trying anything like that with me. He knows he would be picked up at once. If he does, it won't be on an impulse—it'll be some very careful, clever plan. At least, that's what he'll think it. He would give an awful lot to get a chance, though. I won't be long."

With that he strolled away, took the turning indicated, saw first a cruising car go by, a very tough-looking customer in the driver's seat, and then, a few yards farther on, he overtook Cy, lounging along with his characteristic slinking gait and his quick and restless sidelong glances, as of a beast of prey going warily on its search for a victim.

"Well, well," Bobby said in his heartiest, cheeriest voice. "So we meet again."

Cy swung round in a split second, and his hand was at his breast pocket, where Bobby knew he always carried a knife—the swift and silent knife he used to boast was worth more than any noisy, clumsy gun that bawled an instant alarm and was as likely to miss as not. Probably he carried another strapped to his ankle. He did not speak, but his eyes were bright and small and fierce as they rested on Bobby and then up and down the street, as if calculating his chances if he struck and fled.

"What a life," Bobby said, watching him carefully, for he knew his man. "Can't hear himself spoken to suddenly, but he's all ready to run or be run in. Don't you get tired of it?"

Cy made no answer. He, too, was watchful and alert, and he could see that Bobby also was ready, every nerve and muscle taut, prepared, so that no sudden blow but would meet with even more sudden response. Cy's expression relaxed. He thrust his hands deep into his trouser pockets. He said:

"Well, what about it? Can't a bloke take a walk without you snooping round?"

"Funny," Bobby said. "Hadn't seen you for quite a while, and now here's the second time within a day or two. Making a habit of it, aren't we? Why, I don't think I had seen you since that day you got sent up for—how long, was it? Anyway, not half as long as it ought to have been. Looking for another spell?"

"Not while I'm alive—or you," Cy snarled, and showed his teeth, and spat, and again his hand wandered to his breast pocket, and again moved reluctantly away, as if it realized itself how closely it was watched.

"Well, that's a tribute to our prisons," Bobby remarked. "Shows you think they are best kept out of—as is intended."

"What's the back-chat for?" Cy asked.

"Oh, that Seemouth business—ugly affair," Bobby told him.

"You can't pin that on me," Cy retorted. "I've an alibi."

"Yes, I know," Bobby agreed. "And a very present help in time of trouble is an alibi. But I wonder why? Looks as if you knew something. That might be what we call 'accessory before the fact', and if we pull you in on that—well, we might get something more somehow. I suppose you wouldn't care to tell me how you knew?"

"By using my nut, same as you're paid to, only you don't, not knowing how," Cy retorted.

"We do our best with the nuts Nature gives us," Bobby answered meekly. "My own guess is that a certain young lady"— he was watching Cy keenly as he said this, but Cy's expression did not change—"told a friend of hers, and it got passed on to you. Cy, when a girl's life may be in danger—" Again he paused, again waiting to see if any sign of a response appeared on those dark and scowling features. None did. He continued: "Cy, you're a bad lot, and you're headed for a messy end. Like to make a fresh start?"

"If it was on your grave, I wouldn't mind," Cy answered, and his voice was as it were consumed by a slow hatred.

"Have it your own way," Bobby said, sorry now that on a quick impulse he had spoken as he had.

For always his chief thought and constant care had been to avoid giving even the least suggestion of a hint that he or any one else had any thought or knowledge of any young woman being involved. Now he had said outright that a girl's life might be in danger, and though he hoped that the reference would be taken as applying to the false Betty Smith at Southam, yet Cy, quicker in thought and more intelligent than most of his kind, might put another interpretation on it, if the second and genuine Betty were really in his hands. Once he came to suspect that her existence was known, and that to find her was the real object of the unusual C.I.D. activity going on, even the faint hope remaining would vanish for ever. Fortunately what Cy now said did not suggest that he had—as yet—read any such meaning into Bobby's words.

"Got a down on me, haven't you?" he complained, and he had now the air of expressing a real and deeply felt grievance. "Tried to pin the Seemouth business on me; only you can't. And if the girl goes the same way as her uncle, you'll be on me again. Well, nothing doing. I'll take care. I'll watch out. Find out who did in the uncle, and then you'll know who may do the niece the same way."

"Tiny Garden, you mean?" Bobby asked, a little relieved at the turn the talk was taking. "Why should he want to get rid of her? She's safe enough till she gets the money."

"If you know it's Tiny, why don't you take him in?" Cy demanded.

"Got to get our case complete," Bobby answered. "We often know more than we can prove."

The cruising car came back and stopped. The driver leaned out. He hardly noticed Bobby. He called:

"Cy. Ally's been picked up."

"Oh, has he?" Cy answered. "Doug, meet Commander Bobby Owen. He'll remember you," and on the instant there followed a burst of expletives, rich and rare in both quantity and quality, but also largely wasted, for 'Doug' gave one gasp of dismay at learning who was Cy's companion, went very pale, jammed his foot on the accelerator, and vanished in a burst of speed that recked but little of the Highway Code.

"Didn't seem to appreciate meeting me," Bobby observed, with mild surprise.

"Blowing last night he was as not a bogey in London knew him from Adam," Cy said moodily. With the touch of self-pity he sometimes showed, he added: "That's the kind of fool I have to work with. Giving himself away like that."

"Your own choice," Bobby told him. "Doug was the name, wasn't it? Let him know I'll make a sketch of him as an addition to our picture-gallery. Sometimes a sketch is even better than a snap for recognition. Quite a break for me. Always glad to meet any friend of yours, Cy."

Cy scowled. Bobby nodded and walked away; nor did he even once look round, though he knew well how Cy's twitching fingers were hovering near that hidden knife of his and how slowly and reluctantly they were being withdrawn.

"I was almost coming to have a look," his driver said as Bobby came up to where he was waiting. "With blokes like Cy you never know . . . got no control of themselves, liable to break loose any moment. What the doctors mean when they talk about 'uncontrollable impulses.'"

"I don't take Cy to be quite like that," Bobby said. "I did think there was one chance in a million he might say something to give us a lead. He didn't, and I hope I didn't give him one. I took a chance, and I'm sorry now. But there's so little time and so little hope. It's like searching for a needle in a haystack that you aren't allowed to touch, only look at."

Indeed, Bobby had never felt his responsibilities weigh upon him more heavily than now, as he was returning to his office. Old Mr Smith's murderers to be brought to justice. The missing girl to be found, or at least her fate determined. Ted Wyllie to be watched, and both he and Ally Hidd to be given protection. Guilty or innocent, they still had that right. The false Betty Smith to be exposed so that not she, but those entitled to it, should inherit the dead man's money.

"And at any moment" he said to himself as he went to his room, "Tiny and Cy and their friends may be starting in on each other—and that'll make headlines all right."

He didn't like the prospect from any point of view, and then on his table he noticed a brief message waiting for him. It came from Fred Ford. With meticulous details of time and place added, it ran: "Begins. Ally speaking. That you, Mr Wyllie? I'm quitting. Too hot for me. She'll be at the same place late to-night. Not me, though. Cy King's on my tracks. And yours. Take my tip and stop out for keeps like me. So long. Ends."

Bobby laid the paper down.

"Same place late to-night," he repeated to himself. "Bit vague? And who is 'she'?"

CHAPTER XXII
"HE HAS NOT COME BACK"

SITTING AT his desk, Bobby grew busy, urging to even greater activity the whole of the great organisation which was at his service. First of all he saw to it that every effort would be made to follow Ted Wyllie to where or what the 'same place' might be. Seldom can more careful, more elaborate plans have been laid to make sure of a successful 'tailing'. And yet the utmost care had to be taken to make sure they were not too conspicuous, and so, by letting themselves be seen, defeat themselves.

Secondly, Southam had to be communicated with. There it was declared emphatically that the presumably false Betty Smith was still in bed, still under doctor's care. She was suffering, he said, from "shock", from a "nervous breakdown", whatever those expressions mean. What it came to was that she needed rest and quiet and must not be disturbed. She had been seen officially in connection with the adjourned inquest at which it had now been decided her presence would be necessary. She had also been visited by her lawyer, Mr Moon. The last interview had, however, been cut short by a violent attack of sickness. The doctor had had to be sent for, and the interrupted interview had not yet been renewed.

"Means," suggested Bobby's colleague who was assisting him in his work, "that this girl can't be the 'she' Wyllie is to meet. So it is just possible it's the other Miss Smith—the one you think is the genuine niece."

"Hope so," Bobby said. "But then 'she' applies to half the human race—the better half in quantity, anyhow. It may only refer to some woman Ally Hidd thought, or pretended to think, might be able to help. Or if Ted Wyllie had anything to do with the girl's disappearance, the 'she' may be an accomplice getting a bit panicky or turned blackmailer, perhaps. Anything is possible in this case."

"Even that we may yet be in time?" the other asked doubtfully, and Bobby left that question unanswered.

Then again, thirdly and fourthly, every effort had to be made to continue the watch on Cy King and Tiny Garden and their associates. A difficult task, for they were all of them slippery customers, almost always able to evade observation when they chose—at any rate for a time, though it was also almost always possible to find them again in their accustomed haunts where familiar surroundings tended to give them a sense of security. Much in the same way as places strange to them seemed to them instinct with a kind of hidden hostility.

Then there was Ally Hidd. Once the flying-squad men had put him down, he had swiftly disappeared. He would certainly not be easy to track. But, then, Bobby did not think it likely he would be of much further use. He had had a bad scare when told that some of Cy King's associates were waiting for him. Probably now his only desire was to get as far away as possible until things quietened down. As well, though, Bobby decided, that a look-out should be kept for him in case he turned up again.

It was at this point that the 'phone rang. Bobby answered it, and then said:

"Bournemouth. They report that Miss Poore has left by the London express. Can Miss Poore be Ally's 'she'? She'll have to be tailed. Suspects and 'tails' tumbling over each other all over everywhere," he grumbled.

So new arrangements had to be made to meet this new complication. They were not successful. There had been delay—delay at both ends in sending as in receiving and in passing on the information; delay in finding a spare man to undertake the new assignment; delay in his reaching Waterloo through a hold-up on the tube, short itself, but long enough to be fatal. A chapter of accidents that resulted in the Bournemouth train having arrived and Miss Poore having departed some five or ten minutes before the plain-clothes man got there. All Bobby could do was to grumble at such bad luck and direct the frustrated plain-clothes man to watch Ted Wyllie's boarding-house.

"She may never go there, though," he remarked as he hung up after giving these instructions. "Quite likely they've arranged to meet somewhere else."

"If it's her that's the 'she' we want," observed Bobby's colleague, "doesn't it rather suggest she may be in it? Might have been as well to have a good look at Mrs Wyllie's cellar, as well as at Cy's. Bournemouth is where the missing girl was going when last heard of, and if Mrs Wyllie knows—well, no wonder she thought she saw things."

"Might be why Tiny went there," Bobby said thoughtfully. "As keen as we are on knowing what's happened, and looking for something to tell him. Awkward for him if the real Betty turns up before they get hold of the money."

"Well, things are on the boil," said his colleague as he rose to depart to his own room and his own special work. "Nothing to do for the moment but wait till you hear something."

Now again, therefore, Bobby had to exercise that most ordinary, exceptional, essential quality a detective needs—patience inexhaustible and unending.

It grew late. Bobby had returned home now, and was sitting as near the 'phone as he could get. Olive was sitting near, occasionally hinting at bed. The wireless, having finished an excursion into swing, was now giving a talk on the fundamental resemblances between the philosophies of Hegel and of Whitehead, with occasional very contemptuous interruptions by a logical positivist. They had forgotten to turn it off, but it didn't matter, as neither of them had heard a note of the 'swing', or a word of the talk.

Olive's hints grew broader. Bobby was still not so much ignoring them as ignorant that they were being made. The 'phone bell went. Bobby grabbed the receiver and put it down.

"Wrong number," he said bitterly. "Never get anything else," he grumbled—indefensibly.

"Well, we do seem to get a lot," Olive agreed, mildly, and was about to abandon her system of hints for direct action when the 'phone rang again.

Though with less alacrity, Bobby picked up the receiver once more, listened, and was on his feet and at the door almost in one movement.

"Miss Poore and Ted Wyllie seen on a 14 'bus," he said over his shoulder. "Expect me when you see me."

He was off. Resignedly Olive made some cocoa, set it to keep hot on the gas and herself to get what rest she could on the couch. At the appointed rendezvous Bobby found a flying-squad car waiting for him.

"Latest report," one of the occupants said. "Suspects seen to alight at Cambridge Circus. Being tailed. Suggest wait Palace Theatre, Avenue side."

There accordingly by the long blank wall where so often the camp-stools stretch as to eternity, Bobby once more waited. Now and again the flying-squad car passed, taking no notice, but ready for any emergency, to all appearance just one car more in the busy evening traffic. An urgent message came. A smash-and-grab raid to take precedence of all else. They delayed a minute, not more, to sign to Bobby that they were called away, and scarcely had they gone when young Fred Ford appeared.

"Jay's Passage, off Lower Street," he said. "Looks as if they were expecting some one. Sergeant James is watching. He told me to report. Lower Street is at the back of Mock Street."

"Mock Street?" Bobby repeated. "Where Jimmy Joe's café is, and isn't there a back way in from Lower Street?"

"The Sarge said so," Ford answered. "By way of a lock-up wardrobe dealer's shop. You jump over the wall from Jimmy Joe's, and the shop door's always on the latch, back and front."

They had been hurrying along as they talked. Now they reached the west extremity of Jay's Passage, one of those dark and secret alley-ways that here and there penetrate the intricacies of the great city, like tunnels bored by some industrious mole through a hillock in a pasture-field.

It was badly lighted—one lamp at one end only, and that not always burning, for there were some of the residents in the vicinity who took steps to see that no inconvenient illumination spoiled for long those pools of darkness into which in times of need they could dive and vanish.

To-night, however, this lamp was burning, and they could distinguish one standing, solitary figure—that of a woman, upright and rigid—about half away along the passage. There was no sign of any one else, no sign of life anywhere, except for one lone light burning high up in an uncurtained window.

"There was a man with her," Ford muttered. "He must have gone off and left her. Sarge must have followed."

They hurried towards her. She turned her head at the sound of their approaching footsteps, but otherwise did not move. Bobby said:

"Miss Poore, isn't it?"

"And who are you, young man?" she demanded, and then, seeming to recognize him: "Oh, it's you. Well?"

"Where is Mr Wyllie?" Bobby asked sharply.

"He went away and he has not come back," she answered. "He said to wait."

"How long ago?" Bobby asked.

"Long enough," she answered. "It might be ten minutes. More."

"Which way did he go?"

She pointed with her umbrella in the direction of Lower Street, at the opposite end of the passage to that by which Bobby and Ford had arrived. Bobby said:

"Did any one follow him?"

"I haven't seen a soul till you came," she answered.

"Where was James?" Bobby asked Ford.

"In a doorway near by where we came," Ford answered. "He can't be there now, though, or he would have seen us."

"Run back and look," Bobby told him, and there was uneasiness in his voice. "See if you can see anything. He may have left a message of some sort." Ford hurried away, and Bobby turned to Miss Poore again: "What was Mr Wyllie doing here?" he asked. "What did he want you for?"

"That's for him to say," Miss Poore answered, and then they were interrupted by a shout from Ford:

"He's here, sir—here, in the doorway where I left him."

CHAPTER XXIII
"CY'S SWEET-SHOP"

BOBBY WENT running when he heard this. Miss Poore followed. Ford, looking in the doorway where he had left the sergeant, had found him there, huddled at the back, unconscious. He had received a heavy blow on the back of his head, inflicting severe injuries. Ford was trying to lift the unconscious man from the doorway to the pavement. Bobby, seeing that the sergeant's injuries were too severe for first aid to be of much avail, told Ford to find the nearest call-box.

"Get a doctor and ambulance," he said. "Urgent. Nothing we can do. Then let them know at the Yard. Hurry. I'll wait here."

Ford disappeared at a run. Miss Poore had joined Bobby. She said disapprovingly:

"What's happened now? Nice goings on."

"A man has been hurt," Bobby said. "Do you know anything about it?" She shook her head. He said: "Did Wyllie do this?"

"Him? Master Ted?" Miss Poore asked indignantly. "Haven't you got more sense than that? Master Ted indeed!"

"Why has he left you?" Bobby asked. "Why did he send for you in the first place?" When she still appeared to hesitate, he said with sudden, sharp authority: "Tell me what you know—everything. And at once. Wyllie's life may be in danger; others too."

"We had a telegram this morning," she answered then; and if still with a certain hesitation, yet none the less impressed by what he said and by the tone in which he said it. "It said for me to come. It said it was important because he had news. We both thought he meant about Miss Betty. So I came."

"What else?" Bobby demanded. "He must have told you more when you met him. Tell me everything," he said. "I must know if there's to be any hope of seeing him again alive, or Miss Betty either."

"He said as there might be a chance of finding her to-night," Miss Poore answered. "If we waited here, a man was to meet us, and he might be able to tell us where she was."

"Ally Hidd?" Bobby asked. "Was that the name?"

"Mr Ted didn't say any name; he just said a man. He was trying to find out why Miss Betty had never come, or written, or anything. He was fretting and worrying his life out about her. Only another job for you, Mr Ted said, but it meant everything to him."

"Another job?" Bobby said angrily. "We're putting all we have into it. Look there." He pointed to the injured man by whose side he was kneeling. "Is that enough for your Mr Ted?" he asked. "Would that convince him we were doing our best? What else did he tell you? Why did he bring you here at this time of night?"

"I couldn't make out rightly," she answered. "I don't think he knew himself altogether. It's somehow mixed up with the old gentleman at Seemouth—him they found dead in his bath. Mr Ted thought it may turn out he was Miss Betty's uncle—the one she always said she wanted to find. Mr Ted said he had found out Miss Betty was met at Euston by some one who said her uncle was waiting for her, because he had heard she was coming, and he was very ill and frail, so she must come at once if she wanted to see him alive. Only now it may be perhaps him that's dead at Seemouth is her real uncle and the other was just a mistake, and she might be coming to-night to make sure, and if we waited here we might see her. Master Ted wanted me to come so I could take her back to Bournemouth. He was that excited and worried you couldn't rightly tell what it all meant."

"I shouldn't have thought," Bobby growled, "that any one out of a lunatic asylum would take that rigmarole seriously. Has Mr Wyllie been handing out good money for it? Why couldn't the fool come to us?"

"If you mean Master Ted," Miss Poore retorted with spirit, "he's no fool, and not like some I could mention who do nothing but stand about and talk and anything happening to Miss Betty all the time and he wasn't saying a word till he knew about Miss Betty and what she wanted."

Bobby took it that this meant that Ted feared the girl might be mixed up in some way with the Seemouth tragedy. He spent a moment or two thinking yearningly of all the things he would like to say to Ted the next time he saw him. He said:

"Why did Mr Wyllie leave you here alone?"

"Well, the man he was expecting never came." she explained, "and Master Ted thought he might be waiting somewhere else instead of here, so he went to look, and he came back and said there were two men he had seen before in a café close by, and he thought one of them was a big man who might be him as broke into our house at Bournemouth, and he was going to wait to find out where they were going because it might be a sweet-shop the man he was expecting to meet here told him about."

"Why didn't you say that at first?" Bobby cried. "Wait here till help comes. I can trust you to do that? Tell them Cy's sweet-shop."

With that he set off running—running with swift, noiseless steps, leaving Miss Poore staring after him, the unconscious sergeant at her feet, she herself so bewildered and flurried that from the incoherent story she told when Ford returned with help, it was difficult to extract much meaning. With delay and difficulty it was at last gathered that Bobby had suddenly rushed away on hearing that the man she and Ted were to meet had not turned up, and that Ted, going to look for him, had seen a man resembling the housebreaker of Bournemouth. Then he had come back to tell her to wait while he tried to follow him. In the hurry and confusion of the swift questions rained on her, she entirely failed to mention those three words, 'Cy's sweet-shop', which, besides, she had only caught imperfectly and without realizing that they were of any significant importance. But her reference to a 'big man'—big as the one seen at Bournemouth—made Ford think at once of Tiny Garden and of Jimmy Joe's café not far distant.

Thither therefore it was that he and another plain-clothes man hurried, finding when they got there everything as quiet, peaceful, orderly and calm as could be desired. Just as Bobby, arriving in that side street where was situated Cy's sweet-shop, found there, too, everything perfectly normal, with no trace or sign to be seen of Cy himself or of Tiny Garden or of any one of their associates.

The shop itself had a deserted air. Closely fitting shutters were over the window. On the door was a notice 'Closed temporarily. Reopening shortly under New Management.' There was no bell, and when Bobby knocked on the closed door, he got no answer. A passer-by, returning late from work and probably an occupant of one of the flats overhead, said to him:

"No one there, mate. Lock-up shop, and been empty a week or two."

Bobby said "Thank you," and walked away, not quite certain what to do next. He told himself uneasily—and very crossly— that whatever happened to Ted Wyllie would serve him right for a blundering, interfering jackass, but that none the less the safety of every citizen, including the jackass variety, was the direct responsibility of the police.

Then again the rather confused story which, according to Miss Poore, Ted had heard from Ally Hidd, had seemed to him at first to be, as he called it, 'rigmarole'. But now, thinking again, he was not so sure. A bogus uncle was no more difficult to provide than had been a bogus niece, and some such scheme, effective in its simplicity, might have been used to get hold of the genuine Betty. Any letter of explanation she wrote to her Bournemouth friends to explain her non-arrival might have been intercepted and a forged reply sent in such terms as to make Betty reluctant to write again.

All attractively simple, and for a time plausible enough. But hardly a deception that could be kept up for long. Betty was no simple, guileless child straight from convent or from school. She had served in the Waafs during the war, she had worked in a lawyer's office in Canada. Sooner or later, and probably sooner rather than later, she would be sure to realize something was wrong. And then what would happen to her, alone in the hands of those already guilty of the murder of a helpless old man, the sole obstacle between them and easy acquisition of a great fortune?

Even if Ally Hidd's story had in it some elements of fact, the missing girl's situation, the urgency of finding her, both seemed as desperate as ever, the pressure of time no less immediate. As well, Bobby told himself gloomily, never find her at all as find her five minutes too late. He thought wrathfully of Ally Hidd sending messages to Ted through Bobby himself, warning him to keep away, and then telling him this long, confused, hesitating story which could only have served to excite him still further.

"If ever I get hold of that little rat of an Ally," he muttered, and knew very well there was nothing he could ever do. Except give Ally a tongue-lashing that would have about as much effect on that gentleman as Sidney Smith thought stroking the dome of St Paul's would have on the dean and chapter.

By now he had wandered round to the next side street running parallel with, and behind, that in which the sweet-shop stood. Here was the site, only partly cleared of rubble, where once had stood an ancient church till one of the last of the flying-bombs to reach London had fallen upon it. Now this vacant plot, marked for the building of a block of flats when labour and material were again available, had become a playground for children and an occasional retreat for courting couples seeking privacy in discomfort. But the hour was too late for children, even in this neighbourhood, where children's hours differed little from those of adults, and, as a light rain had begun to fall, the most ardent lovers were not likely to be lingering there to-night.

Cautiously Bobby began to pick his way across that sad memento of the waste of war. Soon he was half-way to the rear of the sweet-shop. By looking over the back wall of the shop yard, he would be able, he hoped, to see if any signs of occupation were visible. 'Reconnoitring', the army would have called it. He became aware that behind him some one else was moving, stopping when he stopped, moving when he moved. With every sense alert, he resumed his way, still cautiously, still silently, telling himself he must be careful not to allow his unseen pursuer to draw too near. He had no desire to share the fate of the unlucky Sergeant James and to wake up in hospital, wondering how on earth he had got there. He reached the yard wall, and there stooped down so as to be hidden in the shadow the wall threw. He moved a little distance to one side. There he stayed, crouching in the shadow so that, unseen himself, he could distinguish even against that dark sky the silhouette of his follower.

"Clumsy lad, whoever it is," he told himself as the noise of a stumbling approach grew louder. "Sounds as if it might be Tiny," he thought. "Big and clumsy," and braced himself for a struggle with an opponent who might be clumsy, and too awkward to make full use of his muscles, but whose physical strength none the less was formidable, and who would certainly resist with desperation.

Whoever it was, Tiny or another, had now reached the yard wall, and there stood for a moment or two, apparently puzzled to know what had become of Bobby—if, that is, he had recognized Bobby, and had not merely been following out of curiosity or else from some more dangerous motive. Now he hoisted himself to the top of the wall and balanced there, half over. Probably he thought Bobby might have climbed over into the yard behind, and was trying to see if he could make out any sign of him there. Bobby straightened up and began to move nearer. His movements were certainly not as clumsy or noisy as had been those made by his follower, but neither were they perfectly silent. Indeed, to move noiselessly on the rough and rubble-encumbered ground would have tried the skill even of the Red Indian of fiction or the well-trained commando of fact. He was heard, for the man balanced on the top of the wall looked round quickly, and dropped back on the ground to be instantly tackled, tripped, and laid flat on his back before he had any chance to know what was happening or to recover his balance. In tones of concentrated fury, Bobby said:

"You again, Wyllie; still doing your level best to mess things up."

CHAPTER XXIV
"ARE YOU ALL SQUIFFY?"

IT WAS with almost equal temper that Ted retorted as Bobby, having relaxed his grip, he struggled to a sitting position:

"Mess up? What are you doing for any one to mess up? Except grabbing me from behind when I wasn't looking? Haven't you anything better to do than dodge around after me?"

Bobby glared. As it was too dark for a glare to be visible this had no noticeable effect. He gathered all the latent resources of his eloquence together in order to tell Ted exactly and precisely what he thought of him. Then, instead of letting loose the full torrent of his official wrath, he paused and said:

"H-ussssh, husssh!"

His quick ear had caught the sound of what he thought was the cautious opening of a door. He crouched down in the shadow of the yard wall. Ted, obeying a fierce and imperative gesture, did the same. Cautious footsteps on the other side of the wall became clearly audible. They came nearer, and fresh sounds indicated that some one had placed a packing-case or something of the sort in position, had climbed on it, and was peering over the wall into that bleak expanse of waste and rubble where a church had stood for many hundred years and now was there no longer. The shadow thrown by the yard wall hid the two crouching in its shelter. The patter of the rain, now much heavier, helped to cover any faint sounds they might have made. Apparently satisfied, whoever it was went back to the shop, and they heard the sound of a closing door.

"Who was that?" Ted whispered.

Bobby did not answer. He had drawn himself up to the top of the wall, and was peering over it in his turn. A faint illumination was visible where a light within the shop shone behind a closely drawn blind. Bobby lowered himself to the ground again. He said to Ted:

"Hurry off. Find a call-box. Dial police and tell them I'm here and want help. Understand? I'm going to climb over and see if I can find out what's going on."

"Cut along yourself if you want to," Ted retorted, though in the same careful whisper. "I'm not leaving here till I know about Betty. It's my job."

This time Bobby's glare ought to have been visible even in that darkness. Unfortunately it didn't seem to be. At any rate, Ted didn't seem to notice anything. Bobby tried to speak, but words simply would not come, smothered as they were by deep emotion. He thought wildly of knocking Ted out with one on the point of the chin, delivered with all the force behind it of the overwhelming emotion he was feeling. But that would have been highly improper and unofficial, and, much more important, could not have been carried out, even successfully, without the risk of resultant sounds that would be sure to betray their presence. Then all the wild and whirling words with which his mind was full turned once again into a whispered 'Husssh,' as once again there became audible cautious sounds indicating a fresh careful opening of a door. A voice said:—

"O.K. No one about. Not likely. Not when it's raining like this."

"Got to make sure," another voice said. "Always make sure."

The second voice had been a woman's, and Bobby felt how Ted strained and quivered to the sound of it. Bobby whispered:

"Did you recognize it?"

"I couldn't tell. It's the rain," Ted whispered back. "I couldn't say."

There was again the sound of a door carefully closed, and again there was silence. Ted muttered:

"It might be Betty. She may be there. I got hold of that man you saw at the teashop, and he promised to help. He told me to meet him here to-night, because if she came it would be along that street where I was waiting, and if I saw her, then I could speak to her. He never turned up, and I didn't see her—only I saw that fellow who answered my advertisement I told you about, but he and another fellow with him only went into a café, so I came on here, where Hidd thought they might be bringing her."

"How much money have you been giving Ally?" Bobby asked crossly. "I suppose you haven't enough sense to understand that if you offer money for information, you get it all right, only mostly made up for the occasion. What else did he tell you?"

"He said Betty had probably been got at and taken off under pretence of seeing her uncle she's been wanting to find for years. But now she may have got suspicious. It's all mixed up with what happened to mother and at Seemouth. I'm going to make sure if Betty is there. God knows what's happening." With a sudden, unexpected spring he was on the top of the wall. He said: "It's all right. I've got a gun. You go and fetch your chaps."

"A gun," Bobby groaned. "It only needed that."

Ted, lowering himself into the shop yard, disappeared from sight. Furious, frustrated, unable to make effective protest of any sort or kind, since an attempt to do so would be almost certain to raise an alarm, Bobby followed. The yard was full of that sort of debris—old packing-cases, wrappings, empty canisters, and so on—naturally accumulating in the back yard of any shop.

Against the wall dividing the yard from the one next to it on the left, stood a small shed. Again there came the sound of a door being carefully opened, and in the rain, now really heavy, a little group of men and women dashed from the back door of the shop across the yard into the shed, wherein they vanished in a hurried scramble. Why this rush to get out of the rain, and the fact that some of the group had umbrellas up, struck Bobby in memory as slightly comic, he did not know. Even murderers, planning fresh crime, may reasonably object to water trickling down their necks.

At the moment, however, he had neither time nor inclination for such reflections. Seizing the opportunity offered by this skurry in the rain and the dark, he darted across into a space left between the back of the shed and the outer wall of the yard. Ted was almost as quick. Any sounds they made passed unnoticed, mingled as they were with others made by those who had so suddenly emerged from the shop. There was a small window at the rear of the shed, and by good fortune a pane had been broken. A rag, stuffed in to replace the missing glass, fitted only imperfectly, so that any light within the shed would be instantly visible and any talk audible at once and without effort. Against this so convenient spy-hole, Bobby stood. Ted pressed as close to him as he could get, and Bobby observed, entirely without sympathy, that a stream of water from a broken gutter was descending upon him. Not that it made much difference, for by now they were both wet through. Besides, Ted was plainly utterly oblivious to any such minor inconvenience.

Inside the shed there was a certain confusion of movement and disconnected muttering as those within settled themselves into position, shook off rain from hair or clothing, put their wet umbrellas aside. A voice Bobby recognized for that of Tiny Garden asked:

"What's the sense bringing us out here?"

"Because," said another voice, lower, thinner, with a kind of hidden snarl in it, rather as if an angry cat had been given human speech, a voice Bobby recognized, too, this time for that of Cy King: "because there's a flat overhead and a bogey comes sometimes. He's the woman's brother, I think. He's a flatfoot, not a busy, but you can't trust him for that. Snoopers, the whole blasted lot. Likely as not they know about me being here, and suppose they've took up a floorboard and put in a dictaphone or something? I tell you straight, I'll take no risk of any one listening in to us to-night, not on your life, I don't."

"O.K.," Tiny answered. "I don't want any listening, any more than you, see? What about a light?"

"And having some one looking out of a window seeing lights in a place supposed to be empty? As likely as not ringing 999 because of thinking it might be burglars."

This suggestion seemed to amuse them all, and there was a sort of general chuckle. Tiny said again:

"O.K. Have it the way you want. All I wanted was to be sure who's here. You wouldn't ever think of planting a pal or two just to be handy like, would you?"

"Don't be a fool," Cy snarled. "We're got to fix things honest and friendly, haven't we? We know you've got the money, and you know we can do you down any time we want. Only we shan't if you act on the square. Do a straight deal with the money when you get it, fair shares, same as said, and everything's O.K. and every one satisfied, and us with our share we've a right to, no more likely to double-cross than you. Can't afford it, either of us, once the deal is through."

"That's O.K., that's all right," Tiny agreed in his heavy, rumbling tones. "Only you being same as you are, you'll do the dirty if not watched, and I'm taking no chances. Who is the other skirt, and what's she come along for?"

"What other skirt?" Cy demanded. "There's only Ma Day and her kid and Gladys." Some one sneezed at this point, and Cy said. "That's her. Shut it, Gladys, you and your snivelling."

"Can't help it if I've got a cold, can I?" Gladys retorted. "Dragging me out in the rain and all," and she sneezed again.

"'There was four," Tiny insisted. "Coming across the yard, I saw there was four. I reckon you had her hid out there in the yard, waiting, and she come in with us to get out of the rain."

"You didn't, it's a lie, you didn't, you couldn't!" Gladys screamed, loud and shrill, "There's only us three, so how could there be another? It's a lie, it's a lie, it's a lie! Isn't it, Tiny? Tell us it's a lie, Tiny."

Gladys's voice, hysterical at first, sank into a kind of frightened whimper. There was a sudden silence, as if the rest of those present were too surprised, too bewildered, by this outbreak, for which there seemed so little reason, to know what to say. Then Cy shouted angrily:

"Shut it, Glad! What's biting you? Shut it, unless you want a swipe across the face. Tiny's fooling. What's the big idea, Tiny? How could you see four skirts when there's only three—and one of them in slacks." He chuckled at this, as if he thought he had said something funny, and went on: "Pals aren't we? If we don't work the job together we'll neither of us get a thing. If we do, it's O.K., and enough for us all, and live respectable long as we want. Don't want to fool a chance like that away, do we? What more do you want—everything being fixed up so we've got it the way we all want, safe as houses?"

"I want to know who it was came in out of the rain along with the other women?" Tiny insisted sullenly, "and don't try to fool me, because I'm not standing for any tricks."

"There wasn't any one," Cy repeated, and added a string of oaths for confirmation. "Better stand up, all of you. Line up against the wall. I'll strike a match, and Tiny can count for himself."

There was a general sound of people scrambling to their feet, taking up their position as directed. Cy struck a match. It threw a faint, uncertain momentary light. It went out. Tiny said hesitatingly.

"I saw someone else. I thought I did. Four coming sudden like out of the rain. O.K. There's only the three of 'em. Must have been the mix-up in the rain. O.K.," he said again, but his voice was still troubled and doubtful.

"There's only us," Gladys said. "Me and Ma Day and her kid. How could any one see four when there's only three? Stands to reason. It's the rain."

"Ain't we had enough of this?" another voice demanded, that of a man. "Can't we get on and get things fixed up reasonable like, all being pals?"

"That's right," Cy said, but now it was his voice that was changed and shaken and hesitant as he said: "God's truth, I counted four—Glad and Ma and her kid, and then I thought there was another with 'em; only then she wasn't."

"It's Cy seeing things now," Tiny said with a loud but not too confident-sounding voice. "Light another match."

"It was the last I had," Cy said. "See. I'll call your names one by one, and you answer, each of you, and then come across and stand behind me. And Tiny, you stand at the door to make sure no one slips out. Glad?"

"O.K. Me," came a shaken, quavering reply, and sounds that showed she was obeying the order to move to where Cy stood.

"Ma Day?" Cy said, and again there came the answer, "O.K. Me," and again the sound of some one shifting position.

The same challenge and response; this time from a younger woman's voice, presumably 'Ma Day's kid'; and next from a man addressed as 'Sunday'; and finally from a 'Bill' whom Bobby, listening intently to all this, took to be the 'Bill Bright', heard of last as Cy's companion at Seemouth.

"O.K.," Cy said once more. "There's five spoke up to their names, and Tiny's at the door, and me and him make up seven, and seven we are, and no more, nor room for any, as all can see. Not so much as where a mouse could hide," he said, and suddenly: "What's that? Who said that?"

A confused clamour broke out. Some were saying they had heard, breathed softly through the air, in a voice they did not recognize, coming they did not know from where, the same words they had all used in turn, 'Me, O.K.'; and some were protesting angrily that they had heard nothing because there had been nothing to hear, and some one else was shouting:

"What the hell! Are you all squiffy?"

"Being funny, some one," Cy snarled in a furious undertone. "Just let me spot which, and I'll cut his inside out and fry it for the cat's supper."

"There isn't no one being funny," Gladys cried very loudly. "It's her, and she's here somehow. She always is. She knows. She was there when Tiny did the job with the old man at Seemouth, and told us all about it, me and Auntie, lying on the bed and saying what she saw."

CHAPTER XXV
"SHE'S BEEN TOLD"

IT WAS Tiny Garden who first broke the sudden silence that ensued upon this outbreak, of which, Bobby guessed, none of the others could at first make head or tail. Someone had struck another match. Now it flickered out and left the interior of the shed as dark as before—darker far than without. But Bobby could distinguish a bulky shadow moving heavily forward, and then he heard Tiny's hoarse, threatening voice:

"You go on talking like that, and I'll knock your block off. See?"

"All right, all right," Gladys screamed "Go on, do it! Knock my block off and she'll know, she'll see; she'll tell it all. Go on, you great beast! Why don't you?"

"Shut it, Tiny!" Cy said. "What are you getting at, Glad? What's the good of talking like that, playing the fool?"

"I'm not," Gladys told him. "It's gospel truth, what I said. Ask Auntie. She heard same as me. I tell you straight. Lying there she was, and saying what she saw and all—Tiny and Sunday and the old man and what they did, like it was television. I bought a book."

"Bought a—what?" asked some one, evidently finding this announcement as bewildering and even incredible as anything previously said. "What for? What book?"

"What are you getting at?" Cy demanded, he, too, taken utterly aback by so unprecedented a statement. "A—book?"

"It says all about it," Gladys explained. She had quietened down, and was speaking in a more ordinary tone. "I mean to say, all about knowing things when you aren't there to see them. It was on the wireless. There was a woman in an aeroplane somewhere, flying miles up, and she could tell about things in a room in a house. This book's all about it."

"That was only a dodge," Tiny said. "They worked it somehow. A code or something. Sort of conjuring trick. Any one but a dope could tell that."

"Who worked it when she knew about Seemouth same time it was going on?" Gladys asked.

"She didn't," Tiny retorted. "You don't get off with a yarn like that. You and Cy. A put-up job. I know you. Bastards both. The deal's off."

"If it is," Cy said, "you know what it'll be—no easy big money and the bogeys out to pick you up, all of you. Swing for Seemouth, the lot of you. That what you want?"

Tiny indulged in an outburst of prolonged profanity, though of a limited and repetitive type. Cy told him to shut his mouth, speaking in a tone that had its effect.

"I'm not standing for any double-crossing," Tiny retorted. "You don't scare me with that sort of spiel. Try it on kids, not on me. See? There aren't no ghosts, so what's the good of trying to put it across there are?"

"Can't be ghosts," declared a fresh voice—that of Bill Bright. "Stands to reason when there isn't anything except electricity, and that's not ghosts."

"I haven't said anything about ghosts," retorted Gladys; "and a good thing for some there aren't, or there's one Tiny and Sunday would be seeing, quick, too. If it had been that old man coming and telling, it might be ghosts. But it wasn't, it was just her, lying there and telling what she saw. They wasn't ghosts in that broadcast, was they? They knew all the same—knew about what they couldn't see same as she saw what the two of you was doing at Seemouth. And some people, this book says, can see cards when not in the same room or same house or street, even. It's all in the book I've got." She paused. "It was as bad as seeing ghosts or worse, listening to her telling it all."

"You didn't ought to be buying books," Cy told her severely. "What do you mean, telling you? How could she, unless some one told her?"

"It was the same night, the same time," Gladys answered. "How could any one tell her what was happening miles away at Seemouth? Ask Auntie."

There was a sudden scream—a woman's scream, loud, piercing as it shrilled through that dark, small, hidden space. Bobby could just make out that one of those present had run forward into the centre of the shed, could just barely perceive hands waved aloft. Wild was the torrent of words poured out, incoherent, without form or reasonable sequence, tumbling into each other so that they could hardly be distinguished one from another. So far as it was possible to attach any meaning to what was being said, the speaker was apparently telling them to give it up or worse would happen to them all, that they were up against things they didn't know about, that it would be the end of them all if they went on, bad luck of the worst if they didn't drop it, and if 'she' could know what they were doing and saying when she wasn't there, perhaps Mr Owen was there, too, and knew just the same as 'she' did. Bobby, listening, almost as puzzled by all this as any of them, finding it as difficult as they did to understand what Gladys really meant, yet indulged in a small grim secret smile as he thought that here at least was the best of guesses.

At first, and for an appreciable time, this wild, screaming torrent of words went uninterrupted. Apparently all her listeners were held still and quiet by sheer surprise. Then Cy shouted:

"Shut your big gob, will you?"

This produced no effect, probably was not even heard. The wild, incoherent screaming continued. Cy stepped forward and slapped the speaker across the face. She fell heavily and lay there, moaning. No one took the least notice. Cy said:

"Come off it, Glad. What's the game? We're all pals here, aren't we? Stick together, honest and fair, and there's easy money for us all, easy as—as gathering nuts in May." He laughed loudly when he said this, as though amused himself by his own quotation at such a time from an old nursery rhyme. But no one else laughed, nor had Cy's laugh sounded very natural. Bobby had the idea that by some odd association of thought Cy had hoped that this scrap of nursery rhyme might help to persuade them, or perhaps himself, that what Gladys was telling them was also only a nursery story. Not that on Bobby it had any such effect—to him it seemed to add only a grimmer, more sinister touch to this talk in the dark of murder past and to come.

"You don't put nothing over on us," Tiny was repeating in his heavy, growling voice. "I'm not so easy to fool as all that."

"You're a fool, and a big one, if you think I could make up anything like this," Gladys said. "The creeps it gave us, me and Auntie, both of us. It's when she's had the stuff fresh. Most of the time she just sits around all funny and quiet and doesn't seem to know anything except what you tell her, like she was sleep-walking. I said to her as Auntie was her Auntie and she never batted an eye, but said Auntie just natural like, only all hazy and dreamy, if you see what I mean. Sitting there all quiet and never moving unless spoke to, and then like it was all a dream. No trouble keeping the doors locked or anything like that. If any one saw her they would only think she was a bit touched. But when she's had it fresh she goes off altogether, so we put her on the bed out of the way, and it's then she'll start talking."

"She didn't ought to be let," Tiny interrupted. "And wouldn't be if you was true pals. She could be stopped, couldn't she? You know how."

"Not yet," Cy said, his slow, snarling voice so odd a contrast to the other's loud, bullying tones, and yet by far more sinister, more deadly. "Not till it's all fixed up, fair shares all round. Then we'll be in the same boat as you. But till then we keep her, in case wanted."

"If we stopped her talking she would know all the same, wouldn't she?" Gladys asked. "Only then we couldn't have told she did. It was last time she had the stuff. In her tea. The night you and Sunday went to Seemouth. She said sudden, but ever so clear, and as if she were ever so far away, but quite plain, like on the 'phone, and she said: 'Why is that big man looking at the door of the bungalow?' So, because of knowing Cy said Tiny knew where was the bungalow they had gone to, and Tiny was following them, Auntie said: 'What bungalow?' and she said there was a name up. Castle Beach bungalows, she said."

"She must have been listening when we was talking," Cy said, quickly. "She couldn't have known else."

"If she did, she heard more than Auntie or me did," Gladys answered. "Listen. I'm not saying this because I want to. I'm scared. See? We're up against what we don't know. Me and Auntie, we knew nothing about castles or beaches, but she did. She said there was an old castle on a cliff high up and the bungalows down below, close to the sea. She said: 'The big man never looks at it or the old castle or anything; only the bungalow. He keeps walking round it, and the other man with him, and they don't speak; only when the other man trips and falls and the big man is angry with him.'"

"Who told her that?" Sunday's voice cried. "How could she know that? She's been told."

"Who knew to tell her?" Gladys asked. "Only you and Tiny! Did either of you tell her or any one? Did you, Tiny? Or you, Sunday?"

Neither of them answered her. Gladys went on:

"She said the other man—was it you, Sunday?—had hurt his thumb and was sucking it and the big man was angry again."

"Like a blessed baby," Tiny said. "There was us with the job we had on, and there was him, sucking away at his thumb. I wanted to land him one, only for its being a job we couldn't leave. Sucking his thumb," and this last was uttered in tones of concentrated contempt.

"Well, I had to, see," Sunday protested. "It was bleeding, wasn't it? It's good luck to leave something of yourself behind you. But not enough for the busies to catch on to."

"Some one must have been watching," Tiny persisted. "Cy, most like. And now trying to scare us so as we'll get out and leave it all to them."

"How could Bill Bright or me been listening," Cy asked, "when we were both at Sidmouth? Ask the bogeys there. They can tell you. Can't you get hold of this? We can't get the money without you, and you can't keep it without us standing in. You've the money, we've the girl. Fair shares. Isn't it that way? So what's the sense of talking? And mind you don't swing for the Seemouth job all along of not trusting pals that's working with you straight and honest."

"You needn't believe it if you don't want," Gladys said. "I'm only telling so as you'll know. There's times I don't believe it myself, only I can hear her still, plain as I can hear any of you. Thin and small and very far away. Auntie heard it just the same. Ask her. I'm saying exact what she said, because of remembering every word as she spoke it, and I'll never forget it either—me nor Auntie, sitting there and listening while she told it same as it was happening miles away at Seemouth. She said: 'They're opening the door. They must have a key, but they don't live there. He's been having supper, and they are looking at him because he has gone to sleep. That's why he doesn't know about them. Isn't it funny going to sleep while you're having your supper? It's a nice supper too. Cold chicken. I wonder if he got it ready himself or some one did for him. But he's all alone now. Oh, they are undressing him. They must be going to put him to bed. He's asleep. They've taken all his clothes off. They've put him down on the floor like that. He'll catch cold, and they aren't paying any attention. Why don't they put him in bed? He's moaning a little. The big man's putting a bottle of beer from the table in his pocket. He must be going to drink it afterwards. He's taking the glass, too, and putting that in his pocket. The poor man without any clothes on is still lying on the floor. They aren't taking any notice or putting anything over him. The other man, not the big man, has gone into the bathroom and turned on the water. They can't be going to give him a bath, can they? What for? I don't think they ought. It's silly to want to give an old man a bath when he is asleep. The water's not hot, and they've left him lying on the floor ever since they took his clothes off. They're picking him up now. The big man has hold of him by the shoulders and the other man by the legs, and they are carrying him into the bathroom. The other man is shaking so he can hardly hold the old man up, and the big man is angry again. They are putting him in the bath and leaving him there. They are going away now. The big man is wiping everything he thinks they may have touched, and they are being very careful not to disturb anything. They are taking the bottle of beer with them and the glass, but they are leaving the old man in the bath. I think they must want him to die, don't you?'"

There was a sudden sound as of the fall of something heavy. Cy bent down.

"It's Sunday," he said. "He's fainted."

CHAPTER XXVI
"GOT A GUN, YOU SAID"

THE CONFERENCE, or whatever it might be called, broke up. There emerged from the shed a small procession. They were very silent as they hurried away through the rain and disappeared into the shop. The man who had fainted was being hustled along between two of the others. Their footsteps sounded dully through the heavily falling rain, and the only other sound was that of a fit of violent sneezing coming apparently from the Gladys woman. As they crowded into the shelter of the shop, Cy was exhorting her to stow it; and Gladys protested hotly that she couldn't help it, it was the second time that day she had got wet through and it wasn't her fault if she had caught cold. The only sympathy she got was advice from Cy to put her head in a sack and keep it there, instead of making row enough to wake the whole neighbourhood. Bobby found himself hoping he hadn't caught a cold like that, and Ted said to him:

"What are you going to do? Can't you arrest them, the whole lot?"

Bobby, in a much more cautious whisper, told him to shut up.

"We've got to get out of here," he went on. "If they suspect anything, our last hope's gone. Get over the wall and back across the blitzed area. I'll follow. Thank God, it's still raining hard, and that'll help to stop us being heard. Don't make a sound. The girl's life may depend on where you tread each time you put your foot down."

Covered by the ceaseless patter of the rain, first Ted and then Bobby climbed silently the yard wall, and then, with equal silent caution, picked their way across the bombed site. Only when they had reached the street beyond did Bobby turn on his companion with an asperity in no way diminished by the fact that he was soaked to the skin and exceedingly cold. It was between two sneezes almost as violent as those that had aroused the wrath of Cy that he said:

"If it hadn't been for you playing the fool, Mr Wyllie, we might have known by now where they've got her hidden."

"What do you mean?" Ted retorted with equal temper. "Why don't you do something? Why don't you arrest the lot of them?"

"Oh, for the Lord's sake!" Bobby said impatiently. "I must find a call-box. Come on."

He ran along to the corner of the street. There he had noticed, for it was his habit and his training to notice things, a call-box. First he rang up the Yard and gave his instructions, and then he rang up his home and told Olive that he would soon be back. He added pathetically that he was wet through and had probably caught his death of cold, so what about dry clothing and a hot bath, and Olive said it was just like him and she would have some warm gruel ready as well. Bobby said hurriedly that that was quite unnecessary, but Olive had already rung off, most likely in order to be sure of getting the gruel ready in time. So all Bobby could do was to give the innocent instrument a malignant look and go out again into the rain. Happy to find some one on whom to vent his extreme displeasure with life in general and gruel in particular, he said to the waiting Ted:

"Got a gun, you said, didn't you?"

"Yes. Why?" Ted asked.

"Got a licence for it?"

"A licence? No. Why?" Ted asked.

"Because unless you have," Bobby told him, "you are committing an offence in carrying it. Hand it over."

"Not me," said Ted simply.

By this time Bobby knew the young man well enough to realize that he would yield only to superior physical force, and that, Bobby supposed, he had no right to apply at the moment. Besides, a scuffle just now would be highly undesirable. So Ted had to be left in possession of his weapon, and all Bobby could do was to say with considerable annoyance:

"All right. You'll get a summons. I'm sorry it'll only be a fine. Six months in goal would keep you quiet for that long, anyhow, and give us a chance to get on without you messing things up every time."

An unjust speech, perhaps, but one delivered from the heart and with considerable feeling.

"I don't see that you've done such an awful lot," Ted retorted, with even greater heat. "What have you done that's any good?"

"Do you think it's so easy to find one among fifty million?" Bobby asked. "If you had gone to ring up the Yard when I told you, our chaps could have been here in time, and there would have been some sort of chance to tail them to where they've got her hidden."

"Hidd told me not to try to bring you into it," Ted said, "till I knew more. He said if they knew the police were getting too near they might easily . . ."

He left the sentence unfinished, perhaps because he could not bring himself to put into words the dread possibility of which he had been warned. A Flying-Squad car came round the corner. A man got out and said:

"We couldn't see any one. No sign of life in the shop. Chap on the beat says he saw a small party go off in ones and twos. Nothing suspicious, and he had no reason to question them."

"Too late for that to be any good," Bobby agreed. "Thanks to you," he added over his shoulder to Ted. "You put a stopper on all that all right. And," Bobby added feelingly, "nothing I could do about it without the risk of being heard and giving an alarm."

"Well, it's up to me to do something, isn't it?" Ted demanded. "You don't seem to be getting anywhere. If it was a girl you knew . . ."

He stopped suddenly, his voice breaking. In a gentler tone Bobby said:

"No, it's not up to you, it's up to us. We are doing all we can. Easier to hide than to find, though. Still, I must say what we heard to-night does seem to clear you yourself."

"Me?" asked Ted. "What of?"

"Of being concerned in Miss Smith's disappearance," Bobby told him.

"What? Me?" gasped Ted. "Me? Good God! if that's the sort of stuff you've had in your damfool heads, no wonder you never get anywhere."

"You've got some information to-night, sir?" the Flying-Squad man asked, almost at the same moment as Ted was spluttering out his indignation.

"Did you really think . . . ?" demanded Ted, still spluttering.

"You've been under observation," Bobby told him, "ever since that first time you came to see me. Common form for the wanted man to come along with some story he thinks will put us off." To the Flying Squad man, Bobby said: "They were having a talk, the whole crew, Cy King and his pals and Tiny Garden and his lot. In a shed in the yard behind the shop. They thought there was less chance of being overheard. But Mr Wyllie and I were there, and we could hear every word."

"I couldn't," Ted interposed. "Only scraps. I couldn't make it out. It sounded as if some one was telling what some one else had seen."

"That's right," Bobby said. "Something some one saw who wasn't there to see it."

"Sir?" said the Flying Squad man, thinking he had not heard aright.

"It's clear from what we did hear," Bobby went on, without trying to explain, "that they've got hold of Miss Smith, and they seem to be keeping her quiet by drugging her. Gladys—Cy King's woman—and some other woman they call 'Auntie'—probably the fat woman who was at the shop for a time—are looking after her. They seem to be keeping her as a kind of hostage. If Tiny doesn't hand over a share of Mr Smith's money when he gets it, then they'll produce her. Very likely try to pretend they've rescued her from Tiny, and claim a reward. Cy has got it all worked out. If Tiny parts and Cy gets what he wants, then Miss Smith will have to disappear. I don't suppose they quite realize what a long job it is to get a big estate like Mr Smith's wound up and the money handed over. It gives us a little more time, if only they don't take alarm. That means"—Bobby was speaking more to Ted now—"not only that we are working in the dark—we are used to that—but that we daren't let it be known we are working at all. There's something else we have to consider. I think we may be certain that Tiny Garden is doing his best to find her. And if he does—well, he has just carried out one rather specially brutal and cold-blooded murder, and he's not likely to hesitate at another."

"Any evidence we can use?" asked the Flying-Squad man eagerly.

"We heard," Bobby said, "at least I did—I don't know how much Mr Wyllie heard."

"I didn't understand," Ted answered. "I couldn't catch it all. It sounded as if some one had been there all the time and told about it afterwards."

"It sounded," Bobby agreed, "like the statement of an eye-witness. About the first time, I imagine, any eye-witness not one of the murderers has been able to describe exactly how it was done. Only how could there be an eye-witness when there was no one there?"

"Sir?" said the Flying-Squad man, more puzzled even than before.

"Some one fainted," Ted said. Then he said to Bobby: "It does show she's still alive, doesn't it?"

"Yes, I think so," Bobby agreed. "Almost certainly. She is being given drugs, but that is all, so there is still time—but how little!"

"If there was an eye-witness," protested the Flying-Squad man, "there must have been some one there, mustn't there?"

"You would think so," Bobby agreed. "It's all only what we heard, and what it means I've no more idea than you."

"What are you going to do?" Ted interrupted. "It's no good talking. You must do something."

"Yes," agreed Bobby, and his voice was slow and heavy. "So we must. Only what? At present all we can do is to go home and get a hot bath. Mr Wyllie, you had better do the same."

Ted at once sneezed violently, though whether this was a result of the thought of a hot bath or was only coincidental, is not certain.

"We shall probably both have pneumonia to-morrow," Bobby commented, and to the Flying-Squad man he said: "Give Mr Wyllie a lift to his hotel. Oh, and tell them to get him some hot gruel."

CHAPTER XXVII
"THE SMALLER RISK"

WHETHER THANKS to the gruel, the hot bath, the hard training in which Bobby kept himself, or merely to his sound constitution may be doubtful, but at any rate he woke up next morning without the least trace of a cold, with no tendency whatever to indulging in any such series of shattering sneezes as had drawn down upon Cy's Gladys the wrath of her protector.

Sitting down to breakfast he was inclined to be a trifle complacent about this. But Olive showed herself a trifle pessimistic.

"It hasn't had time to come out yet," she said. "Besides, you've been in bed. Wait a few hours before you are so sure. Colds take a little time to develop."

Slightly subdued Bobby said anyhow he felt all right, and then quite suddenly the full force and implication of Olive's remark flashed upon him. He gave a kind of muffled yell and sprang to his feet.

"Now what's the matter?" asked Olive severely.

"I ought to have thought of that before," he lamented, "if I hadn't been the complete idiot."

"Yes, I know," said Olive. "Only what?"

Bobby, however, was already at the 'phone, agitatedly ringing up the Meteorological Office. He explained what he wanted to know and how urgent it was. He received a promise that the information required would be obtained at once and passed on to him without delay. Olive had been listening, and as he had given her a full account of all that had been said and done in the back yard of Cy's shop, she realized at once what had caused this sudden interest in the weather. When he came back to a loathsomely cold plate of porridge—though he was too excited to pay that detail any attention, as Olive had been too excited to think of putting it to keep warm—she asked at once:

"Is there really any hope that that will help?"

"Well, it's the first time we have got even a hint of any line to follow," he answered. "I suppose we mustn't build on it too much, but it does give some chance of finding her before it's too late."

"Suppose," Olive said, "suppose Tiny Garden has noticed it, too?"

"I shouldn't think there's any fear of that," Bobby said. "The danger there is his finding out in some other way. Not much the underworld doesn't know about it's own activities. He might get a hint any moment. Still, that doesn't seem to have happened yet."

He became silent then, lost in deep, uneasy thought. Olive watched him. She knew him well enough to be able to guess what heavy decision he was struggling to arrive at. She said softly:

"I think you must risk it now. I think it is the smaller risk."

He was looking at her with the same, heavy doubt, apparently not realizing that it was his own unspoken thought to which she was responding.

"It may mean her murder right away," he said. He was silent again. Olive waited. Then he spoke, briskly and firmly, doubt put aside. "Yes," he said, "it's the smaller risk. They must realize by now that we know a lot and they must have a good idea of what we are doing. We shall have to come out more into the open. All we can do is to try to put up a show of working chiefly on the Seemouth case and of thinking the genuine niece may be still in Canada. But it must be wearing thin by now. Forced our hand, what's happened recently. I hoped we might have more time—till the estate was wound up."

He had finished his breakfast by now, and he hurried off to the Yard, where he found waiting for him the weather reports he had asked for. They seemed to him hopeful. He became busy setting in motion these new activities from which he hoped so much. Then he borrowed Sergeant Kitty Yates from the women's section, and set out with her for Southam, where he left his car and asked for the help of a uniform man. This obtained he went on, accompanied by Sergeant Yates, who was of course in plain clothes—a natty little three-piece utility suit—for Acres Lane and The Haven. At a discreet distance behind, so as to avoid attracting unnecessary attention, followed the uniform man. When Bobby knocked at The Haven door, it was opened by Mrs Day, who greeted him with a smile that was only too plainly a very forced effort, gave Miss Yates a glance of obvious and deep suspicion, and said if it was business, Mr Moon was attending to everything.

"Do you know," said Bobby contritely, "I had almost forgotten Mr Moon. I shall have to get in touch with him as soon as I can. But just at present it's Miss Smith I would like a chat with."

"She's in bed, poor soul," Mrs Day said, shaking her head. "That broke up you wouldn't believe. It's all been a sad blow to her, losing her uncle she was devoted to. Keeps saying if only she had been there it wouldn't ever have happened. Sort of reproaching herself. Nervous shock, Dr. Green says."

"I can quite understand that," Bobby answered. "But I'm afraid I'll have to see her all the same."

"Doctor said particular she wasn't to be disturbed," Mrs Day told him, looking very grave. "He said he wouldn't answer for it if she was disturbed and I was responsible. It's brain-fever he's afraid may come on."

"Dear, dear, that does sound bad," Bobby said. "You're on the 'phone, I think? I'll just ring him, if I may, and ask how long it's likely to be before it'll be all right. I'll have to get his opinion confirmed by Dr. Atkins, too—the police surgeon, you know."

It was very clear that Mrs Day didn't at all like this suggestion. She tried to raise other objections. Bobby said, interrupting her:

"By the way, where were you in all that rain last night? Didn't get wet, I hope?"

Mrs Day gave a kind of jump, and made no attempt to answer. Nor did she make any attempt to interfere when Bobby walked past her and, accompanied by Sergeant Yates, proceeded upstairs. She watched them for a moment, and then went back into the kitchen at a sort of run, as if her one thought now was to get out of Bobby's sight. On the landing above Bobby stood and listened intently. He nodded when Miss Yates pointed to one of the doors. Both she and Bobby had heard faint sounds coming from behind it to suggest the room had an occupant. Miss Yates went to it and knocked. A voice from within called:

"Who's there?"

Without answering, Miss Yates opened the door. The pseudo Miss Betty Smith was in bed. Bobby followed Miss Yates. He said:

"It's only us. We just want to ask you a question or two, if you don't mind."

"Go away, go away," screamed the occupant of the bed. "How dare you? Go away at once."

But instead of obeying this injunction both Bobby and his companion came farther in. The pseudo Miss Smith, staring at them over the bed clothes she held tightly up to her chin, shouted to them again to go away and how dare they? Both Bobby and the sergeant were smiling. The sergeant said:

"You may as well get up, my dear. Any one can see you're fully dressed." The girl made no answer to this beyond looking extremely sulky. Miss Yates went on: "The commander wants to ask you a few questions."

"I don't know anything," came this time a mumbled response. "I wasn't there."

"Oh, of course, we know that," Bobby said; "but there are a few things you may be able to tell us, Miss Smith. Or shall I say Miss Day? The lady downstairs is your mother, isn't she?"

"If she is, you know more than I do," the girl answered; but now she had thrown off the bed-clothes and was standing up and groping for her shoes—all she had removed before seeking refuge in bed. She found them and put them on. "I don't know anything," she mumbled again. "I can't tell you anything."

"Oh, I think you can," Bobby retorted. "Quite a lot, probably," and suddenly she began to cry.

"I never had anything to do with it," she sobbed. "I never knew what they meant. I liked him. He was good to me. I liked it here. It was so safe and quiet and you weren't ever afraid and everything so—so respectable." She paused to wipe away the tears running down her cheeks and she made an effort to control her sobs. "Respectable," she repeated, and managed to make the word sound like a lost Paradise. "It was lovely," she said—"shopping and helping in the house, just like any one else, and never waking up with awful headaches or being pushed around or anything, and no beastly men messing you about, and having him to look after, and now he's dead—I never, never knew that was what they meant."

"What did you think they meant?" Bobby asked.

"What they said when they told me about it," she replied. "Get him to give me money to start a business or something like that. But then afterwards they said we must try to keep it up till he died, and it wouldn't be long, because he was so old, and why couldn't I get him to make a will leaving me his money? I didn't see any harm. Why shouldn't he leave me his money if he wanted to?"

"You knew you were no niece of his?"

"It was just the same as if I was," she defended herself. "If there was a real niece she wouldn't know and wouldn't miss what she never had, and I was doing just the same for him. I liked him," she repeated. Her tears began to flow again. "I never would have stood for it if I had known what they meant." Then she said: "They'll kill me when they know what I've told you. I don't care now if they do. I hope they do," she cried desperately, and with that broke down completely.

"Look after her," Bobby said to Miss Yates. "Bring her downstairs as soon as she's pulled herself together a bit. Tell her she'll have to answer our questions, though, and I think she had better come away with us. I think she may be in real danger if she stays here."

Bobby left them together and went downstairs again. Mrs Day was still there. If she had had any idea of departure she may have noticed the uniformed policeman pacing patiently up and down outside. When she appeared from the kitchen in answer to his call, Bobby said to her:

"Well, would you like to say anything?"

"I don't know anything," she protested sullenly. "I don't know what it's all about. I'm only the housekeeper here. If there's anything wrong, it's nothing to do with me. I wasn't near Seemouth. Never been there in my life."

"Is the girl upstairs your daughter?"

"She came here as poor Mr Smith's niece, that's all I know."

"Do you know a man named Tiny Garden?"

"Never heard of him that I know of."

"Is a man known as 'Sunday' your son?"

Her face had become ghastly now, and her closely twisted hands, her restless feet betrayed her agitation. It was only with difficulty that in answer to this last question she managed to stammer out:

"No. Who is he? Never heard of him, either."

"A mother denying her son," Bobby said. "I wonder if you thought of that the day you bore him?"

"Shut up," she mumbled. "Let me alone. I told you, didn't I?"

"Why do you think he fainted last night?" Bobby asked, and now Mrs Day nearly fainted herself.

They had been standing in the entrance passage but she went back into the kitchen and sat down there, as if she feared her legs would no longer support her. Bobby followed her. She looked up at him. She said:

"Who told you?"

"Who told Cy's Gladys everything that happened at See-mouth?" Bobby asked in return.

"Some one must have been watching," she answered after a pause, a little calmer now. "I don't know. I'm not saying another word. You've no right. You did ought to have told me I had no call to say a word if I didn't want. It's not right."

"Sounds as if you had some experience in these things," Bobby remarked. "Do you know where the real Betty Smith is or what has become of her?"

"No, I don't, and that's God's truth," she answered. "I don't know anything about it. I'm the housekeeper here. That's all. If there's been anything crooked, I didn't know."

"You had better think over your position," Bobby warned her. "You may find yourself charged with being an accessory to Mr Smith's murder. Or, supposing there is a real niece, with conspiracy to defraud. Or even with conspiracy to murder, if there is such a person and anything has happened to her. We shall have to send to Canada and try to find out. Meanwhile any time you care to make a statement, let us know. Up to you to decide, but it might be the best thing you can do for yourself."

CHAPTER XXVIII
"THEY WILL KILL ME"

THE ONLY response to this suggestion was an even angrier, more sullen scowl. Bobby went back into the entrance hall. He had heard the sound of descending footsteps. Sergeant Yates was coming down the stairs, followed by the pseudo Miss Smith, who had on her outdoor things and had just given her real name as Ada Day.

"Ada says she will come with us," the sergeant said to Bobby.

"Good," said Bobby. "Best thing all round."

Mrs Day had followed Bobby into the hall. She said:

"What are you taking her for? She's done nothing."

"We may be coming back to take you," Bobby said cheerfully. "You haven't told us yet where you were in the rain last night."

Mrs Day returned with some haste to the kitchen. It was a question that very clearly frightened her badly. Bobby used the 'phone to ring up the police station to ask for his car to be sent to the top of Acres Lane—with a plain-clothes man for driver, if possible. He followed the sergeant and her companion down the garden path to the road. The uniformed man saw them, turned his back, and strolled carelessly away in the opposite direction. Onlookers would have seen no more than two women out together and a tallish, youngish man walking along behind with his hands in his pockets and apparently not a care in the world or a thought in his mind. At the corner of the road the car was waiting. The driver got out. The sergeant opened the door, but now Ada drew back.

"I'm not going," she said. "I won't. You can't make me."

Sergeant Yates said nothing, but still held open the door. It was an invitation that was a little like a command. Bobby was getting into the driver's seat. He did not speak either. Ada said:

"I won't go." Then she said: "They will kill me if they ever know."

"Yes," said the sergeant. "If you give them the chance."

"I don't want to be killed," Ada said, and got into the car, and as Bobby started off he could hear her crying again.

At the Yard when they reached it, Sergeant Yates alighted first. She said to Bobby:

"Ada is ready to make a statement."

"Well, she had better have a rest first," Bobby said, "and something to eat, and a chance to powder her nose or whatever it is you ladies do to yourselves. Besides, I want my lunch. What about four o'clock, Ada? That all right with you?"

Ada gulped and gave a miserable little nod of assent. Bobby felt that at any moment she might try to run away or else turn obstinate and refuse to say a word. The more friendly, the more everyday sort of atmosphere he could create, the more likely, he thought, she would be to talk freely. Also he was very anxious to hear if any results had been obtained by the new activities he had set in motion. He hurried off to find out. The C.I.D. man, Mark Miller by name, whom he had left in charge had however nothing of interest to report.

"I've checked what the Met. people told us with Bradshaw," he said. "There are seven districts where according to the Met. people sudden showers would have been liable to catch any one making for a London train."

"A lot of ground to cover," Bobby remarked. "More than I like. Two-mile radius from each railway station. Work that out in square yards and it comes to quite an area."

"We want to get a line somehow," Miller said. "If we could hear of Cy or Tiny or one of their pals being seen anywhere, it would help. I'm trying to arrange for a look-out to be kept on any newcomer—car, rail, bike or 'bus. Difficult."

Bobby had picked up the sheets of paper on which Miller had been collating the times of the rain-storms reported with the times shown in Bradshaw. Rather different, he reflected again, from the popular notion of the detective with a powerful magnifying-glass discovering almost imperceptible clues in almost invisible dust and deducing therefrom precise and conclusive detail. Yet this work of collation that any competent clerk could have performed had its own dramatic significance as it helped to draw ever tighter and closer the widespread net of justice.

The door opened and the Assistant Commissioner put his head in.

"I heard you were back, Owen," he said. "Any news?"

"We brought the sham Betty Smith back with us," Bobby said. "Her real name seems to be Ada Day, but she doesn't seem anxious to claim Mrs Day as her mother. She says she is willing to talk. She's badly frightened, both of us and of her friends. Says they'll kill her if they get hold of her."

"Quite likely," agreed the Assistant Commissioner. "They've killed once at Seemouth, and it often seems to come easier the second time. What about Mrs Day?"

"I left her in possession," Bobby said. "I hope she's busy 'phoning that we aren't sure if there is a real Betty Smith and that we are sending to Canada to find out. That's what I tried to get across. Cy King is sure to hear we've picked up the Ada girl, and then he and his friends might panic and decide their only chance was to get rid of the genuine Betty at once. But if they hear too that it's the Seemouth murder we are working on, and we don't even know if there is any other girl, they may be more likely to continue holding her as a kind of hostage till they see how things are shaping. Contrawise, I hope when Tiny Garden and his lot hear we've picked up Ada they may panic and then their panic may prevent them from going on trying to find out where Cy has got the genuine Betty."

"A sort of two-way panic," the Assistant Commissioner remarked. "No panic for Cy in case he acts in a hurry. Panic for Tiny to stop him from acting at all. Quite subtle, Owen."

"All I could think of," Bobby said, somewhat dejectedly. "Heavy odds against us. We are walking in the dark, and the least slip may be fatal."

"Yes, I know," agreed the Assistant Commissioner gravely. "What's all this about heavy rain-showers yesterday near railway stations? I've been reading your report, and I don't quite see where you get that."

"Well, I didn't at first," Bobby said, "and so I didn't stress it. I did just mention Gladys had a bad cold and kept sneezing and that when Cy grumbled at her she said it wasn't her fault, it was because of getting wet through. The point is that a cold does take some time to show itself. Therefore it's a fair guess Gladys got her wetting earlier in the day, that she had come out without an umbrella or mac because it looked settled till a sudden storm blew up, that it was in the country with no taxi or bus at hand, and that she couldn't shelter or turn back because she had a train to catch."

"Rather a lot to build upon a sneeze," the Assistant Commissioner said doubtfully.

"Oh, not a sneeze," Bobby protested. "Volleys of 'em."

"Never heard before of sneezes helping to solve a case," the other remarked. "Or save a girl's life, perhaps." He went on: "There's another thing. I didn't quite get what you mean by the account you overheard of the Seemouth murder. Sounds as if you thought it was made by an eye-witness?"

"That was what was claimed," Bobby answered. "But what eye-witness can have been there likely to tell Gladys in such detail exactly what did happen?—according to her story at the moment it was actually happening many miles away."

"Well, what do you make of it?" the Assistant Commissioner asked.

"One of them made enough of it to faint," Bobby answered. "That is all that I can say."

"It comes to this," insisted the other. "Some one must have been watching. Stands to reason." Bobby said nothing. The Assistant Commissioner said: "As for ghosts or clairvoyance or this thought-reading business that's all the fashion, I don't believe a word of it. Poppy-cock."

"In any case," Bobby pointed out mildly, "no use to us. Hearsay evidence only."

The Assistant Commissioner grunted. He was a plain man with a strong sense of discipline, and he only accepted facts that fitted into the accepted scheme of things—if they didn't he didn't believe they were facts and anyhow were an offence to discipline and best ignored. In a somewhat discontented tone, he said:

"What are you thinking of next?"

"Well, I'm thinking of lunch at the moment," Bobby explained. "I haven't had it yet. I'll leave Miller in charge, in case anything turns up."

"Oh, lunch," said the Assistant Commissioner in a somewhat deprecatory tone, for he had had his, and a good one. But Miller looked wistful, for he hadn't, either good or bad. "Let me know if there are any developments," the A.C. added.

Therewith he went away, telling himself discontentedly that police work was coming to a pretty pass when suggestions about thought-reading and all that sort of thing could make their appearance in an official report.

"Be a psychic department soon," he grumbled to himself, "with a medium as Superintendent-in-Charge."

CHAPTER XXIX
"IT WAS FUNNY IN A WAY"

PUNCTUALLY AT four, Sergeant Kitty Yates brought Ada, the erstwhile Betty, to Bobby's room, where he had a tempting tea waiting for them. Ada had taken full advantage of those amenities which Bobby in a lordly sort of way had simplified under the general heading of 'powdering your nose'. But her eyes were still red and bloodshot, and in them showed all the restless fear she felt, nor could all the lip-stick in the world disguise the nervous trembling of her lips.

She accepted the cup of tea and one of the cakes Bobby offered, but at this she did no more than nibble, and soon it was lying neglected on her plate. The tea she drank thirstily, and asked for another cup. When Bobby said something trivial by way of starting her talking, she made no attempt to answer, only looked at him doubtfully and then towards the door, as if instinctively wondering whether even at this late hour she might not somehow manage to escape. Sergeant Yates said:

"Ada has been telling me about herself. When she was very little she lived with a woman she called Auntie Jane, who made her living partly in Piccadilly and partly shop-lifting. She used to send Ada out to see what she could get in the open-access stores."

"It's easy," Ada said. "When they are busy. Saturdays chiefly. Even if they see you, you can get away in the crowd. They don't make a fuss if they can help it. You get caught in the end, but you say it's the first time, and you cry a lot, and as often as not they let you off. I was pretty good at it. I had to be, or I got a thrashing at home if I couldn't show anything worth while. Then Ma Day came and took me away."

"What happened then?"

"It wasn't so long before she had me on the street," Ada answered simply. "I ran away once, but what was the good? There was nowhere to go. I didn't see much harm in it, anyhow, and then Ma fell ill and we had to have money somehow. It wasn't much fun, and your man beat you up if you didn't bring back enough. A girl has to have a man behind her. Then you got drunk to forget it, and you feel awful bad next day and don't want to turn out and you get beaten up again. Ma told me to get another man, but the one I had said he would cut my nose off if I did, and I expect he would. Then he and Ma got mixed up in a big bank job that didn't come off and he was killed when the car crashed he was trying to get away in, and Ma Day never came home. I didn't hear of her for nearly a year, and then she sent to say I was to come to Jimmy Joe's place. Tiny was there and a boy Ma said was my brother."

"Was that true, do you think?" Bobby asked.

"I don't know," Ada answered. "I had never heard of him before. I don't know if she was my Ma. When she had been having a drop she used to say she wasn't sure I was the same kid she gave Auntie Jane to look after, or whether that kid hadn't died and Auntie got me instead so as Ma would go on paying. Auntie Jane's dead, so no one will ever know."

It was a sad and pitiful little story, but one that in its essentials both Bobby and Kitty Yates had heard before. Bobby said:

"There is a sort of family resemblance between you three— not very strong, but it's there."

"Ma asked Auntie once if that was why she picked me when the other kid died? If that's what happened," Ada said. "Ma may have been only talking. She hadn't paid what she promised, and Auntie Jane said she was making it all up for an excuse, because of being behind. But they both lied natural like, so you couldn't ever believe anything. It's no catch belonging to Ma and Sunday, but it's better than nothing. You don't feel so lost like."

"What was it they wanted when they sent for you at Jimmy Joe's?" Bobby asked.

"It sounded a bit of all right," Ada said, "and no harm to no one, seeing as no one wouldn't ever know. Ma was being house-keeper to an old gent, because of having to lie low after the bank raid hadn't come off, and the old gent—it was Mr Smith—hadn't any one belonging to him, only for a niece in Canada he hadn't ever seen and didn't know anything about, so why couldn't I be the niece? Ma had been trying it out already, she said, saying how nice it would be if he had his own flesh and blood to look after him and how he didn't ought to be all alone with no one of his own with him. Ma said it was beginning to work, and how about me going over to Canada and writing him from there about being his niece and I was coming to England on a visit and might I come to see him while I was here?"

"What did you say?" Bobby asked when she paused.

"Well, it sounded a bit of all right and dead easy," Ada answered. "You see, I never reckoned on getting to like him. Him and me, we got on a treat. He was ever so good to me." There were tears in her eyes again now, but slow, reluctant tears, very different from her former violent, unrestrained sobbing. "No-body had ever been good to me before," she said simply. She added after a pause: "It made me want to be good to him, too, only I wasn't let."

"You agreed to go to Canada?" Bobby asked.

"Ma had it all worked out," Ada explained. "She said he had written to the Mayor of the town where his niece had been years before and asked if he could give him her address or any news of her, only Ma got hold of the letter and tore it up, and instead she and Tiny wrote themselves to the Mayor to ask about some-thing or another, and she said when they got an answer they would have note-paper printed just the same and a faked letter to say his niece had been found and she was writing to him. That was me, of course, I was to write as soon as I got there, and say how nice it was to hear from him, and I was coming over to England to see him, only I shouldn't be able to stay long because of having such a good job in Canada, and all my friends I didn't want to leave. That was to make him keen, and not suspect anything, and Ma said it was up to me to make him want me to stay on. Ma had had a look at all his letters and things to find out all she could about him, and I was to study up all about Canada and everything when I was there so I could talk about it convincing like."

"A clever little scheme," Bobby said. "Did you never think of what it might lead to?"

"No—not what happened," she answered in almost a whisper. "I swear to God I never did—not for ever so long I didn't. I wouldn't have stood for that, not ever. I don't think at first they meant—that. Not at first. The idea was to get money from him to start me in business here so I wouldn't go back to Canada, or to make up for what I was giving up there or something like that. Ma kept saying we ought to be able to get a thousand or two out of him quite easy like and even if he found out he wouldn't ever want to prosecute because of looking such a fool. I don't think they meant more than that—not at first. I'm sure Ma didn't. Not at first."

"Not at first," Bobby agreed. "It's always such a lot easier to start than to stop."

"It's always like that," Kitty Yates said. "You don't mean to and then you think you must."

"I never thought what it might mean," Ada went on, "when Mr Smith said he would make a new will and leave me all his money if I would promise to stay on. I only thought it would make it easier still, only just waiting a little. I told Ma, and I remember now she did look queer like, and she went to tell Tiny, and he came one night and asked questions and I think that was when I began to be afraid. Only I wouldn't let myself think, and I asked Ma, and she said I was a fool. All we had to do was to wait and we should get it all without any risk or bother at all. She said it was big enough even for Tiny to be willing to wait, and he came special to say the same. But I was still being frightened underneath, only there wasn't anything I could do."

"You could have told the truth," Bobby said.

"I never thought of that," Ada said as simply as before. "Besides, I knew they would get me if I tried. And then Cy came into it."

"How was that?" Bobby asked.

"Sunday talked," answered Ada. "It was too much for him, see? Went to his head like, all that money we were going to get so easy. He got dropping hints about the big job we were going to pull off, and if you talk like that, there's plenty want to find out what it is, so they can share, only most were too afraid of Tiny to try. You got yours quick if you got across Tiny. Only there was Cy King, and he and Tiny always hated each other like poison and Cy soon knew it all. He's clever. He sent Gladys to Canada to find out. It was funny in a way. He told her to go straight to the police. She didn't want but he said she had to."

"And did she?" Bobby asked. "Bit of cheek, too. Getting the police to help."

"It was funny in a way," Ada repeated. "She let on she had a cousin, Betty Smith, she thought lived there and could they help her find her? And they said maybe it's the Miss Betty Smith who works with the Turner law firm. Very nice young lady, they said, and they would ring her up at once. Gladys didn't want that of course, but she didn't see how to stop them, and they did and it was her, the real Betty Smith, I mean and she said how exciting it was and she would come right over and Gladys must lunch with her and tell her all about it. Gladys couldn't get out of it, and Betty asked her a whole heap of questions, and Gladys had to answer them all, and Betty got more and more excited and said it was near her vacation and she would ask if she could have a week or two extra and come to England because she had always wanted to find her uncle. It put Gladys on the spot all right and she didn't know what to do so she let on she had to go to New York on business, and she wrote to Cy to tell him Betty was coming to England to see her uncle and it was all up. But Cy got the idea of getting hold of Betty as soon as she landed and only letting her go when Tiny had shared equal like. Only now I don't think perhaps he ever meant to—let her go I mean. Because of it's being such a lot of money and enough for all without working any more, and it went to their heads like with Sunday, so there wasn't anything they weren't ready for. And Cy got up a pal of his to look like you and they went to Mr Smith's to find out more and let Tiny see they meant to join in and have their share."

"Why like me?" Bobby asked, very indignantly indeed.

"It was a line Cy had been working quite a while," Ada explained. "One of Cy's gang, Bill Bright was his name, he really was like you and a lot more when made up. When Cy knew about some blokes had pulled off a good thing, Bill would go along, got up as you, to make inquiries like, and then, when they were in a bad scare, Cy would tell them that if they would share up equal with him, he knew how he could switch you off, because of having a pull with one of your men who could work it with you."

Bobby got very red and so angry he would have liked to kick something round and round the room for quite a long time.

"I'll take jolly good care I'll settle up with Mr Cy for that," he growled. Then he added: "Only fools would fall for such a cracked yarn."

"Well, they mostly are," Ada said. "That sort. Fools I mean. If they weren't, they wouldn't be what they are. If you see what I mean. But it generally worked. First there was you as they thought nosing around and then there was you again, saying there wasn't evidence and you would have to shut down on the case. It seemed O.K. Cy didn't get much out of Mr Smith though. He was only grumpy with them. And I don't think it turned out with Tiny the way Cy wanted. Tiny began to say now Cy was trying to push in, there wasn't any time to lose and no good waiting, and he talked about finding out where Cy had Betty hidden. And I asked Ma about it and Ma said to shut up. She didn't know anything and I had better not either. And she said it didn't matter anyhow, what Tiny meant, because he would never find her, Cy being much too clever, and it looked as if the whole thing was going to be a wash-out. I was glad, only sometimes I was frightened, too."

"You have no idea where Betty can be?" Bobby asked.

"No," Ada answered. "Maybe she isn't anywhere any more. Russky might be able to help."

CHAPTER XXX
"SHE'S RUN AWAY"

"Russky?" Bobby repeated. "Russky?" he said again, startled, vaguely uneasy.

It was the name, he remembered, by which was known the strange old man whose patronage of his café had at one time made Jimmy Joe so uneasy that he had appealed for police help—an assistance which the police, though highly amused at the request, had been unable to accord. For there was no complaint against the old man's behaviour. All he did was to ask for some modest refreshment or another and to sit quietly consuming it. He could hardly be held responsible for the behaviour of other customers, who, when he appeared, tended to depart forthwith or, if they saw him already there, to retire with some promptitude.

"He has the evil eye," had declared Jimmy Joe, who was of Italian descent, but the evil eye is not officially recognized in this country, and so Jimmy Joe was informed, and informed also that he was bound to serve all comers.

Fortunately for Jimmy Joe, Russky was no regular patron, and indeed wandered in and out of the Soho underworld at his own good pleasure and often at long intervals. Sometimes he would disappear for months at a time, especially during the summer, when he was said to take to the open road, and then again, when the fine weather broke, returning to the Soho streets. No one seemed to know how he lived or where, and somehow he had managed to make himself regarded with an odd mixture of fear and respect. It was not only Jimmy Joe who believed that he brought bad luck to those who crossed him, and he was credited with strange powers. There were rumours that he peddled drugs, but there had never been the least evidence of this or any discoverable grounds on which to take action.

"Russky?" Bobby repeated once again. "Where does he come in?"

"Ma says it might be him gives Cy what he's using to keep Betty so she won't know anything what's happening," Ada explained. "It's something Russky has that makes people funny in the head and say just what you tell them. Ma knows about it, because once Russky asked her to get him some honey when it was on points and he hadn't any or any ration book either."

"What did he want honey for?" Bobby asked.

"It's what he uses for mixing," Ada answered. "It has to be done just right. He told Ma what he mixes the honey with comes from India, only the Russians have found out how to make it a lot stronger and how to control it. It's not honey they use but something else, Russky doesn't know what, and it's what they give you to make you confess when you are being tried for something you don't know anything about."

A vague memory was stirring in Bobby's mind into which had come suddenly a picture of his tutor's room in an Oxford college and of an essay he had produced on Greek history. The tutor had not been pleased with it. But then tutors seldom were pleased with Bobby's efforts even though in the end he had managed to take his degree. On this occasion in that distant year the talk had been about Xenophon, and had Xenophon not recorded how some Greek soldiers had been given honey to eat, with very odd results? Bobby's troubled and confused thoughts were struggling in his mind to reach a conclusion always evading them. He went to the window and stood there, looking out. Ada and Sergeant Kitty watched him curiously, wondering what was disturbing him so. A familiar quotation came into his mind:

'For he on honey-dew hath fed.'

Was this honey dew of the poem other than the familiar honey dew of our gardens, and was the reference to something possessing strange qualities of its own, something of which the poet had acquired a knowledge in the course of his wide reading? No use though, Bobby told himself, letting his mind wander into such vague speculations, and then what he had been trying to remember came back to him and he turned away from the window to his chair and sat down and said loudly and abruptly:

"Datura."

The word evidently meant nothing to either of the other two. Bobby's memory was stirring again. Years before there had been a curious law-suit in the English courts. A Hindoo had laid claim to a great position and great wealth in his native land, alleging that for years—since his childhood, indeed—he had been kept under the influence of a decoction of datura, so that until he had been rescued from those who had subjected him to this treatment he had had no memory or knowledge of his true identity, but had been purely passive in their hands, docile to all their wishes. It was a civil case in which Bobby's interest had been no more than that of any other newspaper reader, and his memory of it was anything but clear. But one thing had become very clear to him.

"This Russky will have to be found," he said aloud.

"You never will," Ada told him—"not unless he wants. If you go looking for him he just isn't any more. All any one can do is to wait and keep a look-out till he turns up some time."

"Time," Bobby repeated angrily. Outside Big Ben struck the hour. "Time," he said again, now with something like despair in his voice. "There isn't any. It goes. We had no time to save poor old Mr Smith, and now I think there'll be no time to save the girl."

"You're awfully upset about her, aren't you?" Ada said.

"Oh, that's professional," Bobby answered, for he did not wish to seem sentimental; and indeed in all his cases he held emotion as far from him as he could, since he knew how easily emotion could disturb the clarity of thought so necessary in his work. "You don't want to fail to bring off what you are trying for," he said. "We would do as much for you if you were in the same sort of fix."

"Not in the same sort of way you wouldn't," Ada told him quietly. "It wouldn't be right if you did. It isn't her fault. Her uncle was good to me as no one else ever was and I wasn't much good to him, was I? I think really I knew all the time, only I wouldn't let me. It's different when it's happened, and you think about it and remember he was kind." Then she said: "I would help you find her if I could. I expect he would want me to if he knew. Only I can't. Ally Hidd might know something."

"Ally has gone off, too," Bobby said. "It'll take just what we haven't got to find him—time."

"There's others might know," Ada said. "I don't know but they might. Perhaps Sunday might. Only he wouldn't dare tell. Tiny wasn't half near doing him in last time he talked and Sunday knows if he did again, he wouldn't ever get another chance. Or there's Russky might have a notion where she's being kept."

"Why?" Bobby asked. "Why should he?"

"If it's right that Cy is giving her Russky's stuff, then Russky has to get it ready the way he knows and no one else. What he wanted the honey for. It has to be mixed just right and it has to be given immediate or it doesn't work proper. If you knew where Russky meets Cy, it's near certain Betty's somewhere near."

"We should have to find Russky himself first," Bobby said. "Time again and so little of it."

He lapsed into silence. It was a new and in some ways a more difficult situation with which this new information confronted him. He had had to arrange for a search for the missing girl to be carried out in each of the several districts where it seemed possible that yesterday's sudden showers might have caught and drenched any one hurrying on foot to catch a London train. 'Wide and vague,' he found himself muttering once again. Moreover some of these districts were outside the Metropolitan police area and the co-operation of the local forces had to be asked for. Now a new search had to be instituted for the illusive Russky who came and went at his own pleasure, and little hope there was that that would be successful in time for any useful result to be achieved. Then, too, fresh effort would have to be made to get hold of Ally Hidd who might well be in Dublin by now, and all this under the imminent and dreadful pressure of time, that ceaseless, everflowing river into which no man steps twice.

Ada interrupted his thoughts. She was saying:

"There's some might know where to look for Russky. Only they wouldn't ever tell you or any cop. They might me, but not now, not when they're thinking I may have turned nark."

"It wouldn't be safe for you to try," Bobby agreed, but he spoke with a touch of hesitation and because he felt he had no right to encourage in any way Ada to undertake so dangerous a task.

Her former associates would certainly all know that she had been taken away by the police and then released. They would be asking themselves what could be the reason for so quick a release and if she began to ask questions, they would think they knew.

"I wouldn't ever dare," Ada told him. "Asking for it," she said loudly.

"Yes, I know," Bobby agreed, once more deep in thought.

"Tiny's been doing all he can to find her, where Cy's got her hidden," Ada went on. "Ever since Cy told him he had her and how about fair shares, or else he would let her go to claim her rights. That's what they met to talk about. But they aren't going to trust each other. Not likely."

"No, I know," Bobby said, still more than half absorbed in his own thoughts.

"She must be safe enough till now," Ada went on, "or it wouldn't be any good. I mean to say, if she isn't, Cy can't bring her out and say all the money's hers by rights."

"It may only be," Bobby said, "that Cy has to make Tiny believe she is."

"Well, I shan't be for long—I mean to say, not alive," Ada remarked, more than a little tremulously. "Not if they get to know I've been talking."

"We'll take care of that," Bobby assured her. "You stop with us and you'll be perfectly safe. Sergeant Yates will see to that."

"I'll stay all right," Ada promised. "I don't want to be done in. I'll be for it all right if Tiny gets half a chance."

"You'll be perfectly safe with us," Sergeant Kitty repeated with a reassuring smile.

But later that night, very late, after Bobby had done all that he could, after he had made all possible arrangements for the morrow, after he had impressed upon all concerned how important it was that inquiries so far without result should be resumed first thing in the morning and pressed with the utmost energy, after indeed he had actually begun to undress, the 'phone bell rang. Resignedly Olive went to answer it for him.

"Most likely it's to say you're urgently wanted the other side of London," she remarked, from long and sad experience, as she picked up the receiver. But when she laid it down again it was to say: "It's Miss Yates. Ada's run away, she says. Climbed out of her bedroom window and gone off. Miss Yates says very likely she's just been having you on all the time."

CHAPTER XXXI
"LISTENING TO A MURDER"

IT WAS hardly an encouraging note on which to end a long and trying and doubtful day, but Bobby had known only too many such disappointments when those who had involved themselves in crime had shown signs of a desire to escape to better things, and then had been unable to cut away the ties that bound them to their former life. He knew how often it is not so much the wish as the will that is weak, the inability, after long indiscipline, to accept the steady control of social life.

Something of this he said to Olive, trying to make light of what was to him a real disappointment, and Olive said:

"I expect the poor girl is really frightened. She just simply daren't. Is she really in danger?"

"Very much so," Bobby agreed, "if they do suspect that she is giving information. It's possible a message or warning has been passed to her by some means. If she could climb out of her window, some one else could climb up to it and tap and beckon, and she might not dare disobey."

It was a picture that Olive did not like to let her thoughts dwell on—this picture of a beckoning hand at the dark window in the dead of night there was no courage to repel, even though it might well turn out to be a summons to die.

Bobby told her to put such thoughts out of her mind—a task in which he succeeded better, for it was one he had trained himself to accomplish, finding it necessary. But next morning he was awake and up the earlier of the two, for, after a long tormented night, Olive had dropped into a sound sleep, so that he had had his breakfast before she appeared.

Yet, early as he was at his office—while, indeed, the cleaners were still in possession—there was little to be done except sit and wait. The search had been resumed with promptitude and was in full progress. Ada's name had been duly added to the lengthening list of those whom it was so urgent to find imme-diately. There was nothing else he could think of that needed attention. So he sat at his desk, waiting, occupying himself with routine matters, and every time the 'phone rang, or there was a knock at his door, he hoped it might mean that at last there was news on which action could be taken.

Ted Wyllie rang up twice; and all Bobby could say was, in the customary official phrase, that everything possible would be done. But the second time it was made this reply produced an expression of such grumbling distrust and impatience from Ted that Bobby told him rather sharply that until there was definite news any attempt at action was only too likely to pre-cipitate disaster.

"These people know a good deal of what we are doing," he said. "If they suspect we are coming too near, they'll get desper-ate." The only reply to this was an impatient snort. Equally im-patiently and perhaps not very wisely, but his own nerves were at breaking point, he added: "You messed things up pretty badly the other night. If you do it again, it'll be the end of every hope we have. But for your infernal meddling—"

"All very well to talk like that," interrupted the distant an-gry voice. "If they know what you're doing, it's more than I do. Nothing much, I should say, that's been any good. Officialism and red tape all the time. If Hidd comes along with anything, I'll let you know, but I shan't sit around and wait for you to make up your official minds."

"Are you expecting him? Have you seen him?" Bobby asked eagerly.

"He rang up, that's all. I've promised a hundred quid if he can get hold of anything useful," and with that Ted hung up, most probably, as Bobby guessed, to avoid being questioned further.

Nor was Bobby pleased. The offer of a hundred pounds was one very considerably in advance of anything Ally Hidd could hope to receive from police sources, as Ally very well knew. Con-sequently, if he did manage to get hold of any useful information it would certainly go to Ted Wyllie first, and on it that obstinate, rash and self-confident young man was only too likely to act at once, on his own responsibility, and to regard letting the police, in the person of Bobby Owen, know what he was doing as quite a secondary consideration.

Another period of waiting, and then Detective Constable Miller appeared to report. Good progress was being made, he thought; the ground was being methodically covered. If the missing girl were anywhere in one of the districts indicated by Bobby—that is, within a two-mile radius, roughly speaking, of one or other of seven railway stations—then certainly it would be only a question of time before she was found. But Miller made it clear—unnecessarily clear, Bobby thought—that in his view the 'if' was a very big one. Nor did Bobby try to make it any clearer than he had already that the question of time was exactly and precisely and most urgently that on which all depended.

The next visitor was Sergeant Kitty Yates, very apologetic and apprehensive, evidently fully expecting to receive what wartime slang used to describe as a 'rocket'—and one of the most explosive kind.

From such fears, however, she was soon relieved, for Bobby did try, so far as was possible to weak human nature, to suppress the natural instinct to point out to others, especially subordinates, how badly they had done and how much better their performance would have been if only they had carried out their task more intelligently.

"Bad we've lost her, of course," he said, "and I know I, for one, got the impression that she had made up her mind to help. She did seem as if she really wanted to make some amends and had really been fond of and sorry for old Mr Smith. Apparently she hadn't—just putting it on—and of course that means she may have done us more harm than good. We have to consider now how far we can trust what she did tell us. It may have been only a lot of hooey. Could any one have climbed up to the window and threatened her, do you think?"

"It's a thirty-feet drop," Miss Yates said. "No gutter-pipe or anything to climb by. Besides, how could any one know which was her room or where she was? She knotted the sheets together to let herself down by."

"I was only wondering," Bobby explained. "We could have put a man on guard under her window. But she might easily have taken alarm at that and turned frightened and sulky. We had to have her confidence and good will if her help was to be of any real value. Anyhow, no good crying over spilt milk."

So Sergeant Kitty went away somewhat consoled, and eager to prove her worth another time, and Bobby resigned himself to fresh waiting and filled up some forms—all wrong—and wrote a letter or two and tore them up again.

He did not even go out to lunch. He contented himself with sandwiches and bread-and-cheese sent in, and still he waited, and thought to himself this was as bad a patch as he had ever known in all his years of service.

Then at last the 'phone rang with at last a piece of news. It was to say that an old man had been picked up the night before on the outskirts of Epping Forest, that he was apparently suffering from exposure and was now in hospital. He seemed to answer to the description of the man known as Russky, but had denied it, and had given his name as Roberts. The doctors had not allowed him to be questioned further, as his condition was thought to be serious. A young woman had called at the hospital and had identified him as her uncle, giving his name, however, as John Day. Unfortunately, the hospital had not attempted to detain her and had not informed the police of her visit until after her departure. Bobby could do nothing more than ask that if the young woman came again she should be held and he himself informed at once. He also arranged for a constable to be on duty at the hospital to report on any other visitors.

It began to seem to Bobby that things were drawing to a climax, though of what nature he could as yet form no opinion. It was fairly certain the young woman must be Ada; and if she knew where Russky was, then again almost certainly that was known to Tiny Garden, and most probably to Cy King and his associates as well. But what developments this presaged, why there was concern about Russky's whereabouts, why he had suddenly appeared in the Epping Forest district, were questions to which as yet no answer could be given. Or any action taken with much hope of profit. All Bobby's instincts urged him to hurry at speed to the Epping Forest district, where now it seemed things were beginning to happen. All his reason told him to be patient still and to wait for the definite lead that might come at any moment.

But it was hard waiting, even though he got rid of some of the nervous tension he was experiencing by using the 'phone to make sure that nowhere was there any relaxation of the intense effort he had demanded from all. But he knew well enough that he could never hope or expect to communicate to others that awful need for passionate speed that he felt himself.

"Talk about frustration," he muttered, glaring at the 'phone on his desk as though that harmless instrument were responsible for all.

Then, as if to pacify his wrath, it rang. A wrong number. He said so with commendable self-restraint. It rang again, and this time when he answered there was a voice he knew:

"Ada Day speaking," it said. "Is that you, Mr Owen?"

"Yes, I'm here," Bobby answered. "I've been hoping to hear from you. Where are you? What made you go off like that?"

He heard her laugh lightly. He thought she sounded excited, and he even wondered if she had been drinking.

"Tell Miss Yates I'm awfully sorry," she said. "I would have liked to see her face next morning, though." Her tone changed again. "Russky's in hospital," she said. "Did you know?"

"You've been to see him, haven't you?" Bobby asked, noticing that she had not told him yet where she was speaking from and yet afraid to press the question lest she took alarm and fled.

She had to be handled with extreme care, and now she was laughing again, and this rather excited merriment puzzled him and made him uneasy, for he had never known her in such a mood before and there seemed nothing to account for it; nor anything in her voice to suggest that she had been drinking, as his first thought had been. She was saying now:

"Oh, you know that, too. You always know everything, don't you? After I was in bed last night I couldn't sleep and I got to thinking again how good old Mr Smith had been to me, like no one ever had before, and how I hadn't been much good to him, and it was just as if he was there, poor old Nunks, and if I hadn't any business to call him that, he liked it, all the same.

I began to wish there was more I could have told you, because I expect Nunks would have wanted his really own niece helped out. Only I didn't want, and I thought it wasn't up to me to go and get killed, trying to find out more, and then there I was up and getting dressed again and I didn't want or know why. And I went to the window and I thought it would be easy to tie the sheets together and climb down, and I did, and it was no good telling Miss Yates because she would never have stood for it, would she?"

"Did you think you could get hold of any useful information at that time of night?" Bobby asked.

"It was being so late made it a better tale to tell," Ada explained, and now again she was laughing. "You see, I could say I had got away from you and been hiding till dark, so as to get back, and I told Tiny things I said you had told me, and he told me things, too. He said Russky had done a bunk, and I said why, and he said Russky was an old fool, but he had got to find him and he expected Russky had gone off to his hide-out in Epping Forest. Did you know?"

"No," Bobby answered. "What hide-out?"

"Every one thought there was one, but no one knew for sure," Ada answered. "They say he has a sort of dug-out, same as in the war, and sometimes he'll lie up there for days, sleeping most of the time. Ally Hidd used to say he thought he knew where, but I don't suppose he ever did, though he was good at picking things up, and some day he'll pick up too much and get outed himself, and now it looks like he has got hold of something, and he's telling Mr Wyllie, so you had better get going before he's for it, too, because of not knowing what he's up against."

"I'll do that immediately," Bobby told her, though it was a warning he did not need, and a task he had no means of accomplishing, since he had neither power nor authority to restrain the rashness of a hot-headed boy—one who had in addition already himself described himself as 'half off his head.' "Why did you go to the hospital?" he asked. "Did Russky tell you anything? Where are you speaking from?"

"They wouldn't let me," Ada replied. "See Russky, I mean." She was laughing again in that odd, new, hysterical way of hers, and her words came sometimes in a gush of speech, all the words run together, and sometimes with long pauses between them, as if she kept putting down the receiver and hesitating. It made Bobby afraid that any moment she might ring off. Nor did he dare put down the receiver on his side even for a moment, lest she should ask some question, and, getting no reply, take quick alarm and disappear. What was the matter with her he did not know, but she was clearly in a strange, exalted mood he did not understand. She was saying now: "The hospital let me see his clothes and what had been in his pockets—such a collection, and money, too, and while they were counting it to make sure I hadn't pinched any, I pinched an old note book of his there was among the torn dirty old papers and stuff he had."

"Anything in it to help?" Bobby asked eagerly.

When she replied her voice had changed again. Now it was brisk, clear and quiet, unemotional, as if she had come to the gist of what she wanted to say and was being careful to say it as clearly and quickly as possible.

"It said about meeting 'C.K.' at a fresh place every time," she was answering, "and always a long way from before, and was it possible that was why the effects seemed different this time? So doesn't that mean they had to bring her in a car to where Russky was waiting with the stuff to give her?"

"It might be that," Bobby agreed. "Where are you speaking from?"

"I am going straight back to Miss Yates's," she answered. "I did think there was some one following me, but I gave him the slip. I thought it might be one of Tiny's lot, and I want to get back where I'll be safe. Listen. At the hospital they wouldn't let me see Russky, but a nurse said he kept muttering about the effect being different, and he didn't know why, but he was going to stop it, and he didn't care what they said, because he had seen her twice when she wasn't there, and he didn't want that any more." She paused. Her voice changed again, so changed that for the moment Bobby almost believed it was another person speaking. "I thought I had given them the slip," she said in that new voice of hers, "but I haven't. They are here now. At the door. I'm trying to keep it shut. I can't. It's opening. Good-bye. Good-bye."

With the receiver to his ear Bobby heard the sound of breaking glass and splintering wood. He heard a scream, the sound of a heavy fall, of blows. His deputy had just come hurrying into the room with news. He cried out: "For God's sake, what's the matter? Why do you look like that?"

"I think I've been listening to a murder," Bobby said.

CHAPTER XXXII
"HURRY! HURRY!"

IT TOOK now only a very few seconds for a general warning to be sent out and received. Nor was it very much longer before a report came back that the body of a young woman had been found near a call-box in the Epping district. That the murder had been instigated, and probably actually committed, by either Cy King or Tiny Garden, Bobby was well persuaded. But in those last few pitiful sentences Ada had managed to gasp out, she had spoken no name. Equally well, it could have been the one or the other, since each might have thought himself betrayed and each have sought thus brutally, protection against further revelations.

Enough information, though, Bobby decided at once, to justify, if not an arrest, at least 'detention for questioning', both of Cy and of Tiny. Such questioning, on a firm basis of what is already known, even though that knowledge may still be short of legal proof, can often produce the further evidence required before a formal charge can be laid. But, as Bobby reflected ruefully, before questioning could begin, Cy and Tiny had to be found, and that, he suspected, was not going to prove easy. Both must be desperate by now; must know by now how hotly pursuit was pressing on their heels and both had many friends and associates willing to provide, through bribe or threat, help and shelter.

Bobby had given his deputy a brief account of that last tragic talk over the 'phone—he was still, in spite of long experience, a little shaken by it, helpless at his desk as he had been, forced to sit and listen, with no possibility of finding relief in action. His deputy broke in upon his thoughts and regrets, saying:

"This girl's murder may help the other girl. Ada can't be passed off now as the heir to the Smith money. Nothing to gain from holding the real Betty any more, so they may let her go, don't you think?"

"They may; let's hope so," Bobby said, but doubtfully, and his face was grave. "Or they may panic, and panic may lead to anything. And we don't yet know who was the actual murderer—Cy King or Tiny."

"Tiny," declared the deputy at once. "She was one of his gang."

Bobby nodded, for that was what he thought also. He went on:

"How will Cy react? Serious offence, kidnapping, and carries a long sentence. Fourteen years for what the lawyers call abduction, but that generally means an attempt to enforce marriage. Kidnapping for fraud and personation should come under the same statute, but I don't know, or what the penalty is. Have to look it up. Ought to be life, but sure to be something Cy won't care about. He's always said he would rather face the gallows than a long term—he didn't like one little bit the short one I got him before, and he may go to extremes, trying to save himself."

"You mean suppress the evidence?" the deputy asked, and when Bobby nodded assent, he added gloomily: "Means suppress the girl?" and again Bobby nodded assent.

"Then there's Tiny," Bobby went on. "What's he going to do? He probably blames Cy for the whole thing. He's right enough there. But for Cy we should never have known anything about it, and but for his sending Gladys to Canada, and for her tumbling on Miss Betty at once and letting such a lot of the cat out of the bag, it's certain Miss Betty wouldn't have chosen this particular time to come over looking for her uncle. Cy's putting his oar in ruined as promising a plot as any one ever hatched. But for him Tiny might well have got hold of the Smith money—the biggest haul ever and they must have thought perfectly safe. And none of us knowing a thing about it. Now he knows he'll never touch a penny and he has committed two murders he must realize we do know a lot about. He can't even tell how much Ada had time to tell us. I don't think Cy King need feel too safe and comfy just now. I should be inclined to put Tiny in the mad dog class at the moment. Still, that doesn't matter much. The main thing is, how much nearer are we to finding the real Betty safe and sound?"

"Do you," the deputy asked, a little doubtfully, "put any stock in the story about Russky supplying some sort of drug to keep her quiet? Is anything of the sort known?"

"Well, there is always datura," Bobby said. "Quite a lot about it in the Adams' edition of Dr Gross's book. In India, it is believed to have the property of destroying all sense of responsibility or personality. What is said is that erring Indian wives give it their husbands who then watch placidly the appearance of the wife's lover and his entertainment, and afterwards remember nothing. I don't know what actual evidence there is for that being a fact. There's the case, too—authentic, it's on record—of a Russian husband whose wife eloped with her lover, and he went with them as the lover's valet. If you like, you can put that down to masochism, which seems to be a bit of a Russian speciality, or it might be datura again. If the communists in Russia have learned how to control the stuff, and even strengthen its effects, it would explain why they are able to pull confessions out of the hat whenever they want to. Then there was something in the papers only the other day about the American discovery of a gas that would destroy an enemy's will to fight—destroy his will and personality, that is, and make him wholly passive and docile. Much the same as what is said about datura. It may be only newspaper talk. You can't tell."

"Russky may be able to say something if we can get hold of him," the deputy remarked, though doubtfully. "Well, drugs—they are funny things. Look at operations. Doctors give you something and you are practically dead, and then you come back to life. But I'm not falling for all these ghost stories going about—I mean the yarns about this girl being seen when she wasn't there. Drugs—well, that's science. But ghosts is just superstition."

"No question of ghosts," Bobby pointed out. "I hope she's still alive, and she almost certainly was alive when Wyllie's mother thought she saw her in the cellar of their house. It may be one effect of the drug if that's what she's been given. Releases the spirit and sets it wandering, so to say. It's a possibility. You can take it or leave it. It might be what Professor Rhine calls E.S.P."

"What on earth's that?" demanded the deputy.

"Extra Sensory Perception. Much the same as thought-reading. A kind of visual impression. You don't see what isn't there. You see a picture in your mind's eye you get by reading some one else's mind. I've been looking it up," Bobby added in half-apologetic explanation. "It seems to hang together in a way."

"All the same, it's not evidence," the deputy pointed out. "Is it? You can't call it evidence, can you?"

"Not even information to act on," Bobby agreed with a sudden return of the sense of strain he was under but that he had relieved a little in talking. "If only this mind-reading or whatever it is could give us a hint where to look or what to do instead of having to sit and wait and wait."

"There's one thing," the deputy said, glad to leave these suggestions of 'E.S.P.' and the like, all so remote from the hard, practical, every-day routine of police work. "I expect you've noticed it. If it's correct Russky always had to meet Cy at different places a goodish distance away from each other, then it looks like a car was used."

"There's another alternative," Bobby said. "Might be a caravan. Caravans don't stop long enough in one place to attract attention, and there are plenty of them. No one looks at them twice, and anyhow country people think them and their inmates a queer lot. I've told our chaps to pay special attention to caravans."

The deputy went away then to take Bobby's place at a conference being held over another case, for Bobby had made up his mind to hold himself in complete readiness to leave all else immediately if and when something definite in the way of information came in. Nor did he think this could now be long delayed. But for the time being all he could do was to sit and wait, hoping every moment to hear definite news. Moodily he reflected that even if his caravan idea was correct, there would be innumerable caravans in the districts where the search was going on. All would have to be found and examined, and probably the very last one to be visited would be the one they wanted, and probably when they did find it, it would be empty, 'without trace'. Indeed, the case was so long a record of disappointment and frustration that his mood was one of such depression as he had not often known.

Then again the 'phone rang. He picked it up. The voice said:

"Detective Constable Fred Ford speaking. As instructed, tailed Mr Wyllie, and saw him meet party answering description of Ally Hidd. Mr Wyllie showed excitement and stopped a taxi. I then spoke to him, showing warrant card and offering to accompany him. Was refused, Mr Wyllie stating that surprise was necessary, and three was too much like a party and would be spotted as soon as seen, especially with me looking like a policeman—as I don't," Ford could not help adding. "I warned him against taking law into his own hands and was told to go to hell. He then said for me to tell you to wait at Honor Broome if you like, at the police station, and he would ring up. I noted number of taxi and," he added in a voice charged with all the emotion he felt but had deemed it would be unofficial to express, "if ever there's orders to pinch him, I hope it's me to do it."

"Never mind that," said Bobby, though fully understanding. "You had better get along to Honor Broome and report there. Wait till you hear from me."

"Very good, sir," Ford answered.

Bobby put down the receiver and wondered if there ever had been a case so bedevilled by outside interference. Tiny Gardner's cunning scheme might well have succeeded but for Cy King; and Bobby was sure that but for Ted Wyllie's meddling, Miss Betty would have been found and rescued long ago. It was very possible that this time Ally Hidd really had got hold of something important, and of course he was going to pass it on first to the man who had promised him a hundred pounds rather than to officials who would have difficulty in getting permission to pay a tenth of that sum. Bobby found himself reflecting that if this time Ted got himself knocked on the head, he, Bobby, would be very willing to subscribe for a wreath to be sent to the funeral. As likely as not, he told himself bitterly, Ted's rash, headstrong impetuosity would precipitate final catastrophe.

The 'phone rang again. Bobby picked it up. The distant voice said:

"Information from contact that Tiny Garden has beaten up Sunday pretty bad and is now proceeding to Honor Broome. Tiny stated to be in bad mood and uttering threats. Reason and purpose not known."

"Good," Bobby said. "Thank you very much."

He slammed down the receiver and hurried away, pausing only to let it be known where he was going and why. Outside was standing ready the car he had arranged should be in waiting.

"Honor Broome, hurry," he told the driver, and a constable came running up.

"Beg pardon, sir," he said breathlessly. "Report just come in from North Nodding. Cy King and a companion seen driving along Road 1593. General warning sent out to intercept, but not so far see again."

"North Nodding?" Bobby repeated. "Isn't that in the Honor Broome district?"

"Two or three miles south, I think, sir," the constable answered. "There's a side road."

"Good," said Bobby again, and, to the driver, he repeated: "Hurry. Hurry."

CHAPTER XXXIII
"IF SHE'S THERE . . ."

THE HONOR BROOME district is one of those odd little pockets of solitude and loneliness still be to found here and there all round London. The greater motor roads avoid it, no railway runs near, the only public means of transport is provided by the very occasional North Nodding bus, whose run is extended to its boundaries. Apart from this the few inhabitants have to depend on a bicycle or a four-mile trudge along a road often damp and muddy, since the Broome rivulet runs by its side and is very apt to overflow. This comparative isolation from the rest of the world is due to its situation at the foot of a high and steep and stony ridge, hostile to all forms of mechanical transport, almost impossible for horses and difficult and fatiguing for pedestrians.

On the high summit of the ridge lies Broome Common, now, as a result of neglect during the war years, largely a tangled mass of silver birch, standing amidst a thick undergrowth of bramble. Here picnickers still come in fine weather, though they seldom risk the sharp descent to Honor Broome village and the consequent stiff climb back again. Here, too, children come in the autumn to gather the blackberry crop. The common land extends down the less steep western slope of the ridge till it reaches the boundaries of Honor Broome parish, and down this slope, too, runs through a wilderness of pine and birch, the Broome brook, with its perennial tendency to overflow. No doubt had not the land been so sterile, steep and stony it would long ago have been enclosed and cultivated. As it is, it has remained much as it has been since the beginning of time. For the task of cultivation has never seemed inviting, not even during the war, when almost every square yard of soil was called upon to do its bit and no back garden anywhere but blossomed with its cabbages and carrots.

The village itself consisted of two or three small farms, a church and a beerhouse, serving respectively the body, the soul, and the thirst of the inhabitants. It was but a sombre prospect that the village offered, though, to the approaching stranger, as it crouched as it were under the heavy and frowning dominance of the great, steep, wooded ridge behind, and to it the sunshine seldom came.

At North Nodding Bobby paused and got no news. Nothing had been heard or seen of Tiny Garden. Nothing was known of Ted Wyllie and his companion, nor was there any reason why they should have been noticed in the busy stream of traffic making its way to or from London and the west country. All along the road watch was being kept to intercept Cy King's car, but so far without result.

"If they were going to Honor Broome they would turn off near here to get there, wouldn't they?" Bobby asked.

"Half a mile along on the right," agreed the North Nodding station sergeant to whom Bobby was talking. "If that's where they wanted to go," he added doubtfully, evidently finding it hard to believe that any one was ever likely to entertain such a desire. "I did ring up Mr Turner to ask if a car had been seen. He said not as he knew of but he would let me know if he heard anything."

"Who is Mr Turner?" Bobby asked.

"Well, sir," the station sergeant explained, "we've no one stationed up there, being short of men and no great need neither they being all quiet and respectable like, so Mr Turner's been sworn in as special constable in case of being wanted. Farms seventy acres of the worst land in England, north aspect, too, but doesn't do so bad what with guaranteed prices and all and when parson can't get there, takes the service, being churchwarden."

"Have you inquired about any caravans being seen?" Bobby asked.

"Cycled up there myself special," the sergeant assured him. "A tidy pull, too, up that road. None known and not likely. No caravan wants to tackle that ridge, and no cause either. Not but that there might be a dozen of 'em hidden on the slope or on the ridge for days at a time and no one know anything about it. Take fifty men a week or more to make a proper search."

"You might ring Mr Turner, will you?" Bobby asked, "and tell him to expect me. I may want his help."

"Very good, sir," said the sergeant, but doubtfully. "He's well over seventy, and what with asthma and his rheumatics being so bad, he can't get about much. But very well thought of."

"Ring him all the same," Bobby said. "He may be useful. Get hold of two of your men to report to me there as soon as possible. Urgent. If I'm not at Turner's I'll leave instructions with him. Tell them I expect them as soon as possible—no, sooner, much sooner."

"Well, sir," began the sergeant, even more doubtfully than before, but Bobby was already on his way back to his waiting car, and from his desk the sergeant watched it disappear at top speed. "Did ought to be summonsed for dangerous driving," he muttered to himself. "Job for the inspector," he added as he reached for the 'phone, "and him most like anywhere but at home and the same for all our chaps. Just like these high ups—seem to think we have all the reserves we want under our thumb, so to speak, and if not then up to us to be in two different places at once."

Happily unaware of these unfavourable reactions, Bobby was urging his driver to a speed it was not easy to attain or keep on this steep, narrow, and winding road. But presently they came within sight of the scattered cottages and farmhouses that made up the village, lying brooding as it were and expectant in the dark shadow cast by the overhanging ridge behind. Bobby's driver said:

"Small car over there, sir, under those trees. Looks as if it had been parked there. Bayard Ten."

"Yes, I see," Bobby said. "We had better have a look. It was a Bayard Ten Cy King was reported using."

The driver stopped their car accordingly, and he and Bobby got out. There was nothing in the deserted Bayard Ten to suggest to whom it had belonged, nothing in it, indeed except two full tins of petrol. At these Bobby looked thoughtfully, and then told his companion to transfer them to their own car.

"May as well drain the tank, too, while you are about it," he added. "We don't want Cy to make any hurried departure till we've had a chance of a chat."

"No, sir," agreed the driver and set to work. The tank drained, he said: "Suppose it belongs to some picnic party? Or a salesman trying to do a bit of business round here?"

"Then," Bobby said, "there'll probably be some language going and a highly indignant letter to the Commissioner—or even 'The Times'. High-handed action of police—Gestapo methods in England. We'll have to put it down to excess of zeal and do a grovel. I'll leave a note in the car to say the petrol has been removed for safety and will be returned on application." Then he said more gravely: "But I think the chances are it means Cy King has got here first and knows just where to go. Not too good."

They drove on, and as they reached the village saw Fred Ford waiting for them by the roadside.

"Mrs Turner has just been to say there was a 'phone call that you wouldn't be long," he explained. "Mr Turner is a Special. I've been making inquiries, but no one seems to know anything about any caravan."

"We saw a car parked by the roadside not far off," Bobby said. "A Bayard Ten. Cy King has been reported driving a Bayard Ten. Looks as if he had come straight here, and for a purpose."

"Oh, well," Ford said; and he looked doubtfully at the dark ridge above them, crowned by its tangle of trees and bramble. "If he's there . . . if she's there . . ." he muttered.

"I must get more help," Bobby said. "I must get on the 'phone. Which is Mr Turner's?" He, too, looked doubtfully and with mistrust at the ridge, and it had to him the aspect of a hidden place where immemorial secrets kept themselves inviolate. "Take a regiment to search it properly up there," he said.

Ford and he hurried then to Mr Turner's farm, and there Bobby spent a few feverish busy minutes, every one of them bitterly grudged, since he knew that every one of them was heavy with the issues of life and death. Such rough plans as were practicable in the circumstances he tried to arrange so as to avoid as much as possible of the overlapping that could hardly be avoided in such hasty improvisation. He tried to make sure, too, that every road was watched, and he left his driver on duty at the 'phone to answer the innumerable inquiries that he knew were sure soon to come flooding in.

"Answer as best you can," he told the dismayed-looking driver. "Say we think Cy King is loose in the vicinity and means mischief and we must find him first if we can, if it's not too late already. Repeat I want Broome Common searched from end to end and all roads watched. Come on, Ford. Remember you'll have to mind your step. Cy is probably armed, and we aren't."

"Yes, sir," said Ford. "I know. Luckily I thought it looked like rain, so I brought my umbrella."

Bobby hardly noticed this remark, and paid it no attention, for he had momentarily forgotten that Ford possessed an umbrella, the handle of which he had carefully loaded so as to make it quite an effective weapon. There was something else that Bobby did notice, though, and that was Mrs Turner hurrying after them. She said to him:

"I heard what you were saying. My grandchildren are coming back home across the common. I must meet them."

"They are in no danger," Bobby said. "How old are they?"

"One seven and the other nine," she answered, hurrying to keep up with them and finding the task impossible, so that soon she was left behind.

CHAPTER XXXIV
"MAN HITTING LADY"

WITH NO clear idea of what he could hope for, with indeed little hope of any kind in his heart, Bobby, Ford close behind, hurried on up the still steeply ascending slope. What, he was asking himself, could two men do by themselves to search all that expanse of closely woven tree and bush with which this approach to the summit of the ridge, and the ridge itself, was so continuously covered? Only here and there were there occasional open glades, only here and there was this tangle of growth traversed by some narrow and neglected path that almost always promptly died away again into invisibility.

Somewhere, he supposed, up there, or perhaps on one side or the other of this track he and Ford were following, lay concealed the caravan he now believed had been the true Betty's prison. Why else, indeed, had Cy King and his companion—Bill Bright probably—come this way with such speed, and with a purpose only too easily, too dreadfully surmised? Nor would they need to waste time in search, for they would know exactly where they had to go. Somewhere, too, within those hidden depths was almost certainly Tiny Garden, desperate and at bay, knowing his life was forfeit. A wild beast in a panic, Bobby told himself, and what form his panic might take who could tell, though all might guess? And Ted Wyllie. For he also had been on his way, and these woods were sure to be his destination, too. Probably, indeed, he was already there somewhere in these green, secret shades.

Difficult, Bobby told himself, to realize that this quiet, deserted-looking stretch of woodland and common, where so few ever came, and those few only for the most innocent of purposes—picnicking in the spring and summer, in the autumn for the gathering of berries for tarts and jams, no one at all in the winter—now hid within itself those who by the compulsion of circumstance and their own deeds had been wrought to such extremity of passion and despair that violence, death, tragedy, of one sort or another had become inevitable.

The air was still and quiet, the light of the fading day growing dim as it filtered through the neighbouring trees. Darkness and gloom were descending on the earth as on Bobby's mind. Now hope had nearly left him of ever achieving that purpose and hope of rescue which for so long had eluded him so persistently. The ascent became a little less steep as the crest of the ridge was approached. Here and there on the rough track they were following appeared a derelict cigarette-packet or a torn scrap of newspaper—those universal stigmata of our civilization to show that others did at times pass that way. There were even faint wheel-tracks visible in places, though Bobby wondered a little how any vehicle could negotiate successfully that cliff-like descent to Honor Broome village. It would need first-class brakes in first-class condition.

A glimmer of hope began to stir within him. Clearly by this way wheeled traffic came and went. Then any such vehicle, caravan or other, seeking to evade notice must either have gone on through the village, where, if it had arrived, it would certainly have been seen and remembered, or else it must have turned off to one side or the other. If so, there would equally certainly be tracks left to show where that had happened.

"You look out your side, Ford," Bobby said. "I'll watch mine. If any caravan is up here there must be tracks where it left the road."

"Right, sir," Ford answered, and only a moment or two later he said: "There's a kiddy behind those bushes—two of them. Look as though they were hiding."

"Kiddies," Bobby repeated in surprise, and he remembered that Mrs Turner had spoken of her grandchildren. He stopped and called: "Hullo, you two! Late for tea, aren't you? Your grannie's come to look for you. She's just behind."

A small boy cautiously emerged, followed by a smaller girl, whom he was holding by the hand.

"We've had our tea," the boy announced.

There was a quaver in his voice, and Bobby, looking at them closely, thought the girl at least had been crying. There was a frightened, hesitating air about them both, so that they gave the impression of being on the point of running away. Bobby said:

"What's the matter? Anything been happening?"

"Man hitting lady," the girl said. "Behind a tree," and the boy added:

"We ran away."

"I was frightened," the girl said.

"I wasn't," the boy boasted, and the girl said:

"Story. You were."

"Grannie's coming to take you home," Bobby told them, speaking as quietly as he could, though his heart was beating violently, controlling his eagerness for fear of alarming more the already frightened children. Perhaps into silence. "A man hitting a lady?" he went on. "I don't think he ought to do that, do you?"

"Bad man," said the little girl.

"So he is," agreed Bobby. "I must go and tell him not to." The child nodded emphatic approval. "Where was it you saw him?" Bobby asked. The boy pointed directly behind.

"The man had a big stick," he said.

"How long ago?" Bobby asked. "Was it far?"

But they did not answer. Probably they did not quite know how to express themselves in terms of time and distance. They stood there hand in hand, looking up at him gravely, an odd little air of responsibility about them, as though they understood more clearly than they could say in words that they had come already face to face with the problems of good and evil that life in time brings to all. On Bobby's side he was fearful that they had witnessed the final culmination of that tragedy he had so long dreaded, so desperately striven to avert. He said:

"Well, I think I must go and find him and tell him he mustn't. What was the lady like? Had you ever seen her before?" They shook their heads. He asked again: "What was the man like?"

"Big," the boy said. "Very big."

"Bigger than Mr Sims," the girl said.

"Mr Sims is awful big," said the boy. "I'll be bigger when I grow up," he boasted.

"Story," said the little girl. "Grannie says you won't, not if you don't eat your porridge all up and you never."

Bobby turned to Ford.

"Sounds as if we are too late again," he said very bitterly. "Sounds as if Tiny Garden has got here before us. Anyhow, we can see he hangs—for all the good that is," he added, still more bitterly.

"We ought to have a good chance of getting him," Ford said, with a hungry look over the children's heads into the trees behind.

"Go back with the children," Bobby told him, "till you meet Mrs Turner, and then back here."

"Wouldn't it be all right, sir, to let them go by themselves?" Ford asked hesitatingly. "She can't be far, and no one will want to hurt them."

"Do as you are told," Bobby said, and his tone was sharp and angry as he vented on the unlucky Ford some of the disappointment, the horror, the bitter sense of frustration he was experiencing. "We may be too late to save the girl," he added more mildly. "I'm not running any risks with the children. Get going and don't leave them till they're safe."

Ford, even discipline did not prevent him from looking as sulky and rebellious as he felt, set off at a trot, the girl on his shoulder, the boy running at his side. Bobby plunged into the undergrowth and all his being had become merged in one great urge to find Tiny, and for Tiny to offer that resistance to arrest which would justify resort to force. That this should be the end of the long and weary trail that had been followed so perseveringly, so persistently, was to him almost unbearable. Time, his enemy throughout, had it seemed at this last moment finally defeated him, for he felt that the story told by the children left little room for hope.

He crashed his way through bush and bramble and saw no sign, heard no sound to disturb the immemorial silence of those deserted woods, till he saw on his right hand a thin column of smoke rising into the quiet air. He ran towards it, taking a savage pleasure in smashing through every obstacle in his path. The smoke grew darker, thicker, it became shot with a sudden uprush of flame. He ran faster still, following that ominous beacon. He broke through a fringe of trees into a wide open glade, and there a caravan blazed, a mass of leaping flame.

The heat was too great for him to get very near. He ran round it. He could see no sign of life anywhere, nor was there any way of checking those leaping flames that seemed as though they laughed in their lust of destruction as they fed full on the dry wood of the caravan, and the petrol with which it seemed all had been soaked. Bobby could only stand and watch and ask himself what dark secrets were there being destroyed for ever before his eyes. He heard some one coming at a run. It was Ford. He came and stood by Bobby, watching like him the roaring furnace that once had been a habitation—or a prison. He said presently:

"Is she in there? Her those kids saw?"

"Likely enough," Bobby said. "No telling. It may have seemed the safest way. But for us no one might have noticed the smoke or thought it worth while bothering about if they did. Might have been years before anything was found."

"Will the fire spread, do you think?" Ford said. "There's been a good deal of rain."

"I don't think so," answered Bobby. "We'll have to take care of that, but it doesn't seem to be catching so far. We had better see if we can find Tiny. He may be around still. You go that way. I'll take this. Don't go too far though. Have you your whistle? Good. Blow it if you notice anything and I'll come. Keep your eyes open."

"Yes, sir," Ford said. "If I do come across Tiny, I expect I shall need help. Awkward customer, sir, and him armed and you not. No use getting killed."

Bobby smiled grimly. He recognized that Ford was going as close as he dared to telling Bobby to be careful, and to suggesting that with such a quarry as Tiny Garden, it would be wiser and safer to have a companion. But there was that in Bobby, a kind of smouldering, fierce rage at the thought of this defeat at the last moment, as made him feel the one thing he desired above all was chance or opportunity to meet Tiny alone and alone to take vengeance. At least, if the story of the children was true and not too much exaggerated. But of that it seemed to him there was small hope.

They separated then, each going his own way. But to little purpose for almost immediately Ford's whistle sounded.

"This way, sir, this way," Ford was calling. "Over here," and when Bobby joined him he was standing by an open oblong hole in the ground, deep and narrow, six feet in length.

"Looks like it had been meant for a grave," Ford said. He stared down into that dark, ominous cavity. He said: "Meant for her, I take it—her those kids saw. And then Tiny thought the caravan was a better bet."

"I should guess this is more like Cy King's work," Bobby said. "This hasn't been dug recently, and it's not likely Tiny has been here before to-day. Cy must be somewhere about, too. That was his car we saw. No sign of him, though, unless it was really Cy those kids saw. But then they stuck to it it was a big man. No sign of him or of Ted Wyllie either."

"I can see why Cy wanted to be ready to get the girl out of the way if he had to in a hurry," Ford said. "But I don't see why Tiny should? Doesn't matter to him now he must know his whole plan has gone west."

"I don't much expect there's any 'why' to what he does just now," Bobby answered. "In a panic and hitting out blindly all round. I think he probably came with some idea of getting even with Cy and if he can't find Cy anyone else will do," and even as he spoke there rang out three pistol shots, fired in quick succession.

CHAPTER XXXV
"THAT'S ALL FINISHED NOW"

THE SOUND of these three shots had seemed to come from some distance but from how far exactly it was impossible to say. The direction was clearly that from which Bobby and Ford had just arrived. Hurriedly then they retraced their steps and as they went, swiftly yet with caution, Ford said in a quick undertone:

"'Ware pistols, sir. 'Ware pistols."

Bobby, hurrying ahead, hardly heard, took no notice, intent solely as he was on what the next development might be, his every nerve and sense strained to the utmost pitch to meet it in time and be prepared. Then a little further on he stopped, signing to Ford to stop, too. He had seen something on his left, at a little distance. The undergrowth hid it in part. He saw though that it

was very still, whatever it was. Stooping, for at least his unconscious was alert and warned by the sound of those pistol shots,
he skirted quickly the baffling undergrowth and then was able to
see plainly where, in another smaller glade, the body of a woman
lay huddled in a formless heap upon the ground. At the same moment Ford, who had followed close behind, said sharply:

"Look out, sir. Some one coming."

Bobby swung round. Through the trees, at a kind of un-
steady, reeling run, came Ted Wyllie, like a drunken man. His
hand was pressed to his side and there was blood there, and
it was dripping slowly to the ground. He saw them, recognized
them. Staggering and reeling forward, he called out:

"She's here somewhere. She ran off. Find her quick."

"Who fired? Did you?" Bobby asked.

"Yes, to stop him, frighten him," Ted answered in short,
quick gasps. "He had hold of Betty. By the side of a hole they
dug. He had a knife in his hand, and I saw it, and I fired. Only
I was afraid of hitting Betty, and the thing jammed. I threw it
at him, and he threw his knife and it got me, and all at once
there was that big chap I saw before. Shouting he was, and Betty
ran away. Find her quick, or God knows what'll happen. I'm all
right," he said, and slid unconscious to the ground.

"God knows what's happening, let alone what will," Bobby
muttered to himself as he bent over the prostrate man. "It must
be Cy stabbed him, and he's seen Tiny, too."

Not very skilfully, hurriedly, for he did not know what might
not happen next, but knew there was great need for speed and
action, he was doing what he could to stop the bleeding. As he
worked he told Ford to see what he could do for the woman lying so still, so near, unconscious of what was passing. Ford ran
across and hurried back.

"She's alive all right, but she's been badly knocked about," he
reported. "Her face is an awful mess, but she doesn't look like
the photos of Betty Smith."

"May be Cy's Gladys," Bobby said. "That may be why Tiny
attacked her. Anything to do with Cy, and Gladys was his chief
helper. What's become of them both? That hole near the cara-

van, Wyllie said. We had better get back again. If only we could see a bit further," he groaned. "All these trees and bushes!"

He had already taken a moment to run across and assure himself it was in fact Gladys who had been the victim of Tiny's frenzied violence. Now he and Ford were rushing back by the way they had come. Smoke still rising in the quiet air served them for a guide to the glade where stood the burning caravan. From it, though the flames were less fierce now, came heat still too great for it to be approached too closely. But the sides and roof had fallen in so that it was possible to see more, such things as the stove used for cooking and red hot, twisted pieces of metal.

Ford, obeying a gesture Bobby made him, had hurried first to where had been dug that hole that to them had looked so like a grave. Both he and Bobby had been aware of a secret terror that now it might have an occupant. It was still empty. Ford picked up a small automatic pistol, presumably the one Ted had had and that he said had jammed. Ford armed himself with a long branch, and, getting as near the burning caravan as the heat permitted, he used it to stir up the fiery mass till the branch itself took fire, and he had to let it go.

"I don't think there's anything" he said. "I mean to say, nothing like a dead body."

"No," agreed Bobby. "The fire wasn't for that. On general principles. To destroy evidence. It looks as if Cy and Tiny have cleared off. Hope so. If they have, it would give us a better chance to find the girl. She may be anywhere. Hiding or anything. I wonder if it would be any good to call to her, if she would show up. We might try that, she can't be far. And we had better try separately. Cover more ground. Only look out. Tiny and Cy may still be around somewhere and they're both dangerous— and desperate as well."

"Yes, sir. Very good, sir," Ford said. He was holding the jammed automatic and he showed it Bobby. "Shall I try to get this thing into working order again?" he asked.

"No, no time to lose," Bobby said.

He took the weapon, small enough to go conveniently into a pocket or a handbag, and yet at close quarters a deadly thing. He slipped the safety catch into position as a precaution in case the pistol freed itself, pushed it into his pocket. Then he went one way and Ford the other, agreeing to work round in a circle so as to meet near or on the track they had recently quitted.

Now and again as he pushed his way through and among the trees, looking keenly around on every side as he went, he called softly:

"Miss Smith! Miss Betty! Are you there? Mrs Wyllie is waiting at Bournemouth. Are you there? Mrs Wyllie. Bournemouth. Is that you?"

He had reached the central track sooner than he had expected. There was no sign of Ford. Probably he had made too short a circuit or Ford had made too long a one. He plunged back among the trees, still keeping near the road, and again when he had gone a little distance he called gently:

"Miss Betty! Miss Betty! Are you there?"

This time a soft voice answered, but within it an odd accent of doubt and hesitation:

"I think that's me. I think it must be."

"Yes, it is, of course it is," Bobby answered, though there was nothing he could see, and though indeed it was all that he could do to speak at all, such was the great upward surge of emotion and relief that he experienced at this moment when it seemed that at last the long secret search was over.

He moved in the direction from which the voice had come. Soon he saw a girl standing very still. She was pale, dishevelled. Her hair was disarranged, and in it were caught dry leaves and bits of twigs, so that there came into his mind an odd memory of an Ophelia he had seen in a recent film production of 'Hamlet'. He held out his hand as in ordinary greeting. As simply and quietly as he could, for he felt it might be better to make everything seem as commonplace as possible, he said:

"Oh, how do you do? Mrs Wyllie has been worrying about you such a lot."

"Mrs Wyllie?" she answered doubtfully. "I think I saw Ted, didn't I? You aren't Ted. It's all so funny. I don't know where this is. Where is it?"

"Broome Common," Bobby answered. "We had better get along to Mrs Wyllie's, hadn't we?"

"There was a man with a knife," she said. "He frightened me. Or was it a dream? I think I've had so many dreams."

"That's all finished now," Bobby said.

"I think I saw him digging in a dream, was it? and when I asked him why, he said perhaps I should know before long, and then he laughed, and so did Gladys. Who is Gladys? There was a man ran after her in my dream. I don't think I know you," she added.

"No, but you know Mrs Wyllie, don't you? She's been worrying her life out about you. She's sent me to find you and bring you to her."

"She's in England," Betty said, and then: "But—but—this isn't home, not Canada, I mean. I can't think. Look there's that man again—the man in my dream with a knife I kept looking at."

"So there is," Bobby said, for he, too, had caught a glimpse of Cy hurrying towards them along the track that crossed the wood. He thought, but was not sure, that Cy had seen them, too, for he had suddenly increased his speed. He was running now—and in their direction. "We'll get out of his way, shall we?" he suggested, though indeed it was gall and wormwood to him to think that he must seek to hide from, and to avoid, a man he felt he would give his year's salary to lay his hands on.

But it was the safety of the rescued girl he had to think of first. He took her by the hand and drew her back with him, farther back into the shelter of the trees and the brushwood, angrily conscious that now from the hunter he had become the hunted.

However, Cy could wait; Cy could be dealt with later. Only perhaps Cy did not mean to wait. It might be that he still saw his one chance of safety in eliminating Betty—and Bobby, too, for that matter. As already he had, Bobby supposed, eliminated the evidence the caravan might have provided.

Impossible to tell how Cy would react to the recent swift fierce huddle of events. But clear to Bobby that his first concern must be the girl's safety and the preserving her clearly shaken mental balance from any further shock, especially now that the effect of whatever drug she had been given seemed to some extent to be wearing off. She was saying now:

"There was another dream I had of an old man in a bath, but that was horrible."

"Never mind that now," Bobby said. "Dreams are only dreams, aren't they?"

"But it was horrible," she repeated, "An old man in a bath isn't horrible, but it was."

"You won't have dreams any more with Mrs Wyllie," Bobby repeated. "You can't imagine what a state she's been in about you."

CHAPTER XXXVI
"I SHAN'T SWING NOW"

THE SMOKE from the embers of the caravan, still rising, though now only in slow, lazily drifting, wandering wisps, served again as a general guide. Indeed, but for its help Bobby would have found it more than once almost impossible to keep his sense of direction and to find his way through the tangled growth around. But the glade itself he avoided as he thought it better his companion should not pass again near that dark and horrid hole, standing by the edge of which Ted Wyllie had said he last saw her.

A little farther on was the smaller glade—so small, indeed, as hardly to be worth the name, where Ted Wyllie had been left. Ted had regained consciousness by this time, Bobby's rough and hasty bandaging having been enough to stop the bleeding. When Ted saw them, he tried to get to his feet, but could not, and indeed nearly collapsed again with the effort. To his companion, Bobby said:

"You remember Ted Wyllie, don't you? Mrs Wyllie's son, you know."

She nodded and stood still. She said:

"I thought I saw him. It wasn't a dream, because he's there." She lifted both hands in a queerly pathetic gesture. "Everything's so funny in my head," she said. "I don't know any more what's real or what's only dreams. You're real?"

"Oh, rather," Bobby agreed cheerfully. "Very real indeed. Difficult, though, to tell sometimes, isn't it?" He was trying to make everything seem to her as normal and 'everydayish' as possible. "Especially when you've just wakened up. Ted's got himself hurt. Careless sort of chap. Do you think you could stay and take care of him while I go for a doctor?"

She nodded again, and went with him to where Ted had now struggled again into a sitting position.

"Betty," he said. "Betty." And then a third time he said the one word: "Betty."

"You're Ted, aren't you?" she said as she knelt down by his side, "and I'm me. Only I don't understand. I don't understand a bit."

"That's all right," Bobby said. "Don't bother about it just now."

"You've found her at last," Ted said. "Thank God for that, thank God!"

"Was I lost?" she asked.

"Never mind all that," Bobby repeated. "And don't talk, either of you. Just stay there. Don't move till I get back. Whatever you do, don't move."

First, though, he went to where Gladys had been left. There was no sign of her. Most likely her one thought had been to get as far away as possible, for fear that Tiny Garden might return. Bobby was not inclined to concern himself much about her for the moment. Other and more pressing matters occupied his mind. No great difficulty in finding her again when she was wanted. Especially in her present condition, for she would certainly need medical care, perhaps even have to ask for admission to a hospital.

The first thing necessary was to find Ford and send him for the help so urgently needed. Then Bobby himself could return to Ted and Betty, for he was by no means easy at having to leave them alone. He hurried back to the caravan glade, and thence towards the track crossing the common. Somewhere near it he hoped Ford would be waiting. Still he hurried on, and now began to remember Cy, and Tiny, both perhaps still lurking near. The last he had seen of Cy was the glimpse he had of him running full speed along the track, as if for some sudden unexpected cause. Bobby wondered what. At the moment he had thought it might be that Cy had caught sight of him and of Betty. But that did not seem likely, since there had been no apparent attempt on Cy's part to follow them. Bobby was near the edge of the track now, separated from it only by a thin fringe of trees. He halted, and from near by, shattering the silence, a great voice roared:

"There you are."

For a moment Bobby stood still, half expecting that this was the prelude to attack. So it was, but not upon himself, for now, a long way away, there burst out into the open track the huge and running figure of Tiny Garden, and from the opposite direction emerged Cy, walking softly, knife in hand.

"That you, Tiny?" he said quietly. "Both up against it, aren't we? Why not talk it over together reasonable like?"

"I'm going to do you in same as her," Tiny said, almost as quietly, his great voice sinking to what was nearly a whisper.

"Don't be a fool, Tiny," Cy said; and both of them were too absorbed, warily watching each other, to be aware that now Bobby had come out through the fringe of trees and was running towards them. Yet it was of him Cy at least was thinking, for he went on: "Bobby Owen's on us both. We've no chance unless—"

But Tiny interrupted. He said in the same quiet, matter-of-fact tones:

"I've got to swing for Ada as I've just done in, and I'll swing for you as well, for it's you as broke us up."

"Now listen," Cy began; but once more Tiny interrupted, and now he and Cy were very close together, and both of them still unaware of Bobby running quickly and quietly towards them, his hand upon the automatic in his pocket; for though he was otherwise unarmed, he hoped he might be able to use it, jammed and in fact useless as it was, to bluff them into submission.

A weak hope, he knew, and if it failed he must trust to his own strength and the bare chance that Ford and his umbrella might arrive in time to help—a slender chance, for it seemed as if Ford must have got himself lost in the confusion of the woodland.

Tiny, his words borne to Bobby on a light breeze that had sprung up, was shouting now:

"Only for you everything would have been O.K. and us all set up for life. Now I've got to swing for Ada, and likely for the old man as well, so I may as well for you, too."

"O.K., O.K., if that's how you want it," Cy said, and faced the big man, knife in hand.

By this time Bobby was not much more than a hundred yards away, running quickly, but with caution. He knew the odds against him were heavy; and that his best, perhaps his only, chance was to take the other two unawares. They, intent upon each other, were still unconscious of his approach. Now Tiny rushed and Cy's knife flashed, flashed and failed. For, either by good luck or skill, or possibly because Cy's nerve faltered under the threat and menace of that tremendous onslaught, and thus the thrust of the knife came less swiftly and less surely than usual, Tiny managed to catch it on the sleeve of his coat, and so by a sudden twist, wrench the weapon from Cy's grasp.

Next moment Cy was taken in Tiny's huge grip, and he screamed as he felt himself lifted bodily high into the air, held there helpless.

Bobby was quite close now. He shouted:

"Stop that, Tiny! Stop it."

Tiny heard. He turned his head, staring from his wild and blood-shot eyes. He said loudly, surprised, still holding Cy helpless above his head:

"Oh, you," he said, and flung Cy sprawling down. "Now I can swing for you, as well," he said and made a rush.

Bobby, who had no intention of letting himself be caught in that huge and bear-like grip, stepped swiftly to one side, and twice hit out with all his force as Tiny went lumbering by. They were good blows, well aimed, well timed. Before them, most men would have gone down, but Tiny seemed hardly to notice them. He turned and came running back, and this time Bobby could not quite avoid him, but did check him with a blow that had all his weight behind it, and that landed full on Tiny's chin. It brought him to a standstill for the moment, so that again Bobby had time to step aside, and, from the corner of his eye, to see that Cy was on his feet once more and again had his knife in his hand.

Equal odds, Bobby thought, grimly enough, on which of them Cy chose to use it first. Or would he simply try to make his escape while the other two fought it out? But escape was a thing Bobby did not mean should happen; and, with a sudden sideways leap, he brought himself face to face with Cy, leaving the slow-thinking Tiny bewildered by his sudden disappearance. Again Cy's knife flashed, again it failed, for that quick sideways leap had surprised Cy, too, taking him unawares, and allowing Bobby, by some tiny fraction of a second, to get his blow in first, though a blow too hasty, neither well timed nor well aimed. Yet it was sufficient to make Cy's thrust ineffectual, and now upon the two of them came Tiny, running and roaring. His great arms were swinging, his tongue hung out and on his lips specks of foam had gathered. From a little distance came the sound of a man shouting, and then, incongruously, came flying through the air a rolled umbrella. It struck Tiny full in the face, but he took no notice, impervious in his massive strength to any but the most massive blows. Yet possibly it did serve to halt his rush for some imperceptible moment of time. Bobby was intent on Cy, anticipating a fresh knife-thrust or, it might be, the deadly trick of the thrown knife. Cy was intent on Bobby, watching him, hesitating between thrust and throw. Before he could decide— for all this was so nearly simultaneous it was quite impossible to distinguish the sequence of events—Tiny was upon him, towering above them both, above Bobby's clear six foot as over Cy's smaller, lighter form. Bobby had just time to leap aside, hitting out as he did so, but with no apparent effect, though afterwards he found his knuckles bruised and bleeding. Cy, less alert, less ready, failed to avoid Tiny's grip. Once again he felt himself caught in it, once again he felt himself swung high in the air, as though a father in play were lifting his laughing child high up above the ground.

For a moment, for less than a moment, for less than the tenth of a second, though to Bobby, as he reeled backwards and steadied himself, it seemed like the passage of interminable time, they remained thus—Cy held up high in the air, head down, legs sprawling upwards; Bobby the yard or two away that he had leaped aside to avoid that final, elephantine rush of Tiny's; farther off, Ford stopping in his run towards them to stare at that tremendous effort of Tiny's strength, holding Cy up there in mid air at the full stretch of his arms.

Then Tiny shouted aloud, in wild, fierce exultation, and, lifting Cy even higher, tossed him away, as you might a discarded cigarette packet.

Cy crashed against a tree by the roadside and fell and lay huddled at its foot. Ford began to run again. Bobby stood still, alert and watching. He was not sure, but he thought that once more he had seen Cy's knife, helpless in mid air as Cy had seemed, flash and fall, and this time not in vain. Tiny stood very still, utterly motionless. Then very slowly, while Bobby still watched, while Ford still ran, Tiny began as it were to crumble, to fall in upon himself, till he, too, like Cy, lay in a huddled, dreadful, helpless heap.

Bobby went to him. Ford, panting heavily, came up. Bobby said:

"Well, that's over. A near thing, but it's over." He, too, was breathing heavily. He said: "While Tiny held Cy up like that, in the air, head down, Cy managed to strike down to push his knife into the back of Tiny's neck."

He bent over the prostrate man. The knife had gone deep. There was nothing to be done. Tiny opened his eyes.

"I shan't swing now," he said, and a rush of blood choked him so that he died.

"There's his epitaph," Ford said. "He won't swing now."

Bobby went across to where Cy lay. He was unconscious, though he was moaning slightly and the position in which he lay was twisted and unnatural. Bobby bent over him, and Ford said:

"We've got him, anyhow."

But Bobby said:

"Looks to me as if his back was hurt pretty badly. I doubt if he'll ever come to trial. He may go on living a year or two."

"Pity to let him," Ford said, and looked as if he would have small hesitation in cutting very short that hypothetical year or two.

"You hurry off and get help," Bobby told him. "Doctor, an ambulance. Hurry up. Don't forget that umbrella of yours."

"Only thing I could think of," Ford said apologetically.

"Oh, it helped," Bobby said. "Distracted attention, and that meant a good deal just then. Hurry up. I must see if Ted Wyllie and the girl are all right. These two can wait. They won't move, either of them; but I wonder what's become of Gladys. I hope she isn't up to any mischief," he added, faintly uneasy.

"No fear of that, sir," Ford answered. "It was seeing her made me late. It thought it might be the other girl wandering off, so I went chasing after her till I saw who it was. She was collapsed when I got to her. She's pretty bad. Face cut open and her nose so flat it looks like it was broken. You couldn't want worse for her, even if it's no more than she deserved."

Bobby, inclined to agree with this remark, observed that the ambulance could pick her up, too, when it arrived. Then he and Ford separated, Ford hurrying away on his errand, Bobby to find Ted Wyllie and Betty and to tell them it was now all over and for them all was well.

So far as the public was concerned the deaths of Tiny Garden and of Ada Day—it had to be assumed that that was her real name—were put down simply to a gang feud. At the adjourned inquest on old Mr Smith a verdict of murder against 'persons unknown' was returned, though the police let it be understood that the questioning of Tiny Garden, on the basis of information by the murdered Ada, had been contemplated. As Bobby had thought would be likely, Cy never came to trial. His spine had been very seriously injured, and he did not live long. Gladys was allowed to disappear. There seemed little point in prosecuting one who had already suffered so terrible a punishment in the disfigurement for life that had been inflicted on her. Nor was it thought desirable to proceed against any of the others. Mrs Day; her son, known as 'Sunday'; Cy's associate, Bill Bright; and the woman who had called herself Gladys's aunt were all allowed to go free. It would not have been easy to formulate against any of them a charge on which conviction would have been certain. Little direct evidence, for instance, to prove that 'Sunday' had taken part in the murder of Mr Smith, and the women could all have argued that they had had no real knowledge of what was going on, and had taken in it no real part. Medical opinion, too, protested strongly against the risks involved in putting, after all she had gone through, Betty into the witness-box, now that she was recovering so well at Bournemouth her mental poise and equilibrium. And again there was the official doubt as to whether a jury could be asked to accept her evidence.

"She would be asked if she could distinguish between her dreams and reality," it was said, "and that would settle it with the jury. Imagine the average jury being asked to convict any one on the strength of dreams."

So far as legal proceedings therefore were concerned, it was decided that the whole matter must be considered closed.

Fortunately Ted Wyllie was an exceedingly healthy young man, and though his wound had been serious, he made a quick and complete recovery—and Mrs Wyllie took exceedingly good care that he, too, should spend the whole period of convalescence at Bournemouth. Nor was it so very long before Olive was able to show Bobby in the paper an announcement of the engagement of Mr Edward Wyllie to Miss Elizabeth Smith. Then two or three days later the two of them appeared at Bobby's flat, explaining rather shyly that they both wanted to say 'Thank you' to Bobby. So Bobby explained that he had his job to do, that he was paid to do it, though on a wholly inadequate scale, and that was all there was to it. But what about that paragraph he had seen in the papers about Mr Smith's will?

"Oh, yes, isn't it lucky?" Betty answered, beaming. "Mr Moon says it's no good, because it isn't clear who is meant. That poor girl who got killed wasn't his niece, so it can't be her, because she wasn't any relation at all, and it can't be me, because it says 'in consideration of his niece's kindness in giving up her employment in Canada to look after him and the care and attention shown him,' and though I'm his niece I didn't do that, so Mr Moon says the consideration fails, and I can't claim, and all the money goes under an earlier will to some musty old museum that used to help him about his furniture collecting."

"Well, if that's your idea of luck," Bobby said.

"Well, you see," she explained, "the museum people are giving me quite a lot of what's left after they've paid all the taxes they have to, and Ted says he doesn't mind that so much. Ted kept saying he wouldn't have me—not with all that money, wouldn't touch me with a barge-pole."

"Oh, come, I say, draw it mild, Betty," Ted protested. "I never said anything like that."

"It was what you meant," Betty told him severely, "and I think it was most awfully rude. You just simply can't imagine, Mr Owen, how frightfully obstinate and stupid Ted can be when he tries."

"Oh, can't I?" Bobby exclaimed, with bitter memories surging up in his mind. "I can congratulate him on his good luck, which is a lot more than he deserves, but I don't know about you. Still, so long as you realize how frightfully obstinate and pig-headed and stupid he can be, I suppose it's all right."

"Oh, come, I say, draw it mild," protested Ted again.

"Oh, I do," Betty declared earnestly; "but then, he's a man, and so he can't help it, can he? Because men are always like that, aren't they? Ask your wife."

THE END

E.R. PUNSHON
CRIME FICTION REVIEWER

E.R. Punshon was for many years a reviewer of crime fiction for the Guardian *newspaper in the U.K. The following six reviews by Punshon were published in* The Guardian *between 1938 and 1939.*

Appointment with Death, Agatha Christie (1938)

The End of Andrew Harrison, Freeman Wills Crofts (1938)

Lament for a Maker, Michael Innes (1938)

The Four of Hearts, Ellery Queen (1939)

Death of his Uncle, C.H.B. Kitchin (1939)

The Reader Is Warned, Carter Dickson (John Dickson Carr) (1939)

Appointment with Death
by Agatha Christie
The End of Andrew Harrison
Freeman Wills Crofts
27 May 1938

A reproach is occasionally made that the detective novel is lacking in human values, and indeed at times there is truth in this, for some authors wish to offer and some readers prefer to accept a problem of which the ingenuity is as distant and aloof as the terms of a mathematical equation.

Yet in fact no class of fiction should be more closely concerned with human relationships than the detective novel, dealing as it does with that crisis of the mind and spirit which leads to the extremity of murder. One reason for the leading position won by Mrs. Agatha Christie is that she deals not merely with the mechanics of crime but treats also psychological problems of universal interest. In "Appointment with Death" she tells of a family entirely under the influence of one of its members, a woman of such dominating personality that those around her have almost lost the power of independent thought. But their tyrant makes the mistake of taking them abroad, and in new surroundings the seeds of rebellion are sown. Will they, or any of them, take actions to free themselves? Easy enough, perhaps, for one or other to break away, but will not such rebellion intensify the bondage of those left behind? Is, in fact, any solution possible except the death of the tyrant; and when that death occurs, was one of them guilty of the murder? The reader hopes not, for all have been drawn as sympathetic, deeply tried characters. There is a young woman doctor, too, a spectator hot with indignation; there is the French psychologist who knows that for one of the sufferers at least it is a question of more than life or death, since sanity is in the balance. There are others, too, and above all, Poirot, resolute that never must murder remain unhidden. For ingenuity of plot and construction, unexpectedness of dénouement, subtlety of characterization, and picturesqueness of background "Appointment with Death" may take rank among the best of Mrs. Christie's tales.

* * *

Mr. Freeman Wills Crofts, equally well known and successful, pursues a different technique. He excels above all in ingenuity and in conveying the thrill and passion of the hunt as inch by inch the trail is followed until at last the truth is reached. It might be thought there would be tedium in the long, quiet process of addition and subtraction by which the essential facts are put together, the unimportant eliminated, but presently the slow, almost mathematical procedure changes as it were into a multiplication of excitement as the true solution begins to appear. In Mr. Crofts's new book, "The End of Andrew Harrison," the story deals with the world of high finance and with the odd things that happen therein, with the death of a millionaire found murdered in a houseboat on the Thames in circumstances that must have passed for suicide had not Inspector French noticed just the one simple point the culprit overlooked. Then follows the long, slow chase, checked here, succeeding there, uncovering many things, till at last the guilt is made plain. The book is one that shows at its best Mr. Crofts's remarkable and distinctive talent.

Lament for a Maker
by Michael Innes
1 July 1938

It is the quaint habit of librarians to divide their books into two classes, fiction and serious—Mr. [Charles] Morgan's "The Fountain," for instance as fiction and "Lives of Light Ladies of France" as serious. In the same way a superstition exists that fiction itself may be divided into two classes, "serious" fiction and detective stories, and indeed only the other day a broadcast referred to the borderland between "literature" and the detective tale as though the latter were in some way of necessity excluded from consideration as "literature."

Obviously, in the higher sense of the word, little current fiction, few of the day's books for that matter, can lay claim to be "literature," but the notion that a detective novel is by its nature inferior is merely a specially silly instance of attaching a label and then using that label to judge by. But since some such idea does seem to exist, the warmest of welcomes is due to Mr. Innes's "Lament for a Maker," which has at least a good claim to be "literature," is at least as worthy of the attention of the intelligent reader as any piece of fiction published for many a long day. It is remarkable for strong and clear characterisation and for power of narrative as well as for those distinctive qualities of the detection tale: suspense and mystery logically developed to a reasonable conclusion. The book gives, too, the somewhat rare pleasure of seeing words treated with a fine sensibility, and there is in addition both humour and that agreeable flavour of scholarship given to a book when there is felt to be behind it a background of culture and knowledge.

The story has its faults: the opening is too long—even too Scottish—and Mr. Innes depends to much upon coincidence and on such base mechanical tricks as conversations overheard to carry on his tale, so that at times the situations seem to be built up artificially instead of arising, as they should, from the natural flow of the narrative. Few readers, however, will forget the portrait of the aged "sutor" or the picture drawn of the old laird, aloof in his solitary castle, as a man driven by the whips of the pursuing fates. In contrast there are the sketches of quiet Scottish village life, with its small, everyday excitements. Comparisons are not only odious, they are useless; but it may at least be said that, as there is one glory of Sayers and another of Crofts, so now there is a glory of Michael Innes.

The Four of Hearts
Ellery Queen
9 May 1939

In every form of fiction, in every work of art for that matter, a primary difficulty is always that of keeping even the balance of general composition. In especial the detective novelist must beware lest his main ingredient, the problem, does not play Aaron's rod and swallow up all those other ingredients that make for a good story.

It is a point that Mr. Ellery Queen, with all his skill in problem-making, seldom forgets, and in his new novel "The Four of Hearts" he stages the problem he offers for our solution against the always fascinating background of Hollywood. Two of the best-known Hollywood stars are to be married in reconciliation of an ancient stage vendetta. They begin to get mysterious warnings, they leave for their honeymoon on an aeroplane in the best Hollywood tradition of publicity and "ballyhoo," and are somehow poisoned in mid-air. There seems to be no motive, no explanation. The son of one victim, the daughter of the other, agree in their turn to marry; begin, too, to receive mysterious warnings, and thence ensues a strange and exciting climax in the air. The reader, if he is as shrewd an observer and logical a thinker as is Mr. Ellery Queen, can solve the problem equally promptly, but one imagines comparatively few will so succeed. Yet the argument is clear, simple, and logical. Mr. Queen has the great gift of inventing a fantastic, almost impossible, sequence of events and then providing a perfectly reasonable explanation.

Death of his Uncle
C.H.B. Kitchin
6 June 1939

Good character-drawing is the necessary foundation of all good fiction and without narrative power the novelist tends to become the essayist. Yet how tremendously important an ingredient is also a good style! Since bad and careless writing is a reproach still often aimed at the detective novel, all the warmer welcome should be extended to those in which literary merit is evident.

Mr. C.H.B. Kitchin's "Death of His Uncle" has, for instance, many and evident faults, and might easily pass as no better than the average. The dialogue is sometimes forced and artificial, the plot has glaring coincidences and improbabilities—it is difficult to believe in that disguise business, and the midnight bathe is a trifle too opportune. Again, the device by which the culprit attempts to ward off suspicion is too familiar. Yet the literary qualities of the book are so high that it becomes something of an achievement, though perhaps the achievement of one whose real gifts are for the reflective essay rather than for the novel of crime and mystery. Readers of the still remembered "Death of My Aunt" will meet once more Malcolm Warren, the stockbroker with a flair for detection. His help is asked when the uncle of an old university friend disappears. He traces the missing man from hotel to hotel, discovers his clothes on the beach, and, though the local police accept the theory of a bathing accident, fears foul play, presently proving his suspicions justified.

The Reader is Warned
Carter Dickson (John Dickson Carr)
8 August 1939

The difference between invention and imagination is a little like that between talent and genius, since both genius and imagination contain, spring from, and far transcend what is yet, in a way, their origin and beginning. It is this power of inventive construction that for the detective novelist, as for the dramatist, is his peculiar need if story or play is to be built up into a logical and connected whole. It is a quality in no way essential to great literature, which may or may not show it; it may well be displayed in quite other walks of life, but without it neither good plays nor detective stories can be produced. It is indeed by the use of this gift that the detective novel is chiefly to be distinguished from other examples of the art of fiction.

That Mr. Carter Dickson possesses in an unusual degree this power of ingenious invention is shown once again in "The Reader is Warned" when from the incredible beginning, telling of the thought-reader who says to others, "At such a moment you are going to die," and it is so, there is built up a perfectly reasonable and credible solution, though to the bewildered reader is seems like only sheer magic and witchcraft can explain such a tangle of strange happenings as Mr. Dickson records. That he possesses also the higher gift of imagination is shown by the manner in which is conveyed an unearthly atmosphere of wonder and of dread, all presently swept aside by the clear, strong common sense of Sir Henry Merivale and by the way, too, in which the whole story—"The Reader is Warned"—carries a moral against yielding to nerves and panic. The ending of the book is a little weak with a too garrulous murderer explaining in a monologue, for the benefit of unseen listeners, exactly the how and why of it all, but in the story as a whole Mr. Dickson displays an imagination as rich and varied as any expressing itself in the fiction of the moment.

Lightning Source UK Ltd.
Milton Keynes UK
UKOW01f1017200617
303734UK00001B/19/P

9 781911 413998